SILENT
ISLAND

BOOKS BY DANA PERRY

The Silent Victim
The Golden Girl
Her Ocean Grave

DANA PERRY

SILENT ISLAND

Bookouture

Published by Bookouture in 2021

An imprint of Storyfire Ltd.
Carmelite House
50 Victoria Embankment
London EC4Y 0DZ

www.bookouture.com

ISBN: 978-1-80019-657-5
eBook ISBN: 978-1-80019-656-8

PROLOGUE

It was a beautiful sunny day on the resort island of Martha's Vineyard when death came knocking at the door.

The man who opened it was thinking about all the things he and his family planned to do on their vacation: Go to the beach. Ride bicycles. Eat seafood dinners. Shop for souvenirs and antiques.

Not knowing that they only had a handful of minutes left to live.

The first blow from the intruder was so unexpected that he didn't even have time to be afraid. He was more surprised than scared. But then there was a second blow and then another and another.

"Why?" he screamed out.

There was no answer – only darkness.

Then the killer moved through the rooms – doing the same thing to the man's wife, his two daughters and infant son.

Five people dead.

But the nightmare wasn't over yet.

There was more death to come on this island.

Much more…

CHAPTER 1

My decision to become a police officer was actually made on my fifth birthday.

That year my parents gave me a tiny police outfit as a present – toy gun, badge, hat. There is a picture I still have of me mugging for the camera dressed like that. "Little Abby Pearce," people used to say. "Isn't she cute? One day though she'll outgrow all that and decide what she really wants to do with her life."

Except I never did.

In school, all the other girls dreamed of growing up to be Hillary Clinton or Serena Williams or Madonna.

Me, I wanted to be Cagney or Lacey.

I graduated from the Police Academy in New York City, I got a degree in criminal justice from Baruch University, I joined the NYPD as a policewoman and later became a homicide detective – breaking a lot of big cases during my time there on the force.

And then – for reasons too complex to get into right now (hell, I'm not sure I even understand them myself) – I returned to my hometown on the resort island of Martha's Vineyard to become a detective with the tiny Cedar Cliffs, Mass. police force.

Which is how I wound up sitting here now on this day in early fall talking with Meg Jarvis about how I'd solved the big roadside-sign caper case. Meg was the administrative assistant to the chief of the Cedar Cliffs force – and she'd worked there for like a million years. I, like others on the force, turned to Meg for comfort and guidance on a lot of things. Professional stuff, sure. But personal too.

"So it turned out to be a bunch of kids stealing the signs?" Meg asked.

"Homesick kids," I said.

In the past few weeks, as kids started heading back to school after the summer, a number of street signs had gone missing throughout Cedar Cliffs and also in towns on other parts of the island. Since the signs weren't worth very much – and presumably had little or no resale value – there had to be another motive for whoever was taking them.

And I found it.

"It wasn't a crime at all," I said. "Well, not really. Some kids from here going off to college wanted to bring a few things with them to remember the island. That's what I meant about homesick. What better way than to feel like you're almost home than to have a street sign from home in your dorm room? Something that says *Beach Street* or *Ocean Avenue* makes you think about the ocean and Martha's Vineyard again. At least that's what the kids told me when I confronted them about it."

"How did you figure it out, Abby?"

"Hey, I'm a detective. I get paid to figure out mysteries."

"What happened to the kids?"

"I reported them to their parents – and put back the stolen signs."

"You could have arrested them."

"For what?"

"Theft."

"Oh, c'mon, would you have done that?"

"No, I guess not." She shook her head. "This is quite a come-down for you though. Not long ago, you were on the front pages and all over TV news for catching murderers and sex abusers. Now you're back to bringing street-sign stealers to justice."

"Tell me about it," I said.

I'd recently been investigating the disappearance of Samantha Claymore, the sixteen-year-old heiress to the Claymore Cosmetics fortune, and I uncovered a series of murders and sexual crimes against teenage girls in the process of getting Samantha home safely. Like Meg said, that case had turned me into a media sensation for a while.

But now I was back investigating the ordinary day-to-day crimes that happened in a place like Martha's Vineyard. Stuff like stolen bikes, traffic violations, loud beach parties and squabbles between neighbors. Even something as common in other places as car theft rarely happened here. I mean how do you get a stolen car off the island? You'd have to buy a ferry ticket for it.

It was fall in Cedar Cliffs now, which meant that in a few weeks the number of people on the island – and, hence, the amount of potential crime – would decrease dramatically. The high point of the tourist season here was in August when the number of people on the island soared. But there was still pretty good tourist traffic in the weeks after Labor Day, and some people said this time in the early fall was the best time of the year to be on Martha's Vineyard. I was one of them. I always loved the fall here.

I was really taking advantage of the beautiful weather. Last week – after a series of sailing lessons – I took my first solo sail out into the open sea, making it to Woods Hole on Cape Cod and back. I also was doing a lot of bike riding, taking in the fall beauty on all the bike lanes and trails that criss-crossed the island. There was still swimming too. The ocean water on Martha's Vineyard remained warm and comfortable in the early fall, and there was a secluded beach not far from where I lived. I spent a lot of my free time there.

Yep, it was all very comfortable for me.

Except for the fact that I was doing all these things alone.

It would have been nice to share it with someone.

A point Meg Jarvis brought up with me now.

"How's everything else going for you?" Meg asked.

"Such as?"

"Your personal life."

"Are you talking about men?"

"Yes."

"Oscar's fine."

"Oscar's your dog."

"Well, he's also the only man in my life right now."

"What happened to the Boston TV reporter?"

That was a good question. A question I did not have a good answer for. Lincoln Connor and I became involved romantically when he came here to cover the murders/teenage sex scandal for his station in Boston. Things were exciting between us for a while. But then he went back to Boston. Which was why I was spending most of my free time with Oscar now.

"Lincoln wanted me to move to Boston," I said. "He said I should try to get a job with the Boston police or maybe the FBI there. I asked him to move to Martha's Vineyard. I said maybe he could get a job with the *Martha's Vineyard Gazette*. We argued about that a number of times, and then he left. I'm not sure if I'll ever see him again."

"It's not that far for you to visit him in Boston," Meg pointed out.

"It's not that far for him to visit me here either. But neither one seems to be happening."

"Do you love him?"

"I'm not sure."

"That's really supposed to be a 'yes' or 'no' answer."

"I may still be in love with my ex-husband."

"Zach? The state trooper back in New York?"

"Uh-huh."

"You think there's a chance you and Zach could get back together again?"

"I was hoping."

"But didn't he just get remarried?"

"Well, there is that…"

It was just another routine day in the Cedar Cliffs police station. Talking about petty crimes on Martha's Vineyard and personal gossip and a lot of other stuff like that. Then Police Chief Barry Wilhelm came barreling out of his office. And in an instant everything changed.

"There's been a homicide at The Beach House," he yelled to me.

"Who's dead?"

"Five people!"

"Five?"

"It looks like a massacre up there!"

CHAPTER 2

I knew this was going to be really terrible. I could see it on the faces of the two uniformed Cedar Cliffs officers standing outside. It wasn't just that the two cops looked horrified or distraught or even repulsed by what they'd seen inside. The expression on their faces was more of… well, disbelief.

The Beach House was a very upscale hotel about a mile outside of downtown Cedar Cliffs. It was on its own little parcel of land, right off of Beach Road on the eastern end of the island. There was a pricy restaurant attached to it, and a big parking lot in front.

"Tell me what you know," I said to Josh Gruber, one of the two cops. He was a young guy who'd just joined the force recently.

"Five people dead in there, Abby. Husband. Wife. And three kids. They were all stabbed. A lot of times. My God, there's blood everywhere inside there."

I could see Gruber was desperately trying to keep it together.

"Do we know who they are?"

"His name is Thomas Lavelle. A doctor from New York City who came up here with his family on vacation. I've never seen anything like this. I mean I never saw so much blood…"

Gruber lost control now. He suddenly turned pale, bent down and began to vomit next to one of the police cars in the parking lot. I stood in front of him as best I could in hopes that the curious onlookers who'd showed up wouldn't see what he was doing.

"I'm sorry," he said, once it was over.

"Nothing to be sorry about."

"I'm a cop, I should be able to deal with something like this."

"You're also a human being, Josh."

Looking at him there, trying desperately to keep his composure and act tough again, the way he knew he was supposed to at a crime scene, I remembered another young police officer who once experienced the same thing.

Me.

During my first year on the NYPD force, I became violently ill like that at a particularly gruesome murder scene. It was the only time that ever happened to me. You never get used to the violence and death you have to deal with as a police officer, but you somehow learn to accept it as part of the job.

"It's okay, Josh," I said softly to Gruber now. "It's okay."

Then I went inside…

Thomas Lavelle was lying on the living room floor, covered in blood. He'd been stabbed numerous times. He was on his back and his eyes were wide open, staring at nothing as we looked down at the body. His shirt, his pants, his face – even his shoes – were covered in blood. It was impossible to know which wounds had come first. Only that the attack seemed to have been carried out in a rage, not a professional kill.

His wife's body was in a hallway leading off the living room. It looked like she was trying to get away from whoever attacked her husband. She had only been stabbed once, but it was a lethal blow to her heart that must have killed her instantly. Like her husband, she was lying on her back.

But her hands were clasped together in front of her, which was eerie looking.

Almost like she was praying in death.

I wondered if that was significant – or simply the way she happened to fall after the fatal stab wounds.

Two of the children – young girls, one who looked to be in her early teens and the other a few years younger – were in a bedroom.

Like their father, they had been stabbed numerous times. And the third child, a little boy who was still really an infant, was killed in his playpen. The tiny boy couldn't have been more than a year or so old.

There was more too.

Whoever did all this had left a horrifying message behind.

On a wall in the hallway, someone had written in blood – presumably the victims' blood – these words:

"No One Here Gets Out Alive"

Teena Morelli, the other detective on the Cedar Cliffs police force, was already there. She and I listened to Dave Bowers, one of the first officers on the scene, talk about what we knew so far about the murders. Which wasn't much.

"The time of death is estimated at some time yesterday afternoon," Bowers said. "No one heard anything, but at that time of the afternoon most people staying here were probably out at the beach or somewhere else. No sign of forced entry, but then a lot of people just leave their doors unlocked on Martha's Vineyard. It is supposed to be a safe place."

"Who found the bodies?" I asked.

"The maid. When she showed up to clean the place this morning."

'What about the murder weapon?" I asked.

"Nothing here. From the wounds, it looks like it could have been a very large knife. Something like a hunting knife. But the killer, or killers, must have taken the weapon with them."

"So all we have to do is find someone walking around with a bloody hunting knife and arrest them," Teena grunted. "That should be easy, Pearce. Especially for a hotshot detective like you."

Teena was trying to act like she was tough, which she usually did. But I could tell she was really shaken up by it. Different people react to something like this in different ways. Josh Gruber threw up behind a police car. Teena made jokes.

"Any idea of a motive?" I asked Bowers.

"Nothing seems to be missing. So it doesn't look like a robbery."

"What do we know about Lavelle?"

"He was a cardiologist in New York. Very prominent doctor. He apparently had a lot of high-profile patients."

I knew I'd need to do a lot of digging into Lavelle's background. The motive for a massacre of him and his family was most likely something from his past in New York City. I didn't figure he brought his family to Martha's Vineyard on vacation and then pissed off someone here so much that they did this. No, the odds were this was something, or someone, that had followed him here.

"And I assume there are no witnesses at all?" I asked.

"Just one," Bowers said.

"Who?"

"The girl."

"What girl?"

"The Lavelles' oldest daughter, Karin."

"She survived?"

"Yeah, it's pretty unbelievable! She was found in the middle of the bloodbath. She's the only survivor… and she wasn't hurt at all."

CHAPTER 3

Karin Lavelle looked pretty much like a typical fifteen-year-old girl. Long brown hair, dressed in jeans and a Martha's Vineyard T-shirt, with a wooden Native-American necklace of some kind that looked like she'd bought it on a trip to one of the stores that sell that kind of thing in Aquinnah on the western end of the island. Yep, your average teenage girl. Except her entire family just got wiped out.

So why not her too?

The officers had taken her away from the crime scene – where the bodies of her family were – and moved her into the manager's office where medical people had done a preliminary examination of her and found nothing wrong. Nothing physically wrong, that is.

"What has she said?" I asked Bowers.

"Nothing."

"I don't understand."

"She's been unresponsive, almost catatonic. All we could get out of her is that she doesn't know what happened. Doesn't know who did anything here or why. Doesn't know anything, she says."

"Do you think she's telling the truth?"

"Why would she lie?"

"To protect herself."

"Are you saying she's a suspect?"

"Well, she's the only one we've got at the moment."

I looked over at Karin Lavelle now. She was sitting in a chair behind the manager's desk. Even though the temperature was in the eighties outside, she seemed to be shivering and someone had put a blanket around her. They'd also given her a cup of something to drink, but the cup sat untouched in front of her.

"No way that little girl could have done what we saw back there," Bowers said. "Overpowered her father and her mother and the rest of her family—"

"Then why is she still alive?"

"Do you really think she did it?"

"I just don't know," I said to Bowers.

The manager of The Beach House walked over to me. Lily Knowlton was a strange-looking, almost scary woman – dressed completely in black, with tattoos and body jewelry.

"Are you with the police?" she asked me.

"I'm Abby Pearce, the lead detective investigating this case."

"You don't look much like a detective to me."

"What do I look like?"

"I don't know. More like a, well… like a stewardess or something."

That was a new one. Many people have said when they first met me that I didn't match their idea of the way a cop was supposed to look. I wasn't a big woman. Just average size, maybe even petite at five feet five and around a hundred and five pounds. I have long black hair. Usually I wear it in a ponytail or in a bun held up in the back with a plastic hair pin, but today I'd let it fall loose down my back. Most of the time people figured me at first for a businesswoman or a real estate broker or maybe even a lawyer. But a stewardess? I didn't even think anyone called women who work on airlines stewardesses anymore – they were all flight attendants. Of course, I could have told Lily Knowlton she didn't look much like a hotel manager, but I didn't.

"Tell me what you know about what happened here," I said.

"All I know is a lot of police suddenly showed up and said there were people dead in one of our rooms. And now you're all here with this girl taking over my office. That's all I know."

It didn't seem like Lily Knowlton was going to be of much help.

"I need to be able to use my office again to do my job," she said. "I need to get back to my desk."

"You're going to have to wait until we finish talking to this girl."

"How long will that be?"

"As long as it takes."

Karin Lavelle sat there staring straight ahead at nothing, seemingly not seeing any of the rest of us in the room. Almost catatonic, Bowers had said. That sure looked like the situation.

I walked over to her now and sat down on the top of the manager's desk, trying to be as casual as I could. I didn't want to scare her any more than she already was.

"Hello, Karin," I said. "My name is Abby Pearce, and I'm a detective with the Cedar Cliffs Police Department. We're here to protect you. You don't need to be afraid. Do you understand that?"

There was a slight nod of her head, but no words.

"We need to find out first who did this. To prevent anyone else from dying. And you are the one who can help us do that. Will you help us?"

Another nod of her head.

"What happened here, Karin? Who did this to your family?"

Nothing this time.

No head nod.

No words until…

"I don't know," she finally said in a soft voice.

"But you were there. You must have seen what happened. You must have seen who killed them. Unless you came afterward and found them like this. Is that what happened? Did you call anyone for help? We need this information from you, Karin. It is vital that you tell us. Please help us and talk about what you remember."

"I don't remember anything."

"Are you saying you're not aware of what occurred here? Someone murdered your family, Karin. Everyone. Everyone except you."

I knew that was harsh, but I was hoping it might shock her into saying something.

Anything.

But she didn't.

"Were you here when they died?" I asked her again.

"I don't know. I don't know how I got here. I'm not sure exactly where I am. I'm not sure of anything right now. Who are you again?"

I kept trying to talk to her, casually at first, then with more intensity as my frustration grew, but I never got any real answers from the girl, so I decided to call it a day and move onto the crime scene.

I'd left Teena behind to supervise the rooms where the bodies had been found. The biggest thing there was to collect any forensic evidence – fingerprints or anything else the killer or killers might have left behind – before anyone contaminated the scene. We could only hope that the first officers who arrived had been careful about what they touched. I mean that kind of thing was standard procure at a murder scene in New York when I was an NYPD detective. But not here. There had been only a handful of murders in the island's history. No one on Martha's Vineyard, except me, was prepared to deal with something of this magnitude.

Other officers had been dispatched to go through The Beach House trying to find someone – anyone – who might have heard or seen something. Except, like Bowers had said, the problem was nobody was likely to have been in their rooms on a sunny afternoon. They would have been at the beach or in town or on one of the bicycle trails. Still, it was part of the police procedure I needed to follow, so that's what I did.

The Beach House itself was sprawling, but it consisted of only about a dozen living areas. Most of them were large multi-bedroom apartment-like places, which is what Thomas Lavelle and his family were in. You didn't come to The Beach House to live crammed into a small hotel room or cottage. It was luxury living, for people who wanted to relax and enjoy themselves on Martha's Vineyard. That's what Lavelle and his family came here to do, but instead it ended inexplicably in tragedy.

At some point, Teena came into the manager's office to report on what she'd done, and to find out what was going on with the girl. I told her about my frustrating experience with Karin Lavelle. She asked if she could question her.

I mean Teena was a lot scarier looking for a girl in this fragile state than I was. She stood close to six feet tall, very muscular from doing regular workouts, and wore a leather vest, jeans and motorcycle boots. I didn't figure Karin Lavelle was going to be more comfortable talking to Teena than me. But I said sure. Why not give it a try?

"Karin, my name is Detective Teena Morelli," she said to the girl. "I'm here to help you. Do you believe that?"

Another nod, but no response.

"If you'll just tell me whatever you know about this…"

Suddenly there was a burst of words from her.

"I don't know what happened! I don't know anything! I'm scared… I'm so scared!"

Then she broke down and began to cry.

I tried to comfort her as best I could, then pulled Teena off to the side.

"Let's get her to Martha's Vineyard Hospital and have her completely checked out," I said. "She's obviously in terrible distress. We need to find out why. Maybe that will also help us get the answers we need from her. I want her under twenty-four-hour security. We need to make sure she's protected at all times."

"You think someone might come after her?"

"They killed the rest of her family."

"And left her alive."

"Until we know why, we have to assume she's still in danger too."

I walked back to where Karin Lavelle was sitting, leaned down and softly whispered to her: "It's going to be okay. Let's go to the hospital now. We'll take good care of you."

CHAPTER 4

I was living in a house in the Chilmark area of Martha's Vineyard. Chilmark is in the central part of the island. There's no low-rent district on Martha's Vineyard, but my house was probably about as close as you could get to it. It was definitely a lot more ordinary than The Beach House or other tourist spots in Cedar Cliffs or Edgartown on the eastern side, or the mansions to the west near Aquinnah/Gay Head where people like the Kennedy family have had their places.

When I got home, I was greeted by Oscar. Oscar is a big brown and tan dachshund who is the last remnant of my marriage when I lived in New York City. I was glad to have him here with me. Oscar was my best friend in the world. Which either said something about the importance of a dog or about the state of my own life.

I played with Oscar for a while. Doing ordinary things like this helped calm me down after everything that had occurred that day.

There was a girl in the hospital in a state of severe emotional shock over what she'd seen and somehow survived. A father and mother and three children who had been brutally, and for no apparent reason, murdered in a posh hotel. Which meant there was a killer out there somewhere who could be targeting other victims too.

Nope, I've got no answers for any of that I thought to myself as I ate some leftover chicken pasta I found in my refrigerator and watched Oscar devour his dog food.

I'd done all the obvious things before leaving the station that night. We staked out the airport, questioned people boarding ferries, checked for private boats into the marinas. We questioned anyone in the area of The Beach House to find out if they heard or saw anything unusual. Ran checks on all the fingerprints and DNA and other forensic evidence we found at the Lavelle crime scene. But, so far anyway, it had all turned up nothing.

I knew what the future was going to bring too.

More questions.

A lot of questions.

Because the media would be descending in full force on Martha's Vineyard to cover this sensational mass murder story.

And one of those members of the media who would no doubt show up here, just like he did last time, was going to be Lincoln Connor. I wondered how that would work out for Lincoln and me. Would this terrible crime somehow lead to us working out the differences that had kept us apart? And, if not, what would my life be like here moving forward without him?

I'd moved back to Martha's Vineyard, the place where I grew up, less than a year earlier. For the previous ten years I'd been with the NYPD in New York City, first as a police officer and later as a homicide detective. I was married too, and I thought my life was pretty damn good.

But then, when it all fell apart, I came home again looking for some kind of restart to my life from some of the dark memories from my past.

One of those dark memories was watching my NYPD partner die on the street in a shootout, when I wasn't able to save him.

The other was the disintegration of my marriage afterward. My husband Zach left me back then. He was now married to another woman.

But the real problem for me, the problem that had seemingly defined my entire life, was my drinking.

I was drinking when my partner Tommy Ferraro died. Well, not that night that he was shot. But I'd been drinking before that. I drank too – I drank a lot – after Tommy died. And I was drinking during my marriage to Zach. Until Zach couldn't take it anymore and left me.

I had a number of pictures displayed on the mantel in my dining room. From my days on the NYPD, my marriage to Zach and even from when I was growing up here on Martha's Vineyard. I'm not sure why I keep them so prominently displayed there. They all make me sad.

Especially the ones of me and my dead NYPD partner Tommy Ferraro. There was a picture of Tommy and me standing in front of our police precinct just a few months before he was shot and killed. Another with him standing next to a police car looking tough and cool – with his gun and badge on his hip – the way Tommy always did. And a picture of Tommy with his wife Rikki and their two kids on the front lawn of their house on Long Island. They sure looked like a happy family in the picture, with no idea of the tragedy that would take Tommy from them.

I had several pictures of me and Zach there from when things were still good between us. Zach dressed in his New York State Trooper's uniform. Zach playing with Oscar. Zach and I on a picnic, at a ball game, dressed up for a formal event. We made a damn good couple for a while back then, Zach and me. Until it all fell apart from my drinking.

I even kept the long-ago picture of a five-year-old Abby Pearce in the tiny police uniform from my birthday party that my father took. When I was growing up, that picture hung on a wall of my parents' house. But, once I grew up and moved away, that picture no longer hung on their wall. I found it buried in a closet when I cleaned out the house after my mother moved into an assisted living facility. My father must have put it there – and I hadn't spoken to him in a long time before he died. I thought about asking my mother about it, but I never did. We do not have a very good relationship, my mother and me.

All of it – my guilt over Tommy's death, the breakup of my marriage to Zach and the unhappy relationship with my parents – is connected in some ways to the thing that has truly defined my life in many ways: my drinking.

I'm not drinking anymore.

But that doesn't mean I won't drink again.

Maybe tonight.

Or the next night.

Or sometime after that.

Sure, it's a one day at a time thing – that's what they teach you at Alcoholics Anonymous – but that could be a long, frustrating process.

I'd tried AA and other rehab stuff, but none of it ever really helped me with my drinking problem. Instead, I'd used a number of other approaches of my own, none of which proved very effective. But now I'd come up with a new idea: confronting my drinking head-on.

Right now, I had a bottle of Smirnoff Vodka – my favorite drink – sitting on the kitchen table in front of me while I ate my dinner.

For a long time, I'd bought into the idea about not keeping alcohol in the house because it was too tempting for me. But that never stopped me from going out to a liquor store or a bar or anyplace else to get a bottle to drink or bring home with me. Nope, just not having it in front of me solved nothing.

So now I left a full bottle of my favorite vodka right in front of me.

Tempting me.

Mocking me.

And all I had to do was be strong enough to deal with the temptation to drink the damn vodka.

Maybe one time soon I would do just that.

But not now.

Now I just stared at it sitting in front of me, a reminder of what my life had become in the past when I had been drinking, and I knew I couldn't do my job if I drank. The drinking was always important to me. But the job was even more important. At least at the moment it was. For a long time, I'd fooled myself into thinking I could have both – the drinking and the job. But now I knew the truth. I had to make a choice.

I thought about the horrible scene I'd witnessed at The Beach House that day; about the teenage Lavelle girl in the hospital; and the idea that a crazed, bloodthirsty killer was somehow loose on our quiet little island paradise.

I thought again about the media onslaught that would be coming to cover the horrendous crime.

And I couldn't help but be a bit excited about the prospect of seeing Lincoln Connor again.

That made me feel a little bit guilty.

But then I've got a lot of things to feel guilty about.

CHAPTER 5

When I worked a big homicide case in New York City, we used to meet in what we called the "war room" to go over the details and evidence in the case.

That's what I was doing this morning in the murder of Thomas Lavelle and his family. Of course, the "war room" in Cedar Cliffs was a bit smaller than the one I'd been used to with the NYPD.

It consisted of me, Teena, Dave Bowers and Meg Jarvis.

We were under a lot of pressure to get results – and do it quickly. The people on this island were scared. Martha's Vineyard consisted of vacationers, summer residents and a handful of townspeople who all came here to escape the crime and other problems of big cities. People left their doors open, their cars unlocked and never worried about walking the streets alone.

Now, with everyone already shocked over the murders that happened here in August, we were in the middle of another massive crime investigation to find the killer who massacred Thomas Lavelle and his family on their vacation here.

"Or killers," Teena pointed out when I said that.

"You figure there was more than one?"

"There were five victims. Plus the daughter who survived. No gun was used, just a knife or knives. Wouldn't one of them have gotten away or fought back harder or called for help somehow while all this was going on? Hard to believe one person could overpower five people – actually six, including the daughter – that easily. I think it was done by more than one person."

There was plenty of coffee around, and I was setting up a whiteboard in front of the table where everyone was sitting to list everything we knew and, more importantly, everything we didn't know about what happened at The Beach House. I posted a bunch of pictures too. Crime scene photos of the victims. And a picture we'd taken of Karin Lavelle, the young girl who'd somehow survived the carnage.

Then I began the discussion by running through a list of all the people we'd talked to so far and the forensic evidence from the scene, putting together a timeline of what we knew about the crime.

I went through it all like this for everyone:

"At 9:16 a.m., the maid – an elderly woman named Betty Kubinski – used her pass key to enter the suite of rooms where the Lavelles were staying. She had knocked first to see if anyone was inside, then opened the door herself when there was no answer.

"Upon entering, Kubinski immediately saw Thomas Lavelle near the entrance. At first, she thought he might have fallen and injured himself, but then she saw all the blood. The maid ran screaming from the room, called 911 and the first police officers from the Cedar Cliffs force arrived shortly afterward. That's when the full magnitude of what happened inside those rooms became apparent.

"Thomas Lavelle's body lay next to a wall on the side of the living room, covered in blood. It was later determined that he had been stabbed seventeen times in the chest and his throat had been cut. There were also heavy bruises on his head. Both arms were broken too, which suggested he had tried to defend himself and his family from the attack.

"His wife – Nancy Lavelle – was lying face up in the hallway which led off of the living room. She had only been stabbed once, for some inexplicable reason. But it was enough to kill her."

I said that I was still intrigued too by the position of her hands, clasped together almost as if she was praying. Or begging for something.

"Maybe that's what she was doing at the time she died," Teena said when I was finished. "Begging for her life and lives of her children."

"Or someone staged it like that for some reason," Meg suggested. "Although I can't imagine why."

"It could have just been the way her hands fell as the life went out of her," Bowers added.

"Maybe," I said.

The three children all had multiple wounds, like the father. The two girls – Janet, thirteen, and Eileen, eleven – were huddled in one bedroom. The boy, Steven, who was only fifteen months old, was found in his playpen in another bedroom. There was a third bedroom, and that's where the first officers on the scene found the lone survivor, fifteen-year-old Karin Lavelle. She was unhurt physically, but apparently in a state of shock – which was understandable given what had happened to her family.

"What about security video?" I asked. "Any cameras on the premises?"

"No luck there," Bowers said. "I checked with the manager. She said the only security camera they had was in the main office and lobby of the hotel, plus some of the parking lot. But nothing that covered the rooms."

"Damn."

"Yeah, a security video that showed someone going in or out of the Lavelle place would have been nice, but that's not happening, Abby."

We talked then about the phrase "No One Here Gets Out Alive" that had been written on the wall with the victims' blood. We'd confirmed that was where the blood came from, even though it seemed pretty obvious.

"It's a line from an old Jim Morrison and The Doors song," Dave Bowers said.

"Which one?" Teena asked.

"It's called 'Five to One'."

"What does that mean?"

"Well, 'five to one' was the approximate ratio of whites to blacks, young to old, and non-pot smokers to pot smokers in the U.S. back then in the sixties. The lyric is: 'Five to one, baby, one in five – no one here gets out alive.' That suggests the killer might be someone older – someone who grew up with that music back then."

"Not necessarily," Meg said. "Younger people still follow a lot of that music from the sixties. Beatles, Stones – my granddaughter listens to The Monkees. So it really could be anyone…"

"But why do something like that here?" Teena asked. "At a mass murder scene?"

"It means this is a 'statement kill'," I said.

"What?"

"These murders weren't about robbery or any traditional, obvious motive. They were about something else completely. The killer wanted to leave a 'statement' of some kind with these deaths. Maybe the same thing too with the way Mrs. Lavelle's hands were clasped together, almost like they were in prayer. If that was staged, it could be part of the 'statement'. Part of whatever message the killer wants to send by murdering five people for no apparent reason like this. We have to figure out what that message is in order to catch our killer."

"Jesus," Bowers said.

"Yeah, the 'statement kill' – where the murderer is on some weird crusade that only he or she understand – is the scariest kind of murder there is. And the toughest kind to solve. But I think that's what we're dealing with here."

We kept going over all aspects of the murder after that, talking about the evidence and everything else we'd found at the scene.

"The pattern of wounds from the attack definitely seems significant," I said. "Multiple wounds during the attack on the father and three of the children. But only a single – albeit fatal – wound on the mother. And no damage at all to the fifteen-year-old daughter Karin. Thoughts on that anyone?"

"The killer ran out of time," Bowers said. "That's why there were so many wounds on most of them, but the killer – or killers – didn't have time to finish with the last two. So the wife was murdered with a single blow to the heart. And there was no time at all left to deal with the daughter. Whoever did this fled the scene. Maybe they thought they heard someone outside. Even if we haven't found anyone who heard or saw anything there."

"Or the killer had some kind of sympathy for the mother and daughter," Meg said. "The murders of everyone else in the family were horrifyingly brutal. But, with the wife, he made it as quick and painless for her for some reason. And even more so with the fifteen-year-old, who he left alive. That certainly suggests some kind of prior relationship with the family. Especially with the mother and the daughter."

"Or the fifteen-year-old did it," Teena said. "She got mad at her family and killed them all in a burst of anger. Maybe she really doesn't remember it, the shock of what she did is so great. But it sure explains why she's alive and without a scratch on her, doesn't it? Look, all I'm saying is that we at least have to consider that possibility."

I nodded. They were all good possibilities. But there was one other one too.

"What if the girl herself was the target of whoever did this?" I said.

"How could she be the target?" Bowers asked. "She's the one who survived."

"Maybe that was on purpose."

"I don't understand."

But Teena did.

"She's forced to watch her family being murdered like that. Maybe he didn't want to kill her. Maybe he wanted to do something worse to her. Put her through this ordeal. It's over for the rest of the family, but not for her. She's living in fear. Fear over what happened to her mother and father and sisters and brother. And fear that he will still come after her next. But he wants her to suffer as much as possible first."

I nodded.

"And that's why she went into shock like she is now. She can't deal with everything she was forced to watch happen to her family, maybe because of her. Maybe because of something she did. She knows this is all about her. And she feels guilty and scared and confused the way any person – certainly a fifteen-year-old girl – would be in such a horrible situation. She's the ultimate victim here. Even if she is still alive. What do you think?"

Bowers shrugged. "Or she's putting on a helluva act to cover up the fact that she did it all – she killed her own family."

Teena stood up now, walked over to the whiteboard where I'd posted a picture of Karin Lavelle – the only survivor of the massacre.

"One thing's for sure," Teena said, "that girl holds all the answers about what happened. We've got to figure out how to get those answers out of her."

CHAPTER 6

"The Lavelle girl's grandparents are flying into Martha's Vineyard Airport," Police Chief Barry Wilhelm said. "Walt and Elizabeth Hood from New Jersey. They're Mrs. Lavelle's parents."

"What about the husband's side of the family?" I asked.

"As far as we can tell, both of his parents are dead."

"How did the Hoods take the news about their daughter?"

"How do you think they took it? Their daughter is dead. Three grandkids too, along with their son-in-law. Their only surviving granddaughter is in the hospital barely able to speak a word. And we don't have any idea what to tell them about why this happened or who did it or any other goddamned thing."

Chief Wilhelm was clearly under a lot of stress. He was a small-town cop. A guy who was fine for normal island crimes like traffic tickets, stolen bikes or mopeds and unruly beach parties. But he was way out of his league on this.

Wilhelm didn't like me very much. And I didn't like him – or at least respect him – much either. But he was the police chief here, and I was a member of his force. So I had to try to make it work as best I could.

"We just started looking into Lavelle's background in New York," I told him. "He was a very prominent cardiologist, so there could be some motive there from an unhappy patient or family member or whatever. Also, we're checking to see if he's been in any disputes since he arrived here that might have led to this. But that seems unlikely, especially since they'd only been here for a few days. Our best bet is still the girl. She presumably knows what happened to her family."

"What's her condition now at the hospital?"

"The same as before. Totally unresponsive. Whatever she knows, she's not able to communicate with us. Or doesn't want to for some reason. So we have to figure out some way to get her to talk to us."

"Any ideas?"

"The grandparents."

"You think she'll talk to them?"

"I figure they're our best bet. She might be afraid of us for some reason. But not her grandparents. Maybe we can use them to get the answers that we need from the girl. At least I want to try."

"Okay. That sounds good. I'll have a cruiser pick them up at the airport, then you can meet them at the hospital."

"No, I'll pick them up. Myself. I want to talk to them before they get to the hospital. They're obviously going to be in shock. And seeing their granddaughter in the condition she's in is only going to make it worse. The earlier I talk to them, maybe reassure them we're doing everything we can to take care of the girl and also to find out who did this to their daughter and family, the better it will be."

"Just be here for the press conference today," Wilhelm said.

We'd put out media bulletins on the murders and the surviving teenage girl and all the rest. But now it was time for the full-scale press conference. The media was already arriving in droves on the island. Technically, it was Wilhelm's press conference. But he hated that role. And I'd become a media star with the big case here earlier. I knew he was going to put me in the spotlight. Once again, I was going to be the face of the Cedar Cliffs Police Department, not Chief Wilhelm.

"I wouldn't miss it," I told him.

*

Martha's Vineyard Airport is located in the center of the island, a few miles south of the town of Vineyard Haven, where I grew up a long time ago.

I knew the airport well. I'd flown in and out of it when I was going to college and later after I moved to New York, whenever I returned to Martha's Vineyard. It was a surprisingly large facility for such a small island, maybe because of all the tourist traffic during the summer.

Walt and Elizabeth Hood were a couple in their sixties. They had confused looks on their faces when they came off the plane, and I imagined they were thinking they were somehow in a nightmare they would soon wake up from. I walked over to them, introduced myself and expressed my condolences as best I could. Then I helped get their baggage and walked with them to my car.

The trip back to Cedar Cliffs took us through some of the most beautiful parts of the island – the wooded areas in the central section and then on to Beach Road, where we drove north with the ocean on our right. I thought about how incongruous it must have seemed to the Hoods to be in such a peaceful, lovely place for such a tragic reason.

"Will we be able to take her back to New York afterward?" Mrs. Hood asked. "When she's better?"

"Of course. Will she live with you now?"

"There's no one else." Walt Hood shrugged.

I didn't say anything. There wasn't much to say. But at least Karin Lavelle would have a loving family around her as she tried to recover from what she'd been through. And the Hoods would have one member of their dead daughter's family to help them get through their ordeal too.

"Did she suffer much?" Mrs. Hood asked now.

"Excuse me?"

"My daughter."

"Your daughter was only stabbed once, Mrs. Hood. We believe she died very quickly."

"And my grandchildren? We've been told they were stabbed numerous times. Do you think they suffered much before their death? I don't know that it really matters, but I would just like to know, if possible."

I tried to answer in the most compassionate way I could. "We think it is very possible that the first wounds were severe enough to be fatal. Which means they could have died quickly, like your daughter."

She nodded. It was the best answer she could hope for.

"Thank you. That's comforting to hear."

I noticed she didn't ask about the husband, Thomas Lavelle. Maybe there was some significance to that.

Or maybe she realized my answer would be the same for him too.

Karin Lavelle was in a room on the second floor of the hospital. There was a police guard outside. I didn't actually think the killer would come back and try to finish the job with the last member of the Lavelle family. But I wasn't taking any chances.

"Your granddaughter is in extreme emotional shock," I told them before we went in. "But she appears to be unhurt physically. Hopefully, you'll be able to get past this condition she's currently in. I'm sure seeing the two of you will be a welcome sight for Karin after everything she's been through. Once that happens, maybe she'll be able to talk to you about everything she knows about the murders of your family. It's very important for our investigation, and very important for you too, that we hear her story."

"I understand," Walt Hood said.

"Our main concern is our granddaughter's welfare," Mrs. Hood said. "But we will try to find out more from her too once we know she's all right. We'll do our best, Detective."

I wasn't sure exactly what I thought was going to occur when I took Walt and Elizabeth Hood into that room.

Maybe they would start to cry and break down at the sight of their granddaughter in the condition she was in.

Or maybe the girl would suddenly start talking finally about everything she saw at The Beach House while her father, mother, sisters and brother were being slaughtered for no apparent reason.

But I wasn't ready for what happened next.

"What's going on here?" Mrs. Hood said when she saw the girl lying in the bed.

"I don't know what you mean…"

"Who is this?"

"That's your granddaughter, Karin."

"No, it isn't."

"Then who is she?"

"I have no idea… I've never seen this girl before in my life."

CHAPTER 7

"Do you know who the girl in the hospital really is?" a reporter shouted out to me at the press conference after I'd given the media an update on the day's shocking developments.

"Not at the moment. She continues to be unresponsive. Either because of shock or fear or for some other reason that we have not been able to ascertain yet."

The questions came fast and furious after that.

"Where is the real Karin Lavelle?"

"We don't know."

"Do you believe Karin Lavelle was one of the killer's murder victims, too?"

"Right now she's missing. That's all I can tell you."

"And probably dead?"

"There's no evidence of that."

"What kind of evidence are you talking about?"

"No body. That's why we're saying she's missing."

"Do you think the girl you have in the hospital committed the murders?"

"We have no reason to believe that at this time."

"Then what was she doing there?"

"We don't know."

"Detective Pearce, you haven't given us very much solid information. What *can* you tell us?"

I talked about the massive search that had already been launched on the island for Karin Lavelle once we realized she wasn't the girl we had at the hospital. How search teams were right now scouring beaches, woods and towns for any sign of Karin Lavelle. But it didn't matter. That's not what the media there wanted to hear.

Instead, the press conference turned into a near debacle after we released the information that the girl in the hospital, who we'd assumed was Karin Lavelle, was unidentified. And that the real Karin Lavelle was unaccounted for.

Yep, the press conference was tough, but the scene at the hospital earlier – with the grandparents, Walt and Elizabeth Hood – had been worse for me.

Mrs. Hood broke down completely when she realized the girl was not her granddaughter. It was all too much for her. She had somehow managed to hold herself together to deal with the murders of her daughter, son-in-law and three grandchildren. But now, after finding out that the granddaughter she believed had survived was gone too, she collapsed in sobs on the hospital floor. Medical people rushed in, were forced to sedate her and she was eventually admitted for observation because of her fragile and unstable condition.

The husband, on the other hand, was angry. Walt Hood began screaming at me. Calling me incompetent and irresponsible and a lot of other stuff for letting them believe the granddaughter was here, when it was instead some girl none of them had ever seen before. I was afraid that he might physically attack me in his rage and frustration.

That would have created an unfortunate situation where we might have had to arrest the relative of the victims for assaulting a police officer. Fortunately, it never got to that point. But he kept yelling at me: "How could something like this happen?" I understood his anger and frustration.

The girl herself saw this all unfolding in front of her, as she lay in the hospital bed. Or at least I believe she "saw" it. It was hard to tell for sure because of her lack of response. She simply stared at the Hoods and at me going back and forth, without any real reaction. I thought I saw a small smile on her face once. But that might have been just my imagination. Basically, she acted like she was watching some episode on a TV show or from a movie that she didn't really care that much about.

I still wasn't sure what to make of her.

Was she a victim too?

Was she faking amnesia to hide secrets she knew about the murders from us?

Or, as incredible as it might sound, was she the one who killed the entire family and then, for some unknown reason, sat there waiting for the police to show up?

I did my best to question her again after the Hoods had finally left the room. But I couldn't find out anything more. The doctors had confirmed there was no apparent physical damage to her that might explain her condition. But she continued to insist she didn't know her name or why she was at The Beach House that day. Most importantly of all, she repeated over and over again that she had no knowledge of the murders that had taken place where we found her.

Despite all the pressure I was under at the press conference, I kept looking around there for a glimpse of Lincoln Connor.

Where was he? Was he standing in the back of the media contingent where I couldn't see him? Did he somehow not get assigned to cover a huge crime story like this? Or did he deliberately not come back to Martha's Vineyard because he didn't want to see me again?

I knew I shouldn't have been thinking about Lincoln Connor at a time like this, but I couldn't help myself. Nope, there was definitely no sign of him.

Meanwhile, the rest of the reporters kept hammering away at me with questions about the Lavelle murders and the disappearance of their teenage daughter.

About the unidentified girl we had from the crime scene right now in Martha's Vineyard Hospital.

About the mystery writing in blood on the wall around the bodies that said: "No One Here Gets Out Alive."

Most of these questions I didn't have any real answers for.

But finally there was one I could handle.

"What are you going to do about Karin Lavelle?" a TV reporter asked.

"We're going to find her," I vowed.

CHAPTER 8

"This is a disaster," Chief Wilhelm said to me. "A friggin' disaster."

"Tell me about it."

"How could we make a mistake like that?"

"It was an easy mistake for the first officers at the scene to make, Chief. There were bodies of the Lavelle family everywhere. And a teenage girl who was alive. The Lavelles had a teenage girl. Why would they assume she was someone else? And she wasn't talking, so they couldn't get any information from her."

"Well, its goddamned shoddy police work."

"I'll take personal responsibility for it."

"You're damned straight you will. I'm not taking the blame."

This was typical for Chief Barry Wilhelm. Wilhelm had made a career out of playing it safe, never sticking his neck out for anyone or anything. That cautious approach had lifted him up in the ranks to the top of the Cedar Cliffs Police Department, for whatever that achievement was worth. He'd never had to deal with any real crime for most of his time as chief.

Until recently. Until I came back to Martha's Vineyard.

"We all understand the microscope we're under again because of all this, Chief," I said. You, me – all of us. Not just with the media either. The whole island is afraid right now. Back- to-back major crimes like this. They wonder what's going to happen here next. And people are terrified to come here, too. The more we talk about all this in the media, the worse it gets. It's like that scene in *Jaws* where the mayor of the town doesn't want to admit there's a monster shark eating people because it will stop people from coming there. There's a lot of reasons we need to solve this case quickly. But none more important than finding the missing Lavelle girl and finding out who did this and why. Believe me, I won't rest until I accomplish that."

"Okay, okay," he said with a sigh. "So where do we go from here? What's going on with the search for Karin Lavelle?"

"I've mobilized everyone on the force for it – including calling back some temporary people who worked for us during the summer. And I've got volunteers out there too looking for her. But the best lead we have is still the girl we found at the murder scene. The one we at first assumed was Karin Lavelle. Whoever she is, she is the key to finding out what happened to the Lavelle family. Who murdered them, where the missing Lavelle girl is, and what she was doing there at the murder scene."

"Do you think she's telling the truth when she says she doesn't know anything?"

I thought again about the look I'd seen on the girl's face in the hospital room when Walt Hood and his wife realized she was not their granddaughter.

"I'm not sure about that," I said.

"Any ideas on how to get through to her, or at least find out more about her?"

"We've distributed her picture all over the island – just like we did with the picture of Karin Lavelle – in the hopes that someone recognizes her. Plus, we'll keep on questioning her at the hospital trying to find out more. Who is she? What was she doing there? What did she see when the murders took place? Sooner or later, we'll find out something about this damn girl, Chief."

I told him too my theory about how the motive for the murders most likely had been something from Thomas Lavelle's work as a doctor – or maybe even something in his personal life back in New York City, not anything that occurred during the brief time they were here in Cedar Cliffs.

"So in addition to the forensic evidence at the crime scene, and the search for the missing girl and information on the one we have in the hospital, I'm going to start looking into Lavelle's background and the medical cases he handled."

I looked at a picture of Karin Lavelle. It was on the missing person poster we'd made up and were distributing all over Martha's Vineyard now in the search for the girl.

She sure looked like an adorable fifteen-year-old girl. Nothing like the girl in the hospital from our other picture. There was no confusing the two of them once you knew they were different girls. Karin had long, straight blonde hair, big blue eyes, flawless, almost porcelain like, skin. The picture was taken at a family barbecue, and it was given to me by the grandparents –after they calmed down and realized I was trying to help them find Karin.

Even though the picture had been taken a few months earlier, I had no reason to believe it was much different than she looked today. In the picture she was wearing some kind of a sundress, and you could see that her body was filling out and she was turning into a young woman. I remember going through that same kind of transformation a long time ago, and all that came with it.

Could Karin have been the target of the attacker, someone who then abducted her for sexual reasons?

If so, maybe the family was killed simply because they had tried to protect her.

It was an unlikely scenario because of the brutality of the fatal wounds to Thomas Lavelle and the rest of his family. I still believed he was the target of the killer for some reason. But maybe the killer then took Karin with him. That kind of made more sense.

But what didn't make sense was the mystery girl we found at the scene.

CHAPTER 9

In addition to the search for Karin Lavelle taking place around the island, we were attempting to backtrack on her and the entire family's movements during the time leading up to the murders.

They had arrived a few days earlier. Driven up from New York City, left their car at a parking lot in Woods Hole on Cape Cod and then taken the ferry from Woods Hole to Martha's Vineyard. The Beach House was within walking distance of a lot of places in Cedar Cliffs, including beaches, restaurants and stores. I guess they figured it was easier to leave their car behind.

We had the Woods Hole Police impound the car at the lot there, hoping against hope there might be some clue to their deaths inside. Guns. Money. Drugs. Anything that could have played some role in what happened to them. But it was all just routine stuff – extra diapers for the youngest child, a few DVDs for the older ones, and extra clothes they must have decided they didn't need to take with them. Nothing at all to indicate they were in any kind of trouble or danger from anyone, simply the kinds of things people took along with them on a vacation trip.

On the night before they died, Thomas Lavelle and his family had gone out to dinner at an Italian restaurant in Cedar Cliffs called Delmonico's. It was a family-type place, which seemed perfect for Lavelle and his wife and their four children. People at the restaurant remembered them because they needed a special highchair at the table for the little boy. Also, they had been asking the waiter and others about antique stores on the island. Apparently, he and his wife were planning to visit some the next day.

Going through Lavelle's credit card records from his days on the island didn't produce any leads either. They were pretty much as expected, too – pizza one night, a grocery store for soda and snacks, beachwear for him, his wife and the kids they bought at a local store shortly after arriving.

I thought again about the possibility that they might have had some kind of interaction with someone at one of those shops or places that inexplicably led to their murders. But it was much more likely that the motivation for the killings had been something – and someone – in Lavelle's past as a doctor.

I knew I would have to take a deep dive into his life and work background in New York City in hopes of tracking down what that might be.

I was able to access the emails of Thomas Lavelle and the rest of his family. Everyone – except the little boy, of course – had phones. A computer and a couple of tablets were also found in the rooms at The Beach House. I started with that: going through all the emails, texts and social media posts we could access.

Fortunately, the devices weren't password protected. Like a lot of people, the Lavelles didn't require a pass code to access them. That made it easy.

But the problem was there wasn't much useful information there.

Lavelle's emails mostly consisted of business correspondence for his medical practice – the exchanges all seemed pretty routine, none of them particularly interesting or significant to the investigation. He had been in touch with his office the entire time he'd been here. But just about appointments when he got back, follow-ups on patients and ordering various medical supplies. There were no threats or warnings, no smoking gun of any kind I could see.

The same with his wife Nancy. Most of her correspondence seemed to be telling people about how beautiful it was on Martha's Vineyard and how excited they were to be all sharing it as a family. Nothing to suggest any imminent danger. She talked in one of the last emails to her mother and father about their plans to go to the antique store the next day, the day she and her husband and three of their children would be murdered.

The two other girls besides Karin, eleven and thirteen years old, seemed to be involved in playing online games with dungeons and warriors and that kind of stuff with a host of other people. Mostly their own age, it sounded like. It was hard to believe that had anything to do with what happened. Hard to believe that an eleven- or a thirteen-year-old girl was capable of doing anything to antagonize someone so much it bought down that kind of violent retaliation against her and her family.

Karin Lavelle's social media presence, on the other hand, proved more interesting.

Mostly because she didn't have one.

No emails, Twitter, Facebook or anything else I could find on any computer or iPad in the Lavelle rooms at The Beach House. Hard to believe a fifteen-year-old girl wouldn't be online anywhere these days.

Did she for some reason delete everything before she disappeared?

Or did someone else erase it all for their own reasons?

The other problem was there was no phone for Karin Lavelle. We looked everywhere for it. Inside and outside of The Beach House. But it never turned up. I'd been hoping that might give us some kind of clue as to what happened to her before her family was massacred. On the plus side, the fact that there was no phone suggested she had taken it with her. Which meant she could have left voluntarily. But why? And why hadn't she returned?

I've covered missing persons cases before. Back in New York City when I was with the NYPD, and here on Martha's Vineyard more recently with the teenage girls' disappearances. They were the toughest cases to do on this job. Especially when they involved young girls like Karin Lavelle, who were vulnerable to so many of the horrors of the world that we all lived in.

The lesson I'd learned from veteran cops in New York City was that missing person cases were even worse than murders. With a murder you had a body; with a missing person you just had unanswered questions. Was the person dead? Were they abducted? Did they leave voluntarily for some reason? Are they injured or incapacitated and need help? I only could hope we could get answers about that for Karin Lavelle.

I knew one thing though.

Something else I'd learned over the years as a police officer.

The longer a missing person was gone, the greater the odds against ever finding them.

When I was a detective with the NYPD, we had what we called the forty-eight-hour window on major crime cases. If it took longer than forty-eight hours to solve the case, a lot of the trail of evidence or leads quickly dried up.

Our forty-eight hours was almost up.

I was running out of time.

And a young girl's life was at stake…

CHAPTER 10

"What can you tell us about your son-in-law?" I asked Walt and Elizabeth Hood.

"Tom was one of the most esteemed and respected doctors in New York," Mrs. Hood said. "He had a flourishing practice, an impeccable reputation, he was in demand as a speaker at medical conferences and he was able to provide a wonderful life for my daughter and their children."

"Was he a nice guy?" I asked her.

"What?"

"What kind of man was he?"

"He… he was a very nice person."

"So he was perfect?"

"Well, no one is perfect."

"Why are you asking all these questions?" her husband said. "My son-in-law and his family – my daughter, my grandchildren – were the victims here. He's not a criminal. Why are you trying to make it seem as if he did something wrong?"

Walt and Elizabeth Hood had calmed down a bit after the scene in the hospital with the mystery girl who they discovered was not their granddaughter. But they were upset again now. I didn't want to do anything to push them over the emotional edge. So I tried to keep them on side as best I could.

"I'm looking for a motive," I told them. "Some reason – no matter how crazy or far-fetched – for someone to do something like this. There is no suggestion of robbery or material gain.

Nothing in the place appears to be missing. But the motive of the attack – I know it's difficult to think about, but it is important to the investigation – suggests this was a crime of passion. An angry person out for revenge. But why? Who would be that mad at Doctor Lavelle? Or anyone else in the family?"

"Anyone else? You're not suggesting my daughter could be the reason?"

"Probably not. Because the attack seemed to be aimed at Doctor Lavelle much more than her. He was stabbed many, many times and appears to have been physically beaten too. She died from a single blow. But I need to check out everything I can about everyone in the family. That includes your daughter."

"She was a wonderful mother to her children," Elizabeth Hood said. "And she had a successful career too. She was a lawyer. She'd work all day at her job with a law firm in the city, then still take plenty of time to be with her children. Until they had the baby last year. She stopped going into the law firm's office every day after that. She worked at home so she could be a full-time mother. That was what my daughter was like. There's no reason anyone would want to kill her."

"Tell us about the children," I said.

"Tell you what?" Walt Hood sighed. "The oldest girl – Karin, the one we're still trying to find – is only fifteen. The other two were eleven and thirteen. And the baby was little more than a year old. How could they have anything do with what happened? You're wasting your time with this line of questioning."

I had one more difficult thing to bring up.

"What was the marriage like?"

"Their marriage was fine."

"How fine? Is there any possibility of extramarital affairs? If your son-in-law was playing around, if he was involved in any kind of romantic entanglement with another woman that might explain—"

"Please stop it, Detective," Elizabeth Hood yelled at me. "Just stop that talk now. My son-in-law was not playing around with anyone. He loved my daughter. He loved their children. He was a fine man, an esteemed doctor, a good husband and father…"

"Right. Like you said, he was perfect, right? Well, maybe not totally perfect. No one is perfect, you told me. Not even your son-in-law. So tell me how he wasn't perfect."

Walt Hood looked over at his wife, hesitating before answering me. She nodded.

"Look, Tom sometimes could be a bit pretentious. A bit pompous and full of himself. It was like he knew more than anyone else. He was never wrong. Of course, no one is right all the time. There were a couple of times when Tom's refusal to back down from something – even when he was clearly wrong – caused him problems."

"What kind of problems?"

"There's been a couple of malpractice suits against him."

"From people he treated for heart conditions?"

"Yes. As you know, heart surgery is not always successful, there's a lot of potential pitfalls and complications. When that happened, patients can get very angry. And the person they direct that anger against in many cases is the doctor who's been treating them. Do you think this could have something to do with what happened?"

"It's certainly possible. The idea that a patient might have been out for revenge for something done to them, or, even more likely, to a loved one is a very credible scenario we need to look at thoroughly."

"But why would they kill our daughter and grandchildren too?"

I shook my head. I didn't understand that either, of course. "Maybe they didn't mean to kill them. Maybe they were just in the way, and they were collateral damage, as difficult as that might be to accept. Maybe they were afraid the family would identify them. Or maybe whoever did this was in such a rage of violence that they wanted to kill everyone there, not just your son-in-law."

"Except for the girl that was there."

"Right."

"Do you have any idea who she is or why she was there yet?"

"Not at the moment."

"Or the whereabouts of my granddaughter Karin?"

"No. But we still have reason to hope she is alive somewhere. We're using every resource we have to look for your granddaughter, Mr. and Mrs. Hood. It is our top priority right now. Along with finding who did this to your daughter and family. You have my word on that."

"What will you do next?"

"We want to talk to your son-in-law's patients. As many of them as we can track down. Can you help us with that?"

Walt Hood looked over at his wife, who hesitated for a few seconds, but then nodded. He turned back to me.

"All right, I'll get in touch with his office and see if I can get them to open up his patient files for you, Detective."

"Thank you," I told him. "I still think that's the most likely motive for these murders. As crazy as that might sound. We just have to pinpoint a disgruntled patient who might be responsible for the murder of your daughter and her family. And to find your granddaughter, Karin, wherever she is."

CHAPTER 11

There was a sign in the homicide detectives squad room when I worked in New York City that said: "Get Your Ass Out of That Seat, Go Knock on Doors!" You see it in a lot of police stations. It was a simple reminder that pounding the pavement is still the most effective way to solve a murder case. It was true in a big city like New York. And I had no reason to think it wasn't true too in a small town like Cedar Cliffs on Martha's Vineyard.

So I decided to go back to the first door on this case.

The Beach House.

I started at the front door of where the Lavelles were staying, pushing it open and walking inside. There had been no sign of forced entry of the door before the murders. That meant that someone, presumably Lavelle himself, had let the intruder into the place. Maybe because he knew them. Maybe because he felt he had no reason to fear them. Or maybe he just opened the door without thinking, presuming there was no danger of crime in a place like Martha's Vineyard.

It wasn't hard to figure out what happened next. Lavelle's body had been found slumped against a wall not far from the door, stabbed seventeen times, with what appeared to be defensive wounds on his hands and forearms. He'd fought back against the attacker, trying to protect himself and his family. But it was no use as he was stabbed over and over and died there.

His wife Nancy must have heard his cries during the struggle and come running to help him. The attacker turned on her then, chasing her down the hall as she ran for her life and stabbing her to death with a single fatal wound. Why one time with her? Maybe the attacker realized she was dead and wanted to hurry and deal with the rest of the family.

There was no way of knowing the exact chronology of what happened next. But the attacker presumably proceeded to kill the two girls in one bedroom, then the little boy in the other bedroom. I figured he probably did the girls first because they might have fled.

I put on a pair of gloves and began examining the blood splatter throughout the house. There was a lot of it, I already knew that. But now I noticed something I hadn't seen before. The blood was splattered around differently in various spots.

And not the way it should be.

There was a lot of blood around the spot where Thomas Lavelle's body had been, which was expected. But there was also a substantial amount of blood on the floor and walls around the place where his wife died, even though she'd only been stabbed a single time, not seventeen times like Lavelle was.

On the other hand, there was almost no blood in the bedroom where the little boy's body was found, even though he had been stabbed a number of times. The only possible explanation I could think of was that the little boy had been stabbed at the same spot where the mother's body lay, then moved back to the bedroom afterward. But why?

There was something else strange I noticed now too. All of the rooms seemed in good order, with no sign of robbery or anything like that. Except one. The room where the two girls had been. It was in complete disarray. Clothes hurled everywhere, drawers open and lying on the floor – like someone was searching for something in there.

There were three beds in the room so it appeared all of the daughters had been sleeping in that bedroom while they were there. But, when I went through the clothes I could find in the mess, it seemed like they belonged to the younger girls. Nothing that would seem to fit the fifteen-year-old who was obviously bigger than her sisters.

So where was Karin Lavelle's clothing? Where was her phone? If all that wasn't here, that meant either someone else had taken it – or she had done that herself. Meaning she might have left voluntarily. Either before or after the murders.

I looked again too at the message on the wall, written in the victims' blood: "No One Here Gets Out Alive." The old Jim Morrison mantra. Except that wasn't true, was it? The girl we found here survived. So, as far as we knew so far, did Karin Lavelle, even if we had no idea where she was right now.

Strange thing is I knew all about the phrase, even before Bowers talked about the background of the Jim Morrison song lyric. My old NYPD partner Tommy Ferraro had been a big Morrison/Doors fan – and he sometimes said it before we went into some hairy situation on the street. "No one here gets out alive," Tommy would say and laugh, and I'd laugh too when he said that. It broke the tension of the moment back then. Now though it didn't seem so funny.

Walking back through the hallway to the living room, I thought again too about the way Nancy Lavelle's hands were clasped together as if they were in prayer when we found her body here. Was that just an accident? Was she praying for her life and the lives of her family? Or had someone staged her hands that way in death, for some sick bizarre reason?

When I was finished with the rooms, I locked the place up and went to the manager's office. The same woman, Lily Knowlton, was there again. She was as strange looking as she'd been the first day I saw her – dressed again completely in black, and with tattoos and body jewelry that gave her a really Gothic look. Her skin was very pale white too, which was even more noticeable in contrast with the black clothing and her own dark hair. Because of all that – and maybe because her name was Lily –she reminded me of Lily Munster from those old Munster Family reruns. I half-expected Herman Munster or Grandpa to pop in through the door at any minute.

Lily Knowlton didn't look happy to see me. She'd seen enough police around there, she told me.

"When can we get in there to clean up and rent those rooms again?" she asked.

"This is an ongoing crime scene investigation at the moment," I said.

"Well, this is costing us a lot of money. Those rooms are just sitting empty. Not to mention the guests in other rooms who are freaked out by police swarming around everywhere and asking them questions—"

"It's an ongoing investigation," I repeated. "We will unseal the crime scene as soon as possible. But right now our priority is to ascertain who did this and to find out the whereabouts of the missing Lavelle girl that was staying there."

She nodded. Reluctantly. But she understood there wasn't much else that could be done about the situation right now. I asked her again about security video. But she said the only security camera was the one here in the lobby and the adjoining manager's office, plus one in the parking lot outside – nothing for any of the rooms. Nothing on those cameras had shown us anything unusual. Lily said they were talking about installing more cameras, but hadn't gotten around to it yet.

I asked her a few more questions about The Beach House, mostly to make conversation, but also to pick up whatever information I could. You never knew when something would turn out to be valuable.

"This place wasn't around when I was growing up on the island," I said. "How long has it been here?"

"Well, the hotel itself was built about fifteen years ago."

"It's a nice place," I said.

"Yes, the idea was to provide luxury accommodations for people who could afford it – but didn't want to rent a house or cottage while they were here. Plus, they get all the amenities. Room service, maids, everything you'd expect in a first-class hotel."

"And it's been successful?"

"It struggled a bit at first when it was just a hotel. But then a few years ago, we opened The Beach House restaurant as part of the complex here. The restaurant helped attract people to the hotel, and vice versa. Best move we ever made was this restaurant."

"And you started the restaurant from scratch?" I knew from my father's restaurant business how hard that was to do. "Impressive."

"Actually, we took over another restaurant on the island, then moved it here and renamed it The Beach House. It was called Anchors."

"Never heard of that one either," I said. "Must have been after my time here."

"It used to have another name. But the owner died and it got sold to the people who opened it as Anchors. That all happened a few years ago."

"What was the original restaurant?"

"The Vineyard Grille. Did you know that one?"

The Vineyard Grille.

I sure knew about that.

The Vineyard Grille was the restaurant my father owned.

Damn, that was a weird coincidence.

CHAPTER 12

Teena Morelli and I were hanging out in the Black Dog Bar in Cedar Cliffs. Talking about the case because finding out the answers – who massacred the Lavelle family, the identity of the girl we found there and, most importantly of all, the whereabouts of the missing Lavelle daughter – was all that mattered right now.

"The thing that's the most shocking about these murders, besides the actual killings themselves, of course, is the viciousness of the crime," Teena said. "These people weren't just murdered, they were massacred. Stabbed repeatedly, some of the wounds presumably coming even after they were dead. Who does something like that? Drug dealers, maybe? Maybe Lavelle was involved in drug dealing and pissed someone off by not paying up or stealing a drug shipment. It could be someone like the Russian Mob or a Mexican cartel boss out for revenge."

"Wait a minute, you think the Russian Mob or a Mexican cartel is here on our beautiful little island?"

"It's possible. Drugs can lead to this kind of violence."

She was drinking a Corona beer, which was her usual drink of choice. I was drinking a Diet Coke.

Funny thing about me and drinking. Even when I wasn't drinking, like I wasn't drinking these days, I still liked hanging out in bars. Sure, I know how strange it sounds to some people to understand how an alcoholic can be comfortable just hanging out in a bar and not drinking. But not for me. I liked the ambience, the crowds, I liked everything about being in a bar. Even if I was only drinking Diet Coke. So I still spent a lot of time in a place like the Black Dog. It didn't matter if other people were drinking, and I wasn't. If I was going to have a drink, I could just go home and down that bottle of vodka in my house.

When I attended AA meetings for a while back in New York City, I remembered one woman telling a story about how she'd stayed sober for two years while working as a cocktail waitress in a bar. Then one day, when she was on vacation and staying at a remote mountain cabin, she suddenly got in her car and drove for ninety minutes in a blinding snowstorm to the nearest liquor store to buy a bottle of tequila.

The bottom line: it doesn't matter where you are. If you're going to drink, you'll drink.

"Okay, let's say it wasn't a Mexican cartel," Teena said. "Maybe it was the Mob. Maybe Lavelle crossed the Mob in some way…"

She sighed.

"Except the Mob wouldn't kill the whole family, would they? They'd just whack him. That's the Mafia code, you know: family is left alone, only the target is hit – no one else."

"Where did you hear that?"

"Uh, I think I saw it on *The Sopranos*."

"Maybe whoever did this didn't watch that episode. He didn't know the rules."

"Anyway, it could be that. Or it could be something else. I mean these kinds of violent killings didn't have to be done out of anger, it might have been about passion. Romantic passion and jealousy or betrayal."

"You think Lavelle was having an affair with someone and it went bad?"

"Or the wife was."

"Okay, maybe the wife could have been cheating, not the husband."

"Sure, I believe in equal opportunity when it comes to adultery."

"Then what about the girl? The teenage girl in the hospital who we have absolutely no idea who she is or what she was doing at the crime scene. How does she fit into this romantic passion murder theory of yours?"

She shrugged.

"Not a clue."

Teena was a colorful-looking character. She was a big woman, who worked out regularly so she had a lot of muscles that made her even more physically imposing. She dressed the part too. Right now she was in her normal attire of jeans, T-shirt with a leather vest, boots and a cowboy hat. Oh, and she also carried a small gun strapped to her ankle under one of her boots in addition to her sidearm.

I was much more traditional looking.

I guess we made kind of an odd couple as partners, me and Teena.

"Do you think the real Lavelle girl is still alive?" Teena asked me at one point.

"Yes, I do."

"Is that based on fact?"

"We don't have any facts to back that up – either way. You know that as well as I do, Teena."

"So it's positive thinking, huh?"

"Yeah, I guess I'm just a glass half full kind of detective." I shook my head. "I don't want her to be dead, Teena."

She asked about the list of patients for Dr. Lavelle that Walt and Elizabeth Hood said they would try to get from their son-in-law's office.

"They told me it was taking a bit of effort to get his office to give up the information. Even for them as his family. And even though they explained to the office that it's for a murder investigation. Patient/doctor confidentiality and all. I mean we could go to court for a warrant or whatever to get all the patient records in

Lavelle's files. But this way seems easier. I think the Hoods will be able to get those names for us very soon. Then we can start checking them all out."

"Great. That still seems to be our best lead to pursue in hopes of finding someone with a motive for revenge enough to want Lavelle and, as inconceivable as it seems, his whole family dead."

I nodded in agreement.

"Yeah, it's not hard to imagine a doctor making enemies. Especially a heart surgeon. Not all people with bad hearts are going to survive, or recover enough to live a normal life. So they – or members of their family or friends – might well be angry about that. And who better to be angry at than the doctor who couldn't cure their problem? That's really the only potential motive we have right now."

I told Teena then about the fact that The Beach House used to be the same restaurant that my father owned here.

"What do you think that means?" she asked.

"Nothing, of course."

"Just a weird coincidence, huh?"

"Has to be."

"I thought you always said that a police officer shouldn't believe in coincidences. That there was always a reason for everything."

"Sometimes coincidences do happen." I shrugged.

CHAPTER 13

We got our first break in the case the next day when we found the murder weapon.

Actually, we found two murder weapons.

Both were in a field of grass and bushes not far from The Beach House. Presumably the killer – or killers – had dropped them there after carrying out the murders inside.

The first weapon was a bayonet. A fancy, chrome-plated bayonet. Like a soldier would carry with his rifle. It was sixteen inches long, and a four-inch grip-on handle was attached to it so it could be wielded by hand.

The second weapon was smaller, but even more lethal looking. A curved knife with a razor sharp, jagged-edge blade that definitely looked like it could do serious damage.

"That's a real combat knife," Dave Bowers said when he saw it. "The curved shape, the jagged edge on the blade – in the right hands that can immobilize a person in seconds."

"How do you know all this?" I asked him.

"I read a lot."

"Seriously?"

"I did a stint in the army reserves. I thought about joining Special Forces at one point. We did a lot of hand-to-hand combat in training. They told us about using knives like these to kill or maim someone. I never have, of course – but I learned enough to know that it can make someone who knows how to use a weapon like this a real killing machine."

"So you think this was the main weapon used?"

"Right. The bayonet was there as a backup. Either for the killer or a second person who helped. They were specifically chosen as the best way to kill these people."

"Why not just a gun and shoot them?"

"This way is more personal," Bowers said. "Maybe that was important to whoever did this."

He was right about that. These killings of Thomas Lavelle and his family sure did seem personal. Everything about them did.

"Fingerprints?" I asked.

"Someone tried to wash the blood off on both weapons, and probably the fingerprints too," Teena said. "Maybe we'll get lucky with something on the fingerprints. A lot of the blood is still there, too. We don't have a specific comparison on the blood yet, but it's pretty likely the blood will match members of the Lavelle family. Not much doubt about it, these are the weapons that killed them all."

"Who found them?" I asked.

"An eleven-year-old boy."

"You're kidding me."

"Nope. Kid was out playing in the field and came across the bayonet. Later, when we went back there to scour the area, we found the curved knife."

"Where's the boy now?"

"In one of the rooms here with his father. You want to talk to them?"

"I sure do."

The boy's name was Jonathan Sievers, and he actually looked younger than even eleven. He was short, kind of scrawny and had tousled blond hair that he kept nervously running his hands through. Being in a police station and getting questioned by cops was a pretty traumatic experience for an eleven-year-old. His father had his arm around him, and was trying to keep him calm.

I tried to make the boy feel as at ease as I could too.

"Thanks so much for helping us out here, Jonathan," I said.

"Uh-huh."

"Can we leave soon?" the father asked. "My son's getting very upset about all this."

"Just a few questions, okay?"

"Okay, I guess."

"Do you want anything to drink or eat?" I said to Jonathan.

"No, I'm fine now."

"You're sure?

"Yes, they gave me a coke and a bag of chips when I first got here. But I already told the other police everything I know. Why do I have to tell you too?"

"Well, I'm the lead detective on this case. And we want to make certain you didn't inadvertently leave out any details that might help us solve the murder. I assume you're familiar with the case and why what you found may turn out to be so important to us."

"He wasn't at first," the father said. "But I explained it to him. And then I was the one who said he needed to turn the weapon into you."

It turned out that the boy had found the bayonet a day earlier and taken it home with him. He kept it in his bedroom during that time. It wasn't until his father found it and asked him what it was – and where he found it – that everything started to happen. That's when the father called us – and we later found the second weapon, the curved knife, in the same grassy area as the bayonet.

"Did you see anyone there? Either when you found the bayonet or even before, in the same area, that might have left it?"

"No, there was no one there. I was by myself."

"Did it look like someone had made an effort to hide the bayonet?"

"Not at all. It was very easy to see there. It was in plain sight on top of some weeds. Anyone could see it there. I guess it just happened to be me."

"And the blood on it? Didn't that bother you?"

He shrugged. "I thought it was just from killing animals or something. Can I go home now?"

I asked the boy a few more questions, but there wasn't much more to find out from him. He was an eleven-year-old kid who found something he thought was interesting. The bottom line though was we now had the murder weapon. Or two of them. Thanks to this kid. Now it was up to us to find out more.

I thanked him and his father for their help. After they left, I talked with Teena about the two weapons, trying to figure out exactly what we had here.

"Doesn't it all seem a bit strange to you?" I said to her.

"Strange how?"

"This is an island surrounded by water. If you wanted to get rid of a murder weapon, why not throw it in the ocean? Or off a bridge into one of the lakes or ponds around here?"

"Maybe the killer was in a hurry to get rid of the incriminating evidence."

"Even so, it was only a short walk from The Beach House where the killings took place to the Cedar Cliffs ferry terminal. They could have dropped the bayonet and the jagged, curved knife into the water there. No one would ever find either one that way. Instead, they're placed in a spot where someone is bound to find them sooner or later."

"I see your point."

"Also, didn't we search the area around The Beach House?"

"Of course."

"So why didn't we find the weapons then? I mean we don't come across them until this kid stumbles across them while he's out playing."

"But we now do have the murder weapons."

"Yes, we probably do."

"I guess we just got lucky."

"Or maybe it was more than luck."

"You think…"

"Yeah, I think someone wanted us to find these weapons."

CHAPTER 14

We had finally gotten a list of patients who'd been treated by Dr. Lavelle from his in-laws, Walt and Elizabeth Hood.

Teena and I started to work our way through the names of patients on it. The idea was to contact them all by phone or track them down online to find out what they might tell us. Bowers and Meg Jarvis were helping us, as best they could. It was a long list. And even if we happened to stumble across the right person they weren't likely to confess to murder over the phone or online.

We had to try to pick up clues from what they said, and maybe what they didn't say, in answer to our questions.

Many of them had good things to say about Dr. Lavelle. There was certainly no question about his qualifications for the job. Definitely a top-flight heart specialist. Several people did say they found his manner off-putting. That he wasn't willing to listen to them or discuss their questions, preferring to tell them what needed to be done without any argument. Sort of like the Hoods had said about their son-in-law. But that seemed a small price to pay to have one of the best heart surgeons in the business treating you. At least that was what most of his patients we talked with felt about Lavelle.

There were some interesting cases though.

One involved a six-year-old boy who had a heart defect. Lavelle urged immediate surgery for the boy. The medical records showed the surgery had seemed to go well, at least in the beginning. But there was also a notation that the boy died six months later.

I reached his father by phone and asked him about the surgery and how he felt about Thomas Lavelle.

The man praised Dr. Lavelle, saying the operation had allowed his little boy Isaac to breathe normally for the first time in his life – and even run and play a bit like other kids his age. Sadly, he said Isaac had other health issues and was very frail. That winter he caught a bad case of flu, which spread to his lungs and killed him.

"But you know what makes me feel better about it?" the man said. "More at peace with his loss? Isaac had six good months before he died. He had some time when he could enjoy being a little boy and have fun. That's all because of Doctor Lavelle. I will always be grateful to him for giving that to Isaac. I can't believe someone would do something so terrible to a wonderful man like him."

Well, so much for that lead.

There were several malpractice cases that had been filed against Lavelle. Not unusual, malpractice suits were a part of the business doctors had to deal with. I knew that from previous cases. Still, I wanted to check all of them out.

One that was still pending involved a Queens man whose wife had died during heart surgery performed by Dr. Lavelle.

"Did I kill the doctor for revenge?" the husband asked when I got him on the phone. "That's really what you're asking me, isn't it? Why would I do that?"

"Well, your wife died while he was operating on her."

"Yes. And I did file a multi-million-dollar lawsuit against him and the hospital over that. We were almost at the point of settling on a deal right now. Until Lavelle died. Why would I jeopardize that money settlement by killing the guy? This is just going to complicate everything with the lawsuit. Besides, I never had any real bitterness or anger against Lavelle himself. My lawyer said filing a lawsuit was routine in cases like this. And the money would be paid by his insurance company, not the doctor himself. I didn't have anything personal against Lavelle in all this. I didn't hate the guy. Certainly not enough to kill him or his family. That's all plain crazy."

"How can I be sure of that?"

"You want to question me, go ahead. Knock yourself out. You're just wasting your time though."

I shook my head after I hung up. This was frustrating. I told that to Teena, Bowers and Meg, who were all making similar kinds of calls. I still was convinced there had to be something in Dr. Thomas Lavelle's background in New York that would give us a motive for these murders.

"It doesn't have to be about a patient," Teena said. "Could be someone with a grudge that has nothing to do with the medical stuff."

"Personal, you think?"

"Why not?"

"Let's go back to the sex idea," I said. "Maybe Lavelle was playing around on the side. Things got ugly. Either with the person he was seeing or a husband or boyfriend who was upset about the affair. I mean we said from the very beginning this looked like a crime of passion. So why couldn't it be about sex? Sex gone very bad?"

"The Hoods said their son-in-law and their daughter were happily married," Meg pointed out.

"If you were having an affair, would you tell your in-laws about it?" Teena asked.

"Teena's right," I said. "We need to look into Thomas Lavelle's personal life too. Maybe it wasn't such a happy marriage."

But, before we had a chance to do that, Dave Bowers came up with another lead from the list of patients Lavelle had treated.

A big lead.

"Jesus!" Bowers shouted.

"What?"

"He operated not long ago on Albert Ruggerio."

"Ruggerio, the big mobster?" I asked.

"The one and only."

"What happened?"

"It looks like it didn't go well. Ruggerio is now an invalid. Stuck in a wheelchair."

"Interesting."

"It gets even better," Bowers said. "Guess where Albert Ruggerio is at the moment? Right here on Martha's Vineyard."

CHAPTER 15

A place like Martha's Vineyard attracted a lot of wealthy, powerful people to it. Wall Street financiers, prominent business tycoons, celebrities – all of them with plenty of money and influence. Not all of them made their mark in the world by being perfect citizens, sometimes they skirted the line between what was legal and what wasn't to get what they wanted. And then there were the ones who went way over that line. Men like Albert Ruggerio.

I'd heard of him before. Big Al Ruggerio. His crime family worked out of New York City, when I was with the NYPD. I'd never had any direct dealings with him or any of his people. But I remembered being intrigued when I heard once he had a summer house on Martha's Vineyard, the place where I'd grown up. But that was my only real interest in him until now. I hadn't heard anything about Ruggerio in a long time. I assumed he'd either retired or was dead. But I discovered instead that he'd been sick.

Ruggerio had a bad heart. They called him "Big Al" not just because he was an important underworld guy, but also because he weighed a lot. That finally caught up with him. He went to Dr. Thomas Lavelle, who recommended open-heart surgery. Apparently, the surgery did not go well because Ruggerio was now supposed to be an invalid living here on the island. Had Lavelle messed up the surgery? And, even more importantly, did Ruggerio believe Lavelle had messed up his surgery? Either way, it could be a motive for him to seek revenge, once he discovered Lavelle was here on Martha's Vineyard.

Ruggerio lived in a big house near Menemsha, an exclusive area on the north side of the island. A lot of important, well-known people lived there. Ted Danson and Mary Steenburgen had gotten married there. A Mob guy like Ruggerio didn't really seem to fit into the neighborhood. But money buys you a lot of things wherever you go, even in a place like Martha's Vineyard.

We talked about what we knew about Albert Ruggerio.

"He's got a lot of rage," I said. "That's what I always heard about him when I was in New York. He supposedly has a terrible temper. The slightest affront can set him off. This is a real vicious, cold-blooded guy."

"Well, no one's perfect," Teena said. She was trying to act calm and cool, but I knew she was pretty shocked over the idea that we might have to go after someone like Ruggerio for these murders. Hell, so was I.

"The worst story about Ruggerio I remember from my New York days was when he supposedly wiped out a group of rival Mob bosses over dinner.

"Ruggerio invited them all to his restaurant in Brooklyn. He talked about brokering a peace deal between the different underworld factions; ending Mob gang wars; sharing in the illegal profits they made equally; and a lot of other stuff like that. They all dined on steak and lobster and fine wine. When the meal was over, Ruggerio handed out expensive cigars for an after-dinner smoke. Just as they were lighting up, Ruggerio excused himself and stepped outside.

"As soon as he was gone, a half-dozen of his men came in with automatic weapons and blew away everyone in the room. All the other major bosses were dead. There's a classic picture from the front page of the New York tabloids of one of them on the floor covered in blood, with the cigar still sticking out of his mouth."

"Damn," Teena said.

"But it didn't have to be Mob business like that for Ruggerio to kill people without remorse or even a real reason. Anything – the slightest perceived slight or insult – could ignite a violent rage in the man. Like one time he got into some kind of a dispute with a neighbor. The best anyone could figure out was the argument was over a garbage can. The neighbor's garbage can was left on Ruggerio's yard. Ruggerio told the guy to never put the garbage can there again. The next time the garbage can was in the same place again. Except the neighbor wasn't. A sanitation worker later found him dumped in a pile of trash a few blocks away. And he was stuffed into the same garbage can he'd had the dispute over with Ruggerio."

Teena shook her head in amazement.

"All over a garbage can?"

"Yeah, like I said, he's the kind of guy that can blow up and get violent over anything, from what I understand."

"If he gets that mad about a neighbor's garbage can, it's not hard to imagine him being pretty damn upset about a doctor who botched his heart surgery, is it? And Ruggerio never got charged for any of this stuff everyone says he did?"

"Oh, he's been arrested. A few times over the years. But the charges never stick. He claimed to know nothing about the Mob meeting massacre in the restaurant, said he'd gone into the restroom when it happened. And he had an alibi for the neighbor's death too, said he was out of town when the man was killed. He's always been sort of like John Gotti used to be – a Teflon Don. Nothing ever sticks to him long enough for a conviction."

"Well, they got Gotti in the end," Teena pointed out.

"But not Ruggerio. Not yet. But maybe this will turn out to be the time he screwed up. By killing Thomas Lavelle and his family."

"And you figure that the Cedar Cliffs Police Department – which means basically you and me – can bring this guy down even though the entire New York City police force has never been able to do it. How exactly do you plan on us doing that? Where exactly do we start, Abby?"

*

The best place to start was by getting more information about Ruggerio from the NYPD. More specifically I needed to get that information from the NYPD's Organized Crime Control Bureau. I wanted to find out everything I could about Big Al from them.

But I didn't work for the NYPD anymore so I couldn't call up the Organized Crime people and ask them. I needed someone who was still with the NYPD to do that for me. So I did what I always used to do when I worked as a cop in New York and needed help – I turned to my partner there. At least the partner there who was still alive.

After Tommy Ferraro died, I was paired for my last year or so on the force with Vic Gelman. He was a decent guy, although a lot different than Tommy Ferraro. Tommy had been a good cop, but a kind of a wild man too. Always pushing the envelope and taking chances, right up until the last time he did it outside a building in Chelsea, which got him shot and killed.

Gelman was a much more "by the book" guy who was steady, if not spectacular. Probably the best partner for me to have after Tommy, and we got along well for that last year, even though I was going through a lot of emotional trauma at the time. Both over Tommy's death and dealing with my drinking and disintegrating marriage to Zach.

I called Gelman up now.

"How's it going up there, Abby?" he asked me.

"It's not exactly what I expected," I said with a laugh, mentioning both the teenage sex/murder scandal not long before and now this new mass murder case. "It's an adjustment from New York in a lot of ways for me, but I'm doing the best I can."

I told him a bit about my life here. My house. How I'd learned to sail. And, most of all, about the Cedar Cliffs Police Department. How my commanding officer, Chief Barry Wilhelm, was kind of a jerk. On the good side though, I said I had a good partner here in Teena Morelli.

After a bit more catch up, I told him what I wanted. He already knew some of the details about the Lavelle case; he said he'd seen me at a press conference talking about it on one of the news channels. He told me he knew someone in Organized Crime and promised to get back to me with whatever he could find out.

"You really think Ruggerio did this?"

"He's my best lead – my only possible suspect – at the moment."

"One thing that I'm sure you're aware of: the killing of an entire family, that just doesn't sound like a typical Ruggerio Mob hit."

"I understand, Vic. But Ruggerio is the only one here I can find with a motive for killing Thomas Lavelle. Plus, there's not a lot of killers on this island. Albert Ruggerio is a killer. And he was on the island when the killings took place. I believe there has to be a connection between him and the Lavelle murders."

CHAPTER 16

The sensational story of the Lavelle family murders, coming so soon after the other big crime case on Martha's Vineyard during the summer, had gotten a lot of national attention on the news channels and elsewhere.

Which meant I was getting a lot of attention again, too.

I heard from plenty of people I hadn't talked to in a while, including ones I knew from the NYPD during my days back in New York. But the one call that surprised me, and I really appreciated, was from Rikki Ferraro. She was the widow of my dead NYPD partner, Tommy Ferraro.

"I wanted to check in and make sure you're okay, Abby," Rikki Ferraro said to me on the phone when she called and got me at the Cedar Cliffs station. "Be careful. Whatever is happening up there sounds very dangerous."

"Tommy always taught me to keep my head down," I told her, trying to hold back the emotion I felt whenever Tommy Ferraro's name came up in my life.

"He would be very proud of you."

"Thanks, Rikki. That means a lot to me. It really does."

I asked her how she was doing in dealing with Tommy's death. It sounded awkward as soon as the words came out of my mouth, but I simply couldn't think of any better way to say it to her.

"It is what it is," she said with a sigh. "Isn't that the phrase people use these days for that kind of thing? Look, it's very painful and I miss him every day. But I know he's gone. And there's nothing

I, nothing any of us, can do about it. I think it's hardest for my kids. Tommy Jr. and Christina have to grow up without a father. But me, well, I try to remember the good times and keep busy with my work."

Rikki Ferraro was some kind of a therapist on Long Island where they lived. I never knew that much about her. She was always nice to me when we met, mostly I suppose because I was Tommy's partner. I'd tried to keep in touch with her for a while after he was killed, but we hadn't talked recently. I think I feared deep down that she might have blamed me for her husband's death. Although she didn't sound that way now.

"I worry about you, Abby," she said. "You're all alone up there. Here in New York, you and Tommy always had each other. You had each other's back, that's what Tommy always said. He protected you, and you protected him. I only hope there's someone like that there now for you."

Except I didn't have his back at the end.

I couldn't protect him.

The call from Tommy's wife brought all those memories rushing back to me.

Who could have ever imagined what happened that terrible night?

Tommy and I had responded to an armed robbery call at a sporting goods store in the Chelsea section of Manhattan. The store owner had been shot and killed. Witnesses said the gunman took whatever money was in the store – it turned out to be a paltry $26 – and fled, possibly into a nearby building where he might be hiding.

We could have waited for backup, but Tommy always hated waiting. He said he'd check out the building. He told me to wait by the car and cover him if anything went wrong. Tommy was a tough guy. He'd served in the army before joining the NYPD, and even did a tour in Afghanistan. He told me once how'd met his wife while he was in the army, and they'd decided being in the military wasn't the best way to raise a family. So he became a police officer instead. But Tommy still had a lot of the combat soldier in him, he was already ready to charge up the hill to take out the enemy.

He was about halfway to the building when I spotted a glint of something in a window. It could have been a gun, but I wasn't sure. And so I hesitated before drawing my own weapon. That moment of hesitation made all the difference. It was a gun, and the person with it opened fire on Tommy – killing him before I could even get my gun out of my holster. The gunman got away afterward. He turned out to be a low-level hood named Richie Briggs. Briggs was eventually caught, but that didn't really seem important to me anymore. My partner was dead, and a lot of people – maybe even including myself – blamed me for his death.

I'd been drinking quite a bit back then, and people in the NYPD knew about it. I wasn't drinking anything that night. But the question was whether my response to a life-and-death crisis had been affected in any way by alcohol. Also, there was still a lot of resentment toward women police officers on the street. For many old-guard people on the force, this was another example of how you couldn't trust a woman to protect a fellow officer in a crisis.

In the end, after an investigation was conducted, a police board ruled in my favor. They said there was no connection between my drinking and what happened that night. No evidence of alcohol in my blood. That I had done everything I could as a police officer, and that Tommy Ferraro's death was unavoidable.

So that should have been the end of it.

Well, not really.

Because I wasn't sure.

What if all the alcohol I'd been drinking then really did slow my reflexes? What if I had responded differently when I saw the glint of that gun in the window? Those were the questions I still had to answer for myself. Would Tommy still be alive today? I wasn't sure about the answer to that then, and I still wasn't sure today.

And so because of that, I guess, and a lot of other things, including the breakup of my marriage to Zach, I left New York City for what I hoped would be a simpler life back here in Martha's Vineyard where I grew up.

I was still a cop here, though.

Just a different kind of cop than I had been back in New York City.

But I wanted to be the best cop that I could be because, as corny as it might sound, I believed that was the best way to honor the memory of my fallen partner, Tommy Ferraro.

When I got home that night, I opened up a drawer and took out a scrapbook of big cases that I'd been involved with over the years.

Many of them were from New York, of course, when I was making front-page headlines as a hotshot female NYPD homicide detective. There was the time I singlehandedly stopped a bank robbery. The time I talked a woman out of committing suicide by jumping off the Empire State Building. The time I busted a big underworld gambling operation and got my picture on Page One of the *New York Post* leading the head of the city's biggest Mob family in handcuffs during a perp walk outside my station house. And the time I tracked down and arrested a man who'd abducted and killed a six-year-old boy on his way to school.

The most recent media coverage came from the Martha's Vineyard case when I'd solved the abduction/murders of a series of teenage girls on the island. That one had gotten me headlines like: "BIG CITY COP COMES HOME, BUSTS TEEN SEX RING ON MARTHA'S VINEYARD."

I looked at a picture of Tommy again too. The picture of him standing by a car, his gun on his hip, looking every bit the ultimate tough, professional cop. I looked at this picture of Tommy a lot. I'm not sure why, I guess it made me feel there was still a part of him there with me. Tommy looked so happy and full of life standing there with me in that picture. I thought again about everything that happened that night in Chelsea. I thought about his wife and children alone back on Long Island. I thought about all the pain and remorse I'd felt about not being able to save him when he needed me to save him.

Then I put the picture of Tommy Ferraro and all the rest of those memories away.

It was time to go back to work.

I had a job to do.

Find Karin Lavelle and whoever killed her family.

That was the only thing that mattered now...

CHAPTER 17

Talking to a mobster like Albert Ruggerio was not going to be easy.

Especially when the topic was murders that he might have committed. But I had no choice. I had to find out as soon as possible what Ruggerio knew – or at least what I could find out from him.

So Teena and I drove out to his house on the western end of Martha's Vineyard the next day.

"You really think Ruggerio did it?" Teena asked in the car.

"He's got to be our best suspect right now. He had the motive, the only motive we've been able to find for anyone. He was mad at Lavelle for the heart surgery that left him in a wheelchair and he wanted revenge for that. Plus, we know about Ruggerio's violent record against people he was mad at for all sorts of lesser reasons in the past."

"There are still some things that don't make a lot of sense about Ruggerio for this. The most obvious one still being the killing of an entire family, kids and all – doesn't sound like a typical Ruggerio Mob hit."

She was right, of course.

"And there are plenty of other questions too. Why would a teenage girl be left there with the Lavelle family if it were a Ruggerio hit? And why was the other teenage girl from the family kidnapped or whatever – since she wasn't there at the time and hasn't shown up in any way since then?"

She was right about that too.

"And why stab them? Why not simply shoot them all, the way most mobster rub-outs happen? You don't see a lot of Mafia hit men using a knife. Certainly not when they're killing five separate people like this. That simply doesn't sound typical for Albert Ruggerio or the Mob."

"Maybe that's why Ruggerio had it done that way," I suggested. "To throw suspicion off of him. He wanted it to look like some crazy person massacred the family, instead of making it appear to be a Mob hit. So he did it with all the blood and gore and overkill, even writing the phrase 'No One Here Gets Out Alive' on the wall in their blood. All to make us think it wasn't him. That's possible, right?"

I wasn't planning to confront Ruggerio head-on with accusations about the Thomas Lavelle family murders. Not yet. I didn't have any real evidence to do that. But I might be able to shake something loose just by showing up at his door.

Except it didn't work out like that.

Teena and I were met by several men at the front gate outside Ruggerio's house when we arrived there. His security detail, no doubt. They didn't show any weapons, but I was sure they were carrying them. They wanted us to surrender our guns. Even after we showed them our credentials as officers with the Cedar Cliffs police and told them we needed to talk to Ruggerio. They said we couldn't carry any weapons beyond the front gate or anywhere on their property. We refused to give them up.

"We are police officers," I said. "We are fully authorized to carry weapons wherever we go. How about you guys? Are you carrying anything? Maybe we should search you."

"Any weapons on this property are legally registered," one of them said.

"Maybe so," Teena said. "But I'm sure we can find some violation of the law here, if we look hard enough. Is that really what you want? To get on the wrong side of the local law? We could bring in state police and even FBI to do a complete search of this place if we wanted. Or you could simply let us in there to do our job. Your choice."

It was a standoff like that for a few minutes.

Eventually, another man came out of the house. It wasn't Albert Ruggerio. This guy was much younger, probably in his forties. He had dark short-cropped hair, was dressed in an expensive suit and was very smooth looking. Clearly, one of the Ruggerio people outside had let him know about our presence here at the front gate.

"I'm afraid you'll have to leave the property," the guy said. "Mr. Ruggerio is not in any condition to receive visitors."

"Who are you?" I asked.

"I'm the head of security for Mr. Ruggerio."

"Do you have a name?"

"That's all you need to know."

"We are the police, you realize that?" Teena said.

He smiled. He knew exactly who we were. And he probably knew why we were there. But he didn't seem very worried. I had the feeling that this man had dealt with these kinds of situations before. Probably in New York. Whatever happened, he wasn't going to let the police intimidate him. Certainly not the tiny Cedar Cliffs police. That was his job. But we had our job to do, too.

"We have questions we need to ask Ruggerio," I told him.

"What kind of questions?"

"About the murder of Thomas Lavelle, his physician. The man who performed heart surgery on him recently. About the murders of Doctor Lavelle's family. And about their teenage daughter who is missing. I'm sure you're aware of the horrendous crime that occurred here on this island."

"I can assure you that Mr. Ruggerio knows nothing at all about any of that."

"That's not good enough. I want to talk to him directly."

He looked over at me now and flashed me a big smile. A phony one no doubt, but a big smile nevertheless. Yep, this guy was smooth.

"Detective…?"

"Pearce. Abby Pearce."

"Well, Detective Abby Pearce, Mr. Ruggerio isn't available to talk to anyone right now. And, as I've already informed you, he knows nothing about any of these matters you're investigating."

"I want to hear that from Ruggerio," I said one more time, even though I knew it was futile at this point.

"You'll need a warrant to do that. Until then, have a nice day, Detective Pearce. And it was nice meeting you."

He gave me one more big smile, then turned around and walked back to the house.

"Well, that was a waste of time," Teena said as we drove away.

"Maybe not."

"You figure we shook him up a bit?"

"That security guy will tell him we were there. That we know about the connection between him and Doctor Lavelle. That should bother him a little bit to know we're out here investigating. And that we'll be back."

"You figure we have enough to get a warrant to force him to talk to us? Maybe even bring him into the station?"

I shrugged. "Not yet."

"So what do we do next?"

"Keep looking for more evidence," I said.

CHAPTER 18

Evidence in a big murder case like this isn't always as dramatic as you see on TV or in the movies or in a mystery novel.

There's not always a smoking gun. Not always a confession. Not always an "ah-ha" moment where it all becomes clear to the investigator. Sometimes you have to put together evidence in a case piece by piece. Without knowing whether or not all the pieces you accumulate are important or not. But you don't want to overlook any of the pieces, or else the entire structure of the case could collapse.

I tried to think about missing pieces from the murders of Thomas Lavelle and his family.

Not just Albert Ruggerio and his connection to Thomas Lavelle.

But everything we knew so far about the case.

We had the murder weapon now, even if that hadn't really gotten us any closer to finding whoever used it to murder the Lavelles.

But what else was out there for us to go back and check on again in this case?

I finally thought of something.

"How about the maid who found the Lavelles?" I asked Teena.

"How about her?"

"Tell me again what she said."

"Not much. Not much more she could say. She let herself into the rooms to clean, she saw the blood-soaked body of Thomas Lavelle, then ran screaming out of the place to call 911 for help."

"Who interviewed the maid?"

"Bowers. I was busy with the crime scene. He got her story."

"Well, let's go talk to her again."

The maid, Betty Kubinski, was from Poland, and she was in her sixties. She'd been a schoolteacher for many years there. But then her daughter, who was also a schoolteacher in Poland, married an American. When the son-in-law got a job on Martha's Vineyard as an auto mechanic, the daughter left Poland to be here with him.

The mother followed her to America. Because the daughter wasn't an accredited teacher in the U.S., she couldn't get a job in any schools here yet. So she was taking college courses in education – commuting back and forth to the mainland on Cape Cod for them so she could get a teaching degree here. The mother took a job cleaning rooms at The Beach House to help pay for her college classes since most of the husband's earnings were needed to pay for the expensive cost of housing on Martha's Vineyard.

Betty Kubinski told us all this as Teena and I sat with her in a room at The Beach House. I let her talk for a while on her own. It was an old interrogation technique to help a person you wanted to interview feel comfortable.

"Take us through everything that happened the day you found the bodies, Mrs. Kubinski," I said finally.

"Call me Betty," she said.

"Of course." I smiled. "So what do you remember about that morning?"

"It's like I told the other officer," she said. "I went to the Lavelle rooms like I would any other rooms. I knocked, got no answer and then used my pass key to get in. That's when I saw… I saw everything that was inside."

"What time did you go to clean the rooms?" I asked.

"The first time?"

"What do you mean?"

"Well, I went once and I didn't go in. Then I went back again an hour or so later. That was about nine or nine fifteen, I think."

I looked over at Teena. She seemed surprised too. We'd never heard about her going there earlier.

"Why didn't you go inside the first time you were there?" I asked.

"There was a 'Do Not Disturb' sign."

"On the Lavelles' door?"

"Yes."

"At about eight a.m.?"

She nodded.

"I figured they were asleep or busy or something like that. So I left and did another room. When I got back, the 'Do Not Disturb' sign was still there. I knocked this time to ask if they wanted their rooms cleaned. When there was no answer, I assumed there was no one there – and they had forgotten to remove the 'Do Not Disturb' sign. That's when I let myself. And I saw him lying on the floor."

It wasn't hard to figure out what probably had happened. The killer had put that sign on the door. Wanted to make sure no one from the hotel came in during the time they were there. Then they left the "Do Not Disturb" sign up on their way out – to delay the discovery of the bodies for as long as possible and give the killer more time to get away.

We interrogated Betty Kubinski a lot more about all this but she said she couldn't really help us with any more details from that day.

"Do you remember anything unusual about the Lavelle family before that?" Teena asked.

"Unusual how?"

"Anything that happened? Anything you noticed that seemed odd or somehow out of the ordinary?"

"No. They seemed like very nice people."

"How about you?" I asked. "Did anything unusual or significant happen to you before that morning?"

Teena gave me a strange look. She had no idea where I was going with this. I didn't really either, but I figured it couldn't hurt to keep her talking. As it turned out, we did learn something interesting from Betty Kubinski.

"Just the usual crap," she said. "The manager, Lily Knowlton, is very tough to work for. She's always complaining about the work any of us do, if any guest finds any dirt in the room – that kind of stuff. But that day I was even more angry at her. I'd lost one of my uniforms. My maid uniform, you know. And then the Knowlton woman said she was going to make me pay for the one I couldn't find. She said she was going to take it out of my paycheck. Can you imagine that? I had a big argument with her about that. So I was pretty upset even before all this happened—"

"How did you lose your uniform?"

"I don't know. But when I went to the maids' area to put it on, I couldn't find it. The uniform was gone."

"Do you think someone stole it?"

"Who would want to steal a maid's uniform?" She laughed.

Someone who wanted to look like a maid, I thought to myself.

CHAPTER 19

"We were never sure how someone got into the Lavelle rooms," I said to Chief Wilhelm afterwards. "Sure, Lavelle might have just opened the door because he was on Martha's Vineyard and felt he was safe. But that might not have worked, he might still have hesitated before letting anyone inside. But not a hotel maid. Or at least someone who looked like a hotel maid. She's come there to clean the place, or so she tells him. He opens the door and lets her in."

"And she lets in the killer with her?"

"Maybe," I said. "Or maybe she was the killer."

"A woman?"

"Not likely, but still possible."

"And the missing maid's uniform wasn't found?"

"No, it never turned up."

"So how does this business about the maid's uniform help – where does that information leave us?"

"One step closer to finding the killer."

Wilhelm just grunted.

"What else?"

I told him then about Albert Ruggerio and his connection to Thomas Lavelle. This was the first time I'd mentioned it to Wilhelm. Mostly because I wasn't quite sure where it was leading. But I knew I had to inform him now about what I knew. I also told him about my trip out to Ruggerio's house with Teena to try to question him.

I could tell Wilhelm was really shocked and rattled to hear about this.

Dealing with someone like Albert Ruggerio as a potential suspect in a mass murder was way out of Wilhelm's league.

It was a lot different from handing out tickets for illegal parking or riding bikes on the sidewalk in Cedar Cliffs.

"You shouldn't have gone out there," he said when I was finished.

"I wanted to see if he could answer some questions about Thomas Lavelle and their relationship."

"Which he didn't."

"I didn't know that until I tried."

"You should have checked with me first."

"What would you have said if I did?"

"I would have said no, I wouldn't have let you go there."

Exactly, I thought to myself.

"He was Lavelle's patient," I said. "Lavelle apparently wasn't successful with the heart surgery he performed on him, leaving Ruggerio in a wheelchair. And Ruggerio is a violent man with a violent temper that has killed people for much less. That sure seems like probable cause to me for trying to question him."

"Anything else you haven't told me about this case?"

"Well, you know about the weapon. Or weapons. I've already told you about that. Except I don't think they're going to be of much help. No fingerprints, no DNA, no nothing from them that helps us. Like I said earlier, I figure someone deliberately left them there for us to find. As a dead end to follow in our investigation."

"Everything you have is a dead end," Wilhelm said. "When are you going to get some results? When are you going to come up with something that can help me solve this case?"

Me?

I wanted to tell him that this was the way a murder investigation worked. Piece by piece, until all the different pieces made sense.

I wanted to tell him that I understood about murder investigations even if he didn't.

But I didn't say that to Wilhelm.

No reason to get him more upset than he already was.

"What about the girl?" he asked. "What about Karin Lavelle?"

"Still missing."

"Make that your priority," he said. "Even if we can't solve the murders right away, we need to find that girl. Everyone keeps asking me about her – and where she might be. I want some answers, Pearce."

There was something else bothering Chief Wilhelm.

I could tell he wasn't finished with me.

I waited for him to figure out how to say it, which took a few more minutes.

"Let me talk to you about something else besides the basics of the case," Wilhelm said finally. "You're the face of this investigation, you're the face of this department right now. And, like you've said, we're under a lot of media scrutiny. I need to be sure that you're not going to do anything to embarrass us."

I understood now where this was going.

"Are you talking about my drinking?" I asked Wilhelm.

"That's right."

Sure, my drinking had been under control most of the time since I came back to Martha's Vineyard, but, when I first returned from New York to join the Cedar Cliffs police force, I had some drinks one night – I'm not sure exactly how many, I lost count – at a bar after I left the station.

I blacked out after that and woke up in my car sitting in a ditch off the highway, bleeding from a cut on my head. An ambulance took me to the hospital for stitches, where they said my blood alcohol was more than double the legal limit. I showed them my police shield and managed to talk my way out of a DUI charge.

Still, Chief Wilhelm suspended me for two weeks and warned that any other public drinking problems like that could lead to my dismissal from the force.

There'd been no incidents since then, but I still don't think he completely trusted me when it came to alcohol.

"I'm not drinking," I told Wilhelm now.

"Good to hear."

"And I won't be drinking or embarrass you or the department in any way, going forward."

"I have your word on that?"

"I promise."

That seemed to satisfy him, although it shouldn't have.

Because one of the things an alcoholic does is lie.

I'm an alcoholic. And I've always lied about my drinking, even to people I cared about a lot more than Chief Barry Wilhelm.

In fact, I've told so many lies about my drinking in the past that sometimes even I wasn't sure what was true and what wasn't.

"I haven't had a drink in a long time," I said.

CHAPTER 20

I didn't agree with Chief Wilhelm on a lot of things, but he was definitely right about one thing he told me.

We had to find Karin Lavelle, the missing fifteen-year-old daughter.

That was our priority right now.

The way I figured it, there were three possibilities of where Karin Lavelle could possibly be at the moment. Well, four if you included the possibility that the girl was dead. But I didn't want to include that option right now. I was still operating on the premise that Karin Lavelle was alive.

That meant she was either somewhere on Martha's Vineyard, or she had gone back to New York or somewhere else, or she had been kidnapped by whoever murdered her family.

We'd already swept the island with search teams looking for her without any results. Checked and re-checked ferry terminals, the airport and marinas to see if there were any reports of a teenage girl that might be her. And we'd gone door to door at places around The Beach House. There was nothing. Martha's Vineyard is a pretty big island, but it would seem difficult for a fifteen-year-old girl to disappear on it that quickly.

If she was gone from the island – at least gone voluntarily – the most likely place she might have gone was back to New York where she lived. The Lavelles lived in Mamaroneck, a town in Westchester County north of the city. I called Nancy Lavelle's mother and asked her if she knew any friends her granddaughter had there. She gave me a few names.

"Do you have any new information on where Karin might be, Detective?" she asked anxiously.

"We're pursuing some leads on it, Mrs. Hood."

"What about whoever killed my daughter and family?"

"We're making progress on the case."

"What kind of progress?"

"I'm afraid that's all I can tell you at the moment."

"I still can't believe this all happened."

"I understand. It is unbelievable."

"And I'm so worried, I'm so anxious about where Karin might be."

She asked me about the list of her son-in-law's patients she and her husband had sent us. "It took a bit of effort to get those names," she said. "Even for us. The people in his office were very reluctant to give anyone access to that. But eventually we got them to turn over his files."

"Thank you for that," I said. "Those files have been very helpful."

I didn't say anymore.

I didn't tell her about Albert Ruggerio.

No point in doing that until I knew something more.

"Will you talk to them all?" she asked. "Everyone on his patient list?"

"As many as we can."

"I hope one of them has some answers about my granddaughter. I can't stop thinking about where she is now and worrying that she might be hurt or dead."

"I'll be in touch with you as soon as I know more, Mrs. Hood."

She thanked me.

But I don't think I relieved her anxiety and worry very much.

One of the friends of Karin Lavelle that I reached said she'd heard from Karin the day before the murders.

"She called me. She said the vacation wasn't going as badly as she thought it would. She said they were actually having a good time on Martha's Vineyard."

"Why wouldn't she have a good time here?"

"Oh, she didn't want to go. I mean she's fifteen now. Who wants to go on vacation with your parents when you're fifteen? I know I don't. And neither did Karin. But her parents insisted. She and her mother had a big fight about it before they left. Not that it was unusual for Karin and her mother to be fighting."

"She and her mother didn't get along?"

"Karin and the old lady were always battling about something."

"What about her father?"

"Her father worked a lot, wasn't around," the girl said. "Her mother used to work too; she was a lawyer somewhere in the city. But then she took maternity leave to have the baby a year or so ago, and she decided not to go back to work full-time in the city. She was going to stay home, work from there and take care of the family."

That's what Nancy Lavelle's mother had told me earlier too.

"Karin's mother hadn't been around much before that, just like her father was gone so much. But now the mother was around all the time. Karin said she felt like her mother was always watching her, giving her a hard time. She found it difficult adjusting to having a full-time mother around.

"But, like I said, Karin told me in that last message they were having fun. She said the mother wasn't giving her a hard time. And they'd been getting along so well, that they even promised Karin they could stop in Woods Hole on the trip back. She was very excited about that."

"What's in Woods Hole?"

"The Oceanographic Institution."

"And…?"

"Karin wanted…" she hesitated, I could tell she realized she was referring to her friend in the past tense "… Karin wants to be an oceanographer."

"Someone who studies the ocean and the sea life in it?"

"That's right. She talked a lot about going to college and studying oceanography and making a career out of the field. That was what some of the arguments with her mother were about. Her mother wanted her to go to law school and become an attorney like her. Or, as another career choice, they pushed her to study for a medical degree and become a doctor like her father. Her parents didn't understand Karin's passion for studying the ocean. That was very frustrating for her."

"But they were going to take her to Woods Hole?"

"Yes. Karin was so excited about it when I talked to her. She hoped her parents finally understood her dream about what she wanted to do with her life. Of course, now…"

I checked with Woods Hole police later to see if there was any possibility the Lavelle girl had turned up there. That would have been nice. But it was too easy to be true. No sign of Karin Lavelle at the Oceanographic Institution or anywhere else in Woods Hole.

The last known sighting of Karin Lavelle had been the night before the murders when the family ate dinner at Delmonico's in Cedar Cliffs.

After I talked to as many people in New York as I could find, I walked outside onto the street and over to the restaurant, which was a few blocks away from the Cedar Cliffs station. There was no indication from the waiters and others I talked to there that anything unusual had happened with the Lavelle family while they were eating there. It seemed like an ordinary family out for dinner, everyone said.

I walked around a bit after that, going into stores and businesses to see if anyone else knew anything. There were a few people who thought they might have seen the Lavelle family. But no one remembered anything substantial or helpful.

I went back to the station and looked at one of the pictures of Karin Lavelle I'd posted on the wall.

She was standing on the street, looking every bit like a normal teenager. She had blonde hair, she was slim and petite, she had nice eyes and a nice smile.

Next to it, I had put a picture of the mystery girl in the hospital.

They didn't look much alike.

One of them was slim, the other heavier. One was a blonde, the other a brunette. And, most importantly of all, one of them was missing and the other was still a mystery.

One was gone, and one was here.

Like a substitute.

Someone had substituted the girl we had for the real Lavelle girl. But why?

CHAPTER 21

Even though we hadn't gotten any help from the security cameras at The Beach House, I hadn't given up on the idea.

There are security cameras everywhere. In buildings. On the street. At intersections. Sure, there's more of these cameras in a place like New York City than Cedar Cliffs. But even here, it would have been difficult for Thomas Lavelle and his family to have avoided appearing in at least some of them while they were on the island.

In New York City, I had a computer/tech team to handle a lot of this. Here in Cedar Cliffs, I had Dave Bowers. Bowers was only a patrol officer, but he was also a whiz with computers and video and social media and all the rest. I took him off his regular patrol duties to help Teena and I with that part of the Lavelle investigation.

"We got three hits," Bowers told me and Teena after spending a lot of time poring over video we'd taken from various spots in town. "One at The Beach House with the Lavelles checking in at the front desk. Another at a restaurant in town. And lastly at a game arcade nearby."

"And we're sure there's nothing from their rooms at The Beach House?" I asked. "Nothing showing anyone going in or out of those rooms?"

"Nope. Only that one camera in the lobby and manager's office, plus the parking lot outside. It only shows the Lavelle family checking in."

I kept hoping for a miracle, but it wasn't happening.

"So let's see again what we've got."

"There's really nothing to see…"

"Dave…"

"Okay, okay."

Bowers clicked a button. The first video, the one from the front desk and lobby of The Beach House, appeared on the computer screen in front of him. The security camera shot covered both the hotel lobby and the manager's office off to the side. You could see the Lavelles checking in at the front desk. The dateline at the bottom showed it was six days earlier. They were dressed in casual attire and carrying numerous pieces of luggage, like you'd expect for a family about to start a vacation.

All of them were there on the video.

I especially checked out Karin Lavelle, the fifteen-year-old. She seemed preoccupied with her phone, typing an email or texting someone on it. I wondered who that was on the other end of the message. But, since we didn't have the girl's phone, the answer to that question remained a mystery. Just like the mystery of where Karin Lavelle was right now. After they checked in, the Lavelles gathered up all of their baggage and headed for their rooms. They soon disappeared from the screen.

"Anything else interesting from the lobby?" I asked.

"I went through all of the video of the lobby from this day right through until the murders. Nothing unusual. I sat with the manager, Lily Knowlton, and watched. Man, she's a weird woman, huh? Anyway, no one came in or out of the lobby that wasn't supposed to be there."

I nodded.

"What else?"

"That's it. Everything from The Beach House."

"No, I mean the two other places – the restaurant where they ate dinner and the video arcade after."

"There's nothing there either, but…"

He clicked another key on the computer, and we saw a video from Delmonico's in Cedar Cliffs. Lavelle and his family were sitting outside eating dinner. They were all in the video again, including Karin. We watched it for a long time, but there really wasn't much to see. Just a family on vacation eating dinner.

The last video came from a game arcade not far away. It was from the same night as the dinner. The three Lavelle girls were there, playing games in the arcade. I remembered seeing a lot of games on their phones and tablets too. Eventually Lavelle and his wife, pushing the little boy in the stroller, showed up at the arcade to leave with them. They walked out onto the street together.

"That's all there is," Bowers said.

"Play it again," I told him.

"The whole thing?"

"No, just the end."

He did. I watched again as the Lavelle family left the arcade. But I wasn't watching them this time. I was watching other people in the arcade. Especially one of them. Because I recognized her.

Yes, there she was.

A teenage girl.

Standing next to the Lavelle family and pretending she was playing another game, but she was really watching the Lavelles intently, not the screen of the game.

I recognized her.

"Zoom in on that girl."

"What girl?"

"The one standing in the background."

I pointed to a girl on the edge of the screen.

"Oh, my God!" Teena said when the girl's face came into focus. "Is that who I think it is?"

"Sure looks like her," I said.

She was the mystery girl from the crime scene at The Beach House who was now in the hospital.

What in the hell was she doing here?

Was she following the Lavelles on the night before they died?

Was she stalking them?

If so, why?

CHAPTER 22

I pushed open the door of the hospital room where the mystery girl was staying. She was sitting on the bed with a television set playing in front of her. The show was one of those *Judge Judy*-type courtroom programs with a celebrity judge of some kind making wisecracks to the defendants. The girl was staring at the screen, but I couldn't be sure if she was actually watching or lost in her own thoughts. Whatever those might be.

She turned and looked at me when I came in. I couldn't tell if she recognized me or not. She still had that same blank expression on her face that I'd seen before.

"I'm Detective Abby Pearce of the Cedar Cliffs Police Department," I said, just to make sure she knew who she was talking to.

No response.

"How are you feeling?"

"I'm okay, I guess."

"Do you remember anything yet?"

"Not really. Why am I here?"

I sat down next to her on the bed and took out my phone. I called up a series of photos on it. Pictures from the crime scene. Pictures of Thomas and Nancy Lavelle and their three children lying there. I held the phone right up to the girl's face and scrolled through the pictures. I figured that maybe I could shock the truth out of her once she saw all over again how horrible it had been.

"Five people died here," I said to the girl now. "Died brutally. The only person we found alive in there was you. Now I'm asking you: What were you doing there? And what can you tell us about what happened to these five people?"

She shook her head.

"I don't know."

I showed her another picture on my phone. A still shot from the security video at the game arcade with her watching the Lavelle family before the murders.

"What were you doing there? Why were you so interested in the Lavelles?"

She shook her head.

"I don't know anything about that. All I know is that I woke up there and saw all the blood and the dead people around me. I was scared. I didn't know what to do. I didn't know what was happening. I didn't know anything. And then the police came barging in. Now I'm here. That's all I can tell you. If I could tell you more, I would. Believe me, I wish I could understand what this is all about too. Just as much as you want to understand."

It was the longest sentence she had uttered, as far as I knew, so that was promising. But it was still frustrating. This girl was the key to finding out everything about what happened to Thomas Lavelle and his family. But she couldn't, or didn't want to, tell us anything. I still hadn't made up my mind about whether or not she was faking her loss of memory or if she really didn't have any idea how she wound up at The Beach House.

The doctors at the hospital had checked her out thoroughly with a battery of tests, and they reported finding no evidence of physical damage to the girl. All her vital signs seemed good. Mentally, they said, she could answer some questions – she knew what year it was and even recognized some current event and pop culture references, but couldn't remember anything about her own past or, more importantly, what she was doing on Martha's Vineyard and at The Beach House.

The doctors said this was not unusual in amnesia victims to be able to remember some things clearly – but be totally blacked out on everything else.

Especially when the person had suffered a shocking experience like being present at a mass murder.

I decided to check her out again myself by asking her a series of questions about current events.

"Do you know who the President of the United States is?"

She gave me the right name.

"Tell me what year this is."

She knew the year.

"Have you ever heard of the Kardashians?"

"That's a TV show, right? A reality program."

But she was a complete blank when I asked her about her own past; how she got here and where did she come from; or anything about the details of Thomas Lavelle, his wife and his children.

"Did you know the Lavelle family at all?" I asked.

"No."

"You never met them. Not here on the island or anywhere else?"

"Not that I'm aware of."

I pointed to the picture on my phone again of her standing next to them at the video arcade.

"That's the Lavelle family. And that's you. On the night before they were killed."

She shrugged.

"What about Karin Lavelle?"

"Who's that?"

"She's their teenage daughter. Probably about the same age as you. But she's missing. Do you know anything about her whereabouts?"

"No."

"If you're holding anything back, I advise you to come clean right now. We've taken photos of you and distributed them to all of the media. Not just around here, but all across the country. This has become a big national news story. Sooner or later, someone is going to tell us who you are. And what you're doing here. Are you sure there's nothing you can give us now?"

"I would if I could. Why would I lie?"

"I don't know. But if you are lying, now is the time to tell us the truth. It's important for you as well as us. This isn't just about finding whoever killed this poor family. It could be about saving your life too."

"What do you mean?"

"You were a witness. You're presumably the only person who can tell us who did all this. That person, or persons, might want to come back and finish the job. To make sure you don't ever reveal anything more. That's why I have a police officer stationed outside your door twenty-four hours a day. To protect you."

Her eyes opened wide. But not in fear or shock, at least as best I could tell. More like she was surprised.

"I'll do the best I can," she said. "Maybe it will all come back to me, or at least some of it. That's what the doctors have told me. I'll let you know if I remember anything at all. I promise. I'll tell you."

I wasn't sure I believed her.

But this girl was the best lead we had to solve the Lavelle family murders.

"I'll be in touch with you regularly," I told her.

CHAPTER 23

I was back at the Black Dog again with Teena. I liked spending time at the Black Dog. It relaxed me. And I sure needed some relaxation with everything I'd been dealing with.

"Captain Wilhelm wants to see me in the morning," I said to Teena. "'First thing… in my office.' Those were his words."

"Doesn't sound good."

"I'm supposed to give Wilhelm a detailed report on all the progress we've made on this case. He's under a lot of pressure – from the media, the mayor and city council, plus a lot of townspeople – to come up with some results. Everyone's terrified because there's still a mass killer running around out there. Not to mention a missing teenage girl."

Teena was drinking her usual bottle of Corona beer; me, I was doing club soda tonight. I alternated back and forth between that and Diet Coke for a bit of variety. Teena's Corona looked damn good, but not for me.

"He's not going to be happy with what you tell him. What are you going to say?"

"I'll promise him that I'll solve the case and make him look good. And, if I screw it up, I'll take all the blame. I think he'll be fine with that arrangement."

"Now that sounds like the Captain Wilhelm I know."

Teena shook her head in frustration.

"That damn girl in the hospital. If we could just get through to her somehow. Get her to talk to us. There's got to be a lot of crucial information inside of her, whether she's deliberately hiding it from us or not."

"I pushed her really hard this last time I was at the hospital, Teena. After she showed up on that security video with the Lavelle family. But she didn't give me anything…"

"Maybe I should go back and try again."

"Knock yourself out," I said. "It's worth a try."

"You think she's lying about the memory loss?"

"I think she knows more than she's telling us."

Teena took a big swig of her beer. Damn, that looked good. I realized I was staring at the Corona in her hand.

"Wilhelm asked me the other day about my drinking," I said.

"He thought you were drinking?"

"He wanted to make sure I wasn't. That's why he asked me."

"What did you tell him?"

"I said I wasn't drinking."

"You're not, right?"

"No, Teena, I'm not drinking."

"Glad to hear it. I like to have a sober partner. It makes the job so much easier. Please let me know if you decide to fall off the wagon."

"You'll be the first person I tell."

She drank some more beer.

"What's the deal with you and Wilhelm anyway? How come you don't get along very well?"

I'd thought about that a lot, too. I knew Wilhelm wasn't comfortable working with me, I think he felt threatened by all my experience at working big crimes as a detective in New York. But he had been forced to take me on the force – a lot of people liked the idea of a well-known NYC detective coming home to the Cedar Cliffs force – so we had this uneasy truce between us.

Of course, after I solved the big case here not long ago and became a bit of a media hero for that, he had no choice but to accept me.

Even if he didn't particularly like me.

Because he knew he needed me.

And now, with the Lavelle family murders putting us back on the front pages and news channels everywhere, he needed me more than ever.

"Sexual tension," I said now in answer to Teena's question about the problems in our relationship. "I can't keep my hands off the guy."

She laughed. Wilhelm was close to sixty, stocky, with close-cropped grey hair.

"Speaking of sexual things, what's going on with you and that Boston TV reporter?" she asked.

"Lincoln Connor," I said.

"Right. Are you still a hot item?"

"Meg asked me the same question."

"What's the answer?"

"I don't know."

"Is he here for this story?"

"I don't know that either."

"Being an investigative detective and all, I'm beginning to suspect that the two of you aren't that close right now."

"He's in Boston, and I'm here."

"I wasn't referring to geography."

"But that's a lot of the problem between us. To do our jobs, he has to be there and I have to be here."

I told her how he wanted me to move to Boston and be with him there. And how I wasn't ready to leave my job here on Martha's Vineyard, even if I could get a job in a big city again in law enforcement. I said I was building a life here, not in Boston. I said we argued about all that, and then one day he was gone.

"Do you think he'll show up for this big story?"

"I expected him at the press conference."

"And?"

"I haven't seen him here yet, Teena."

"Maybe you should try someone new," she said. "Someone who is here on the island. You shouldn't be without a man."

"Look who's talking. What about you?"

Teena's husband had died suddenly of a heart attack five years earlier. That had prompted her to make a big lifestyle change and join the Cedar Cliffs police force. I'd never seen or heard anything about her being with any other man since her husband's death.

"I had a man," she said now.

"The key word being 'had'."

"They'll never be another man for me like Nick."

"But he's gone, and you're here."

"Let's just worry about you," she said. "For whatever it's worth, I don't think you and Lincoln Connor are finished yet."

"I hope you're right," I said.

CHAPTER 24

"Damn, Albert Ruggerio is a real piece of work," Vic Gelman said to me. "I knew about him, of course. But I never really was aware of all of it until I talked to my friend in Organized Crime. This guy is a stone-cold killer."

There'd been a message from Gelman when I checked my phone after leaving the bar with Teena. I called him back right away. I wanted to know everything he'd found out about Ruggerio. I sat there now listening to what he had to say. I'd been pretty sure I knew what kind of stuff it was going to be. But, like Gelman had said, the information about Ruggerio was far worse than I ever imagined.

"There's killers and then there's people like Ruggerio. Not all of his victims were about Mob war business. Sometimes he had people killed for hardly any reason at all. My friend told me some shocking stuff about what's he's done over the years."

One of the stories Gelman told me about involved the owner of a bar in Queens where Ruggerio attempted to supply the place with his own liquor. Ruggerio generally didn't ask for someone's business, he demanded it. And few people ever turned him down. But this one said he was going to stay with his current liquor supplier, not switch to Ruggerio despite any strong-arm tactics he was being threatened with by the mobster.

It was a courageous – albeit suicidal – response.

"The day after he gave Ruggerio his final refusal, the bar mysteriously burned to the ground," Gelman said. "A week after that, gunmen burst into the bar owner's home in what was supposed to look like a robbery. But before they left, he and his family were all shot dead. Law enforcement was never able to connect Ruggerio directly with any of it. But it was clear that it was done by Albert Ruggerio to send a message to others not to cross him."

There certainly was one element about this particular Ruggerio crime that jumped right out at me.

"His family? They murdered the guy's family too?"

"That's right."

"Were there… were their kids involved?"

"No children. It was his wife and his brother, who lived in the house with them. The children were at school when the shootings happened."

"Do you think Ruggerio would have killed the children too if they'd been there?"

"I think Albert Ruggerio would kill anyone he needed to in order to get revenge against someone."

Like a one-year-old boy and two young girls, along with a wife, the way it happened in the case of Thomas Lavelle, I thought to myself.

"Sounds something like your case, huh?"

"Right."

"As I said, the guy's a stone-cold killer. There are no rules for him when it comes to murder. He sure could be your guy."

He asked again about my life in Martha's Vineyard and about my new partner here. I told him about Teena.

"That's important having a good partner," Gelman said. "I know you and Tommy had a good, a special relationship. We got on fine too, Abby. But I know how bad it hurt when you lost Tommy."

"I heard from Tommy's widow not long ago," I said. "She called me after seeing me on the TV news. We talked about Tommy. That was nice to hear from her like that. Even though I was a bit surprised."

"Why surprised?"

"I don't know. I always thought maybe deep down she blamed me for Tommy's death. I mean I was his partner the night he got killed. I was the one who didn't save him. So it was good to hear from her."

"You didn't do anything wrong that night, Abby. You know that as well as I do. We've talked about this a lot before."

"I guess, but I'm glad you said that again."

"Why?"

"Because I want to make sure I keep believing it, too."

Before we hung up, Vic Gelman told me something else about Ruggerio and the Organized Crime Task Force.

"There was a weird thing that happened when I was talking to this guy I know in Organized Crime," he said. "At first, I simply told him I was interested in Ruggerio, without telling him why. We were just kind of chatting about him. Not really in an official capacity, more like off-duty cop conversation.

"But then I said I'd been contacted by someone in law enforcement in another part of the country about Ruggerio. After that, everything suddenly changed. He stopped talking so freely. In fact, he pretty much clammed up on me. When I asked him why, he only said there might be something going on with Ruggerio now, something big, and he didn't want any other police interfering."

"Did you mention my name?"

"No. It had nothing to with you. He simply didn't want anyone to compromise whatever they've got going on at the moment."

"Did you tell him that he may have murdered five people – three of them children?"

"I told him."

"What did he say?"

"Nothing. But he made it clear that nothing – even a mass murder like that – was more important than their investigation into Ruggerio. What do you make of that?"

Well, the answer was pretty clear.

Albert Ruggerio was on the NYPD Organized Crime Bureau radar for some reason right now.

It had to be for something really big.

Maybe even bigger than a mass killing on Martha's Vineyard.

One way or another, it looked like Albert Ruggerio was the man I was after for the Lavelle family murders.

All I had to do was figure out a way to prove that.

CHAPTER 25

"Please tell me you've come up with something on the Lavelle case," Chief Barry Wilhelm said to me.

"We're pursuing a number of promising leads, Chief."

"Do you know who the girl in the hospital is yet?"

"No."

"Or what happened to the real Karin Lavelle?"

"No, but—"

"Or who in the hell did these killings and why?"

I shook my head.

"Then you don't have anything, do you, Pearce?"

Like Teena had said, Wilhelm wasn't going to be happy with me. Not until I'd solved the case.

"We have to find that missing girl," he said "Where is Karin Lavelle? A fifteen-year-old-girl doesn't just vanish like this. The media is going to be all over us – all over me – until we find her. What are you doing about that?"

"We're working with the FBI, the Massachusetts State Police and other law enforcement agencies, Chief. Looking for Karin Lavelle throughout the area, throughout the whole country – not just here on Martha's Vineyard. Every resource we have available is being put into this search."

"We better come up with some results pretty soon," he grunted.

I started going through all of things we'd done so far on the case.

I started by telling him about how the girl – the teenage girl we found at The Beach House crime scene, the one we at first assumed was Karin Lavelle – showed up on the security video from the game arcade that Karin and the Lavelle family were at the night before the murders.

"This mystery girl is still the best lead we have to finding out what happened to the Lavelle family," I said. "Who murdered them, where the missing Lavelle girl is and what this other unknown girl was doing there at the murder scene."

"Any ideas on how to get through to her or at least find out more about her?"

"We've already distributed her picture all over the island – like we're doing with the picture of Karin Lavelle – in the hopes that someone recognizes her. I took her fingerprints too and sent them to the FBI database to see if there's any match. Not very likely that a girl that young would have fingerprints in the FBI database, but I still want to check. I still haven't heard back on that. Plus, we'll keep on questioning her at the hospital trying to find out more. Who is she? What was she doing there? What did she see when the murders took place? Same questions we've asked her over and over, but sooner or later we'll find out something about this damn girl."

He nodded.

"What else?"

I told him about my conversation with Vic Gelman – and the new details about Ruggerio's violent criminal acts in the past.

"Everything points to Ruggerio as our best potential suspect. He's the only one we've found that had a motive for revenge against Doctor Lavelle – because of the unsuccessful heart surgery he performed. Plus, there's Ruggerio's long history of murders and violence against people who made him angry. And Ruggerio's right here on the island when Thomas Lavelle and his family was killed. So…"

"But you still don't have any hard evidence linking Ruggerio to the murders – or anything else."

"Not yet."

"So what are you going to do?"

"Keep trying."

Wilhelm sighed.

"What else?" he asked.

I reiterated how we'd done a complete sweep of everyone living or working in or anywhere near The Beach House to see if they knew anything about the Lavelle family in the time leading up to the deaths; about checking all the ferries and passengers for clues; how we'd gone through logs at airports and marinas looking for anyone suspicious coming to or leaving the island; and how forensics had gone over the crime scene virtually inch by inch to document any fingerprints or DNA or other evidence that was there.

Thus far, none of this work had turned up anything significant.

But I wanted him to know that I was doing everything I needed to be doing in the investigation. It helped me to confirm too to myself that I was doing everything possible to get answers.

"Teena is back at the hospital now trying one more time to get something from the mystery girl about what really happened."

"The girl hasn't talked to anybody about it yet," Wilhelm grunted.

"Teena can be very persuasive," I said. "Maybe we'll get lucky this time."

Except we didn't get lucky.

Instead, things got even worse.

I found that out a short time later when Teena called after getting to Martha's Vineyard Hospital.

"The girl's gone," Teena said to me.

"What? Gone where?"

"Just gone. There's no sign of her in the hospital room. Bowers was supposed to be watching her on this last shift, but he doesn't know. None of the staff have any idea either about what happened to her or where she went or how she got out of here. The girl just disappeared, Abby."

I couldn't believe this was happening.

"That girl was the only damn lead we had…"

"Yeah, and now we don't even have her."

CHAPTER 26

I soon caught up on what had happened at the hospital.

Patrolman Dave Bowers had been assigned to guard the girl as part of a rotating set of officers I'd assigned to do that. I was concerned for her safety. She had somehow survived a mass murder. There was no reason to think that whoever did that might not return to finish the job by murdering her too.

As part of that security stakeout at the hospital, Bowers made regular checks on the mystery girl every fifteen minutes to make sure she was all right. He also screened everyone who entered the girl's room.

The last time he'd opened the door to look in on her was 11:15 a.m. No one had gone in or out of the room during the period after that. But at 11:30 when Bowers opened the door to look again, the girl was not there. There was an adjoining bathroom with a closed door. Bowers pounded on the door, then smashed it open. A small window inside was open. The room was on the second floor, so the girl had apparently been able to squeeze through the window opening and jump to the ground below. We later found some bed sheets tied together that she likely used to break her fall and get away safely.

A massive search of the area turned up nothing. But the hospital was very near the town of Cedar Cliffs, so she could have walked into town and disappeared into the crowds of tourists there.

My main concern was to not let her get off the island. Unlike the murder of the five members of the Lavelle family, which had taken place nearly twenty-four hours before the bodies were discovered, this incident was very fresh. The girl been gone for a very short time, and it was crucial to find her as soon as possible. The clock was ticking, and every minute that passed gave her a chance to get further away from us.

The most recent ferry at Cedar Cliffs had left at 11:00, which was before she disappeared. The next ferry didn't leave until 1 p.m. So we were able to check each and every passenger before they got on board. She wasn't one of them.

We did the same thing at the ferry terminal in Vineyard Haven and, of course, at Martha's Vineyard Airport. We also talked with people at the marina to see if anyone resembling her was there or had recently left on a private vessel of any kind. But there was no sign of the girl.

Which meant she was very likely still somewhere on the island.

That was good.

But, no question about it, it was a helluva black mark on the department to let her slip through our fingers like that.

Especially now that she was running away.

Why would she run?

Well, the one obvious reason was she was running because she was the person who killed all five members of the Lavelle family.

As hard to believe as that might be, that a young girl could do something like that, it had to be considered as a real possibility at this point.

It also had to be significant that she'd fled soon after I confronted her at the hospital with pictures from that security video showing her apparently following the Lavelle family on the night before they were murdered.

And, even if she hadn't been the one who killed them, she may have run because she knew the secret of what really happened that caused that horrific massacre of five people – and, for whatever reason, didn't want to reveal that to us.

Or why we found her sitting there calmly amid all that death and horror.

Either way, it had made a bad situation even worse for me and everyone in the Cedar Cliffs Police Department.

"Are you going to fire Bowers for letting her get away?" Teena asked me as we monitored all the search activities at the Cedar Cliffs station.

"Would you fire him?"

"I'd fire him."

"No, you wouldn't."

"Okay, I wouldn't."

"I didn't think so."

"But Bowers really messed up here."

"It's not all his fault. I didn't assign him to prevent her from escaping. That's not really why we had her room staked out at the hospital. I wasn't worried about that. I was worried someone might try to harm her. Bowers was looking for people going into that room, not her sneaking out."

"Do you think we can find her?"

"We have to find her."

We'd taken a number of pictures of the girl. We began distributing these – like we had earlier pictures of her – throughout the island in hopes of finding anyone who might have spotted her after she fled Martha's Vineyard Hospital.

We got a few potential leads that way.

One person saw a girl that looked like her playing video games at the same arcade in Cedar Cliffs where we'd seen her on the security footage along with the Lavelle family on the night before they were killed. Another person reported a teenage girl hitchhiking on the road west from Cedar Cliffs heading toward the central part of the island.

None of these leads or tips seemed very legit. But we checked them all out. Martha's Vineyard is a pretty big island – more than thirty miles long from the east coast to the west – and we were going to need to check every part of that until we found her. We'd done that for Karin Lavelle, now we were doing it for this girl too.

I looked through the pictures we had of the mystery girl now.

She was probably pretty, although it was hard to tell from the pictures since she wasn't wearing any makeup and her hair was uncombed and messed up. She'd been in a bad state when we found her at The Beach House. And she'd made no effort to take care of herself in the hospital, even though the nurses tried to clean her up and comb her hair and do things like that to take care of her.

Now she was gone – and with her went our best hope for solving the mystery of the Lavelle family massacre.

"Who the hell are you?" I said silently to the picture of the mystery girl that I held in my hand.

CHAPTER 27

The fallout from the girl's disappearance was quick and intense and overwhelming.

Everyone, including the media, the Cedar Cliffs mayor and city council and the townspeople themselves, were up in arms about it.

Wilhelm blamed me for what happened, of course. Yelled and screamed and said I might have ruined his career. He said he wasn't going to take the blame for this. Then he got a bit of revenge by making me face the media at the press conference to answer questions about the missing mystery girl, instead of him.

It was a no-win situation for me.

There was nothing I could say to the press that might explain how this whole thing had happened.

And so the press conference itself quickly went downhill, right from the very first question for me.

"Do you have any idea where this girl you found at The Beach House crime scene is right now, Detective Pearce?" a reporter asked.

"We believe she is still on Martha's Vineyard."

"But you have no idea where?"

"Not at the moment."

"Has there been any disciplinary action taken against the police officer who let her escape?" someone else said.

"That's an ongoing internal matter and not something the Cedar Cliffs police force is going to share with the public at this time."

"Did you made any progress at all at determining the identity of this girl while she was at the hospital?" was another question.

"We still have not determined who she is or where she came from. She claimed she did not remember anything. We were not able to tell whether she was telling us the truth or not about having amnesia. Her sudden flight from the hospital certainly makes us question the credibility of her story. But that's all I can tell you at the moment."

And the questions just kept getting tougher as the press conference went on.

But the worst moment for me came when one reporter stood up and said:

"Detective Pearce, the Cedar Cliffs Police Department first mistook this girl as a member of the murdered Lavelle family; you say you still have no idea who she is; now you've let her escape from the hospital where you were keeping her for questioning. And, worst of all, you don't seem to have made any progress whatsoever in the investigation into who killed the five members of the Lavelle family, or what happened to their missing daughter, Karin. Don't you think it's reasonable to ask if the Cedar Cliffs Police Department is capable of carrying out this investigation any longer? Have you considered bringing in the FBI or the state police or another outside law enforcement agency that would be better equipped than you to handle a case of this magnitude?"

I'm not exactly sure what I said in response.

Because I was pretty shocked when the reporter asked me that.

Not so much because of the question itself.

But because of the reporter who asked it.

It was Lincoln Connor.

CHAPTER 28

I hardly ever went back to the house on Martha's Vineyard where I grew up. Too many bad memories. Same with the high school I attended. But I drove there now, on my way home that night after the press conference.

I parked in front of my house and school for a while and stared at them.

Thinking about what had just happened.

I was confused by Lincoln Connor's sudden appearance here on the island.

And I was hurt.

Hurt that he hadn't even bothered to tell me he was here.

I'd been hurt before, of course.

Looking at the home where I grew up and then later at the high school where I went – well, all the memories of those teenage years there came rushing back to me.

On the night of my high school prom, I'd been raped. That horrific event continues to traumatize me to this day. I thought I knew during all the years since – and my parents let me believe I knew the truth – about who had raped me. I was sure it was the boy who took me to the prom. I was angry at my mother and father for a long time because they had never done anything about it.

I took my first drink back then on the night the rape happened, and I've been pretty much drinking ever since. Maybe I would have become an alcoholic anyway even if the rape had never occurred. But the nightmare of that long-ago night has shaped my life in so many ways since then.

That and the way my parents – especially my father, but my mother too – let me down when I was a naïve teenage girl who needed their help the most. They never did anything about the boy I was convinced had raped me. They never made him pay the price for it or answer for it in any way. I was confused and hurt and furious by this. And so the relationship between my parents and me was irrevocably broken for reasons I never could really understand.

But then, last time I was here, my mother finally revealed the real story of what happened to me that night of my high school prom. It wasn't the boy who took me to the prom who raped me, as I had believed; it had been someone else – a family friend who I trusted very much. And I found out for the first time how she and my father – who died a few years ago – had lied about it to me back then and all of my life.

I felt betrayed and angry and violated all over again when I found out the truth.

And I learned my father's reason for lying to me – and how my mother helped him to hide that lie from me for so long – about what really happened on that long ago high school prom night.

"I've told you the truth," my mother said to me. "Can't you forgive me? Why do you still hate your father so much, Abby? Why do you hate both of us?"

The answer to that was a very complicated one. I wasn't sure I actually hated my mother. Or even my father. But I had been angry with both of them for much of my adult life. And now – although my father was dead – I was even more angry at the two of them than I had ever been before.

Maybe someday I will be able to forgive my mother, but not yet.

No, we weren't likely to have any warm, fuzzy mother-and-daughter moments, my mother and me.

And somehow the pain I felt now about Lincoln Connor brought back all that old pain for me too.

I needed to talk to someone about this. About Lincoln. About my frustrations over the missing mystery girl. About trying to figure out how Albert Ruggerio fit into this whole puzzle. About everything. I needed a patient, sympathetic ear to pour out my feelings on all this. And so I turned to the one sympathetic, patient ear that had always been there to listen to my problems.

"I really like Lincoln Connor," I told him now. "I mean I really, really like him a lot. Or at least I thought I did. But I don't hear from the guy for weeks, then he suddenly shows up here unannounced at today's press conference. Doesn't relate to me personally at all, instead he just stands up and shocks me by asking a really hostile question. Like we never even knew each other or something. Like we hadn't slept together, for God's sake. I mean what's that all about, huh, Oscar?"

Oscar stared at me. Probably expecting me to take out his leash or dog dish next.

I went through the case with him too. Everything I knew – and didn't know – about the Lavelle murders, the missing Lavelle daughter, the mystery girl who ran away from the hospital, the Albert Ruggerio Mob connection and all the rest.

"So what do you think, Oscar?" I asked him. "Got any answers for me on this damn case?"

He barked loudly.

I sighed, then took him out for a walk. Which is all Oscar really cared about, I suppose. Men, they're all the same – they only care about themselves. There were some heavy woods behind my house and lots of small trails that were a perfect place to walk. For Oscar and for me too.

I let him off the leash now and walked behind him as he ran through the trees and bushes, sniffing with his nose to the ground most of the way. A few times he spotted a squirrel or bird and chased after them. I wasn't sure what would happen if he ever caught one, but fortunately they were all too fast for a nearly forty-pound dachshund.

While I walked, I couldn't stop thinking about all the confusing pieces in the Lavelle murder case – as well as the ones in my relationship with Lincoln.

In the past, I might well have tried to deal with all this by turning to the bottle. I thought about the bottle of vodka sitting back in my house. A few belts of that, and I wouldn't worry about any of it. The Lavelle murders. The missing Karin Lavelle. The mystery girl. Albert Ruggerio. And even Lincoln Connor.

Nope, none of it would bother me after a swig or two of vodka.

Vodka always made a lot of things better for me.

Yep, I used to believe that for a long, long time.

Except I knew now that wasn't true.

The vodka only made me think things were better.

Instead, my problems got worse after the vodka.

Much worse.

I couldn't do that now. I had a mass murder to solve and a missing girl – actually two missing girls to find. That was the most important thing for me now. Too important for me to spend time brooding about my love life.

But sometimes things just work out when you least expect them to.

Which is what happened.

Back at the house there was a knock on my door. When I looked out the window to check who was there, I saw Lincoln Connor. I opened the door.

"I was in the neighborhood so… well, I wanted to explain to you about what happened at the press conference today and… oh, what the hell, Abby, this is what I really came to see you for."

Lincoln leaned over and kissed me.

I impulsively kissed him back.

"That was nice," he said to me.

"Let's do some more of it then…"

CHAPTER 29

"What in the hell has been going on with you?" I asked Lincoln as we lay in bed afterward.

One thing had quickly led to another after the kissing at the door. The sex part was fun after all that time apart. But now we still needed to deal with the issues that had kept us separated for so long.

"How come you weren't here with the first batch of media for that initial press conference? Why weren't you covering the story from the very start? And why did you ambush me with that killer question at the press conference?"

"I didn't come here to do the story in the beginning because of you. I wasn't sure how to handle being around you. But then I decided I wanted to see you again. I thought asking you that question might be kinda romantic – and a way to break the ice."

"Huh?"

"Yes, I know it sounds crazy, but remember that's how we met on the other case? I asked you a really obnoxious question, you got mad at me and then we wound up together. I guess I was trying to replay that moment. But then, after I saw your reaction, I decided to come talk directly with you."

"Why didn't you just do that when you first came back to the island?"

"I wasn't sure if you'd be happy to see me or not."

"Well, I am."

"I know that now, but I didn't then."

I smiled.

"I understand that the rules for relationships have changed a lot in today's world," Lincoln said to me. "That a guy needs to realize his job is no more important than the woman's job. That he should do whatever it takes to make sure she is happy and fulfilled in her career. Even if he might have to make some sacrifices in his own career to do that. A guy should be big enough, caring enough to understand all that. I get it, Abby, I really do." Lincoln sighed. "Unfortunately, I'm not that guy."

"I'm not that woman either," I told him now.

"What do you mean?"

"You've got a big, glamorous, high-paying job as a Boston media star. I should understand that better. Understand that you can't just walk away from it and come live with me in a small town like Cedar Cliffs. I wish I could understand that, accept that, better than I have. But I guess I can't really do that anymore than you can."

"So where does that leave us?"

"Apparently in bed at the moment."

"Not too bad, huh?"

"For now anyway."

"But where do we go from here?"

"What do you want out of this relationship, Lincoln?"

"Not much. I guess I'd like to start by having you move to Boston so we could be together."

"Then what?"

"Maybe marriage."

"Wow!"

"After that, a family."

"Kids?"

"Sure, all that good stuff."

The mood was broken when Oscar suddenly jumped onto the bed. Oscar has been trained to not be on the bed during sex. I wasn't sure if he could understand exactly what was going on when that happened, but he knew to wait until the lovemaking was over. After that, well... it didn't take Oscar long to join Lincoln and me on the bed.

He happily kissed and licked me, then did the same with Lincoln. He and Lincoln really seemed to get along. That was a positive sign. It's good when your dog likes the guy that you're with.

"Can I tell him a joke?" Lincoln asked.

"You mean like I do?"

"Yes, I've been thinking about that."

I'd said when we first met how I told jokes to Oscar a lot. Not that Oscar understood the jokes, of course. But telling a joke is supposed to make your dog feel better. The dog reacts to the emotion in your voice and mannerisms. So if you're happy telling the joke, it makes him happy too. Or something like that. Anyway, it seems to work pretty well on Oscar.

"It should be a really bad joke though," I said, laughing. "Those are the kind I tell him."

"Oh, this is bad."

Lincoln turned to Oscar, looked him in the face eye to eye and told his joke.

"A guy goes into a doctor's office, gets his physical and the doctor tells him afterward he's got good news and bad news.

"'What's the bad news?' the guy asks.

"'You've only got six months to live,' the doctor tells him.

"'Jesus,' the guy says, then remembers the rest of it. 'What's the good news?'

"The doctor smiles. 'I had sex with my nurse this morning.'"

Lincoln laughed loudly, and Oscar licked his face.

There sure were a lot of good things about Lincoln. My dog liked him. He was good looking. Smart. Funny. And he seemed to be in love with me. I was probably in love with him too. He was an easy guy to fall in love with. So why was I so reluctant to drop everything in my life right now and run off to live happily ever after with him?

"Look, Lincoln, I might want to move to Boston with you at some point. See if I can get a job with the Boston police or the FBI there or some other law enforcement agency. But not now. Right now I need to be here."

"Because of this big murder case?"

"Yes, that's important to me. But it's more than that. This island is scared, the people are in a state of shock over what's been happening here. This is supposed to be a quiet little vacation paradise. Now we just had this huge crime case that happened here over the summer. Then quickly afterward a massacre of five people on a family vacation at one of the ritziest places on the island. People are afraid to go out, they don't know who to trust anymore. I can't leave now. I owe them, I owe this island where I grew up myself, something. So I'm here for the time being."

I looked over at Lincoln.

"Which means right now we still have a problem. Same problem as before. You're assigned to cover this story, I'm the chief investigative officer on it. That's a tricky situation. Not good for you as a journalist or me as a police officer if people find out that we're sleeping together."

He shook his head sadly. "I know."

I brought up the marriage idea again at one point as we talked. I didn't want him to think I wasn't interested in the prospect. But I was afraid too. Afraid of how that would turn out. Not because of him. Because of me. It was me I couldn't trust.

You see, I'd found the perfect man to marry once before. Or at least I thought I had. With Zach, my former husband. Zach was good looking, smart, funny and he loved me too. Just like Lincoln now. And I'd messed that marriage up with my drinking. I told Lincoln about all that now.

"I'll help you deal with your drinking problem," he said when I was finished. "I can handle it."

"Zach thought he could too… but in the end the alcohol was too much for him."

"But you're not drinking anymore…"

"Not right now."

"Do you think you'll start drinking again?"

That was a tough question. The easy answer was no, my drinking was behind me. But I knew it wasn't that simple. "One day at a time," I told him.

He nodded. "The Alcoholic Anonymous motto."

"It's the only way to deal with it, Lincoln."

He leaned over and kissed me.

I kissed him back.

Then it was time for Oscar to get off the bed again.

"And what about us?" he asked.

"Same deal."

"Huh?"

"One day at a time," I said.

CHAPTER 30

Teena and I were driving out to the western end of the island again to Albert Ruggerio's house the next day when we got a call from Meg Jarvis.

I wasn't planning to directly try to talk to Ruggerio a second time about his possible involvement in the Lavelle murders. At least not at the moment. I still didn't have enough to do that.

But, when all else failed, I sometimes felt it helped for me to check out something in person. In this case Ruggerio's Martha's Vineyard house. Just to see if maybe I could shake something loose just by showing up one more time to let Albert Ruggerio and the people inside – especially Ruggerio's security chief – know they were still very much on our radar for these murders.

But those plans changed when Meg called us.

"Someone thinks they might have just seen the girl who escaped from the hospital down on South Beach. Said she was about fifteen or sixteen, looked confused and kind of out of it, might have matched the description of the mystery girl we put out... anyway, she was on the west side of the beach."

"Who saw her?" I asked. "One of the lifeguards?"

"No, there aren't lifeguards there in the fall anymore, Abby."

Of course. I used to know that when I grew up here. But it had been a while. And this was really my first fall back on Martha's Vineyard. I had a lot of catching up to do.

"Then who saw her?"

"A guy who was surfing near there. He's waiting to talk to you now. At the restrooms over near the main parking lot. He said you should be able to recognize him pretty easily. He'll be the one…"

"Carrying a surfboard?"

"Right."

Even though it was fall now, South Beach – the biggest and most popular beach on Martha's Vineyard – was still packed with people. The ocean water stayed warm here for weeks after Labor Day, so it was even more comfortable for swimmers than it was in the early summer when it could still be very chilly.

The surfer waiting to talk to us turned out to be a middle-aged guy. He seemed sincere about trying to help by calling the police right after he saw the girl. But I wasn't sure it was going to be of much use. His description of the girl was vague. Only that she seemed to be confused and out of it.

Sure enough, when we found her a little later sitting on a dune about a half-mile down the beach, it was not the mystery girl from the hospital. Or the missing Karin Lavelle either. She was the right age, but that's about all. She didn't look like either one of them.

The girl said her name was Jill Holtzman and she had run away from home after an argument with her parents about getting a tattoo and having her nose pierced. She said she'd been hanging out here on the beach ever since then trying to figure out what she should do next.

"Are you going to arrest me?" she asked anxiously.

"No, we just want to make sure you get home safely," I said.

"My parents will be furious with me."

"I bet they'll be glad to see you."

"You don't understand…"

The thing was I did understand. I'd been through enough of my own teenage angst here to know what this girl was going through.

I didn't have any answers for her any more than I had answers for myself when I was her age, but I understood.

Once we got her back home, we kept on driving west toward Albert Ruggerio's home.

On the way, Teena asked me about Lincoln Connor. She'd obviously seen the tense exchange between us at the press conference. I told her how he'd showed up unexpectedly at my door that night.

"What happened then?"

"Uh, we had sex."

"And afterward?"

"He spent the night, went back to his hotel in the morning."

"That's it?"

"Well, he did kinda ask me to marry him."

"Jeez! Was he serious?"

"I'm not sure."

"But you're going to keep seeing him?"

"I think so."

When we got to Ruggerio's house, it looked the same as it did the last time we were there. We parked outside and waited. I wasn't sure what we were waiting for. At one point, the good-looking, well-dressed security chief came out the front door, looked at our car, waved at us and then went back inside. I guess he must have recognized our car from last time.

But, after that, nothing. No one went in or out of the house. No one came over to give us the secret Mafia handshake. Big Al did not tell us he wanted to confess.

"Sooner or later, he's got to come out of there," Teena said.

"Maybe not. They could spirit him off the island secretly. Then it would be even tougher to get to him once he's out of our jurisdiction."

"What about a warrant to bring him in for questioning?"

"We don't have enough evidence against him for a warrant. It's all circumstantial. He was a patient of Doctor Lavelle's, he's got a violent history, etc. But that's a long way from pinning the Lavelle family murders on him. Even though I'm pretty sure he must have been behind it all somehow."

"So how long do we just keep sitting out here?" Teena said.

Before I could answer, my phone rang. It was Dave Bowers at the station. He sounded really excited.

"You better get back here right away," he said when I answered. "Big news on the mystery girl from the hospital. I'm getting an ID. I'm waiting for the email right now from the FBI. It's supposed to arrive any minute."

Bowers, of course, was the man responsible for letting the unknown girl slip away from the hospital. I knew he felt bad about that and was doing everything he could to try to make up for his mistake.

"I've got the name!" Bowers yelled now as I heard a ping over the phone when an email landed in his mailbox and he opened it. "Susan Kirwin."

"Where did you get that?" I asked.

"The feds. Remember we sent all the fingerprints we found at The Beach House crime scene to them to run through their data bank? They just got back to me on it. There was only one they could identify. That was her. And they sent her picture. It's the same kid we found there, Abby."

"Why is a fifteen-year-old girl's fingerprints in the federal data bank?"

"Apparently she committed some kind of crime and got fingerprinted for it."

"What kind of crime?"

"Hold on a second… I'm still trying to read through all this."

He went through the rest of the email now.

"Jesus!" he suddenly yelled out.

"What? What did she do?"

"Susan Kirwin was arrested for killing her entire family."

CHAPTER 31

"Susan Kirwin is sixteen years old," Dave Bowers said. "A year older than the Lavelle daughter who's missing. Originally from Morristown, New Jersey, she's moved around to a lot of different foster homes over the past several years."

"Foster homes because…"

"Right. Because her parents were dead."

"And she killed them?"

"That's never been officially confirmed. Which is why she wasn't still in some kind of juvenile institution. She was initially arrested, but then the charges were dropped for lack of evidence. She was only thirteen years old at the time her mother and father died. Here's what happened…"

Susan Kirwin's parents died in a fire. They were trapped in their house when the blaze broke out and couldn't escape. Thirteen-year-old Susan somehow managed to get out though and was unhurt, even though the house behind her was an inferno of flames. Firemen and police arriving at the scene found her sitting, dazed and confused, in front of her burning house.

Dazed and confused?

Sort of like she was at the Lavelle crime scene at The Beach House here, I thought to myself.

She wasn't able to give them any new details about what happened. All she remembered, she said, was being outside, seeing the flames from the blaze and then hearing the sirens of fire trucks and rescue units and police arriving.

At first, the assumption was that the fire had been accidental. It was determined to have been started from a space heater device that had been placed too close to a curtain in one of the bedrooms – and the curtain caught fire, which then quickly spread throughout the rest of the house.

But the more details authorities found out at the fire scene, the more disturbing questions they found.

For one thing, the space heater had just been bought a few days earlier. And it was bought by the girl herself at a nearby store. She said that she had been cold at night, asked her parents if she could have the extra heater and they said yes. Still, it seemed like an improbable series of events that led to the fatal blaze.

Young Susan also gave a lot of confusing answers about how she managed to get out of the house and her parents did not. As a result of that, authorities soon became suspicious of the thirteen-year-old girl.

Then came the most disturbing revelation. Both parents died in the same room, the bedroom next to Susan's where the heater had been placed. An examination of the room indicated the lock on the parents' bedroom door seemed to be locked from the outside.

It also appeared that some kind of glue might have been used on the lock to make it difficult to open too. Which meant someone had deliberately trapped the parents in the room. Presumably after setting the fire in the other bedroom with the space heater. And the main suspect – as incredulous as it seemed – had to be the thirteen-year-old daughter.

"She locked them in to die?" I said in amazement. "A thirteen-year-girl could do something so monstrous."

"Like I said, no one could ever prove that," Bowers said. "But yes, that seemed to be what happened, according to the local police and fire officials in Morristown who investigated the parents' deaths."

It turned out that Susan was the only child in the family at the moment. But there had been a younger brother when she was growing up. He died when he drowned in the family swimming pool when he was eight and she was eleven. The only other person in the pool with him was Susan. She said she tried to save him, but there was some speculation by authorities afterward that she might have drowned him herself.

That's because during a counseling session with a school psychologist – after some earlier behavioral problems – young Susan had told the counselor she hated the brother and: "I want him to go away. I don't want him around anymore. Whatever it takes, I want him gone. I'm going to make sure that happens."

It was also revealed that she had been fighting with her parents in the days and weeks before the fire and they had taken away her phone and computer and grounded her as punishment for some of her behavior. Friends said she was furious over that – and vowed she'd get back at them.

In the end though, the authorities were forced to conclude that there was no real hard evidence that she had deliberately set the fire or prevented them from getting out of the flaming building.

And so, after a period in juvenile facilities, she was sent to a foster home as part of the child welfare process.

"Wait a minute," I said. "They think she might have killed her parents. So they put her in a house with another set of parents. Foster parents. Does that seem logical?"

Bowers shrugged.

"What were they going to do with her?"

"Did they tell the foster parents about her background?"

"Presumably."

"Then why did they agree to take her in?"

"From what I understand, there's a lot of money to be made by taking in foster kids. Some of these families take in multiple foster children. It's supposed to be a real money machine if you know how to play the child foster care system right. Maybe that's all they cared about. Or they didn't think she was really any danger. Or they figured they could control her? Who knows?"

"Still…"

"She did move on to a series of foster parents. So there must have been a lot of problems with her along the way. She ran away from the last family. They said they hadn't seen her in days until she showed up here at our crime scene."

"Let me ask you the obvious question. Were Thomas Lavelle and his wife ever one of the families that took in Susan Kirwin to live with them?"

"No. There's no record of the Lavelle family ever taking in any foster children. All of the children in their family were their own."

"Damn."

"You didn't think it was going to be that easy, did you, Abby?"

"One can always hope…"

CHAPTER 32

"Let's look at the security video again," I said to Teena.

"We already watched all of it from anywhere around town that we could find footage."

"No, I mean the security video at The Beach House."

"But they didn't have any cameras there, except for the lobby and manager's office and the parking lot. We've looked at that. Nothing there."

"Then let's go back to The Beach House and look through it all again. Maybe we missed something."

Teena and I were sitting on a bench outside the station, near the town beach. We'd got some takeout sandwiches at a deli and were trying to grab a quick lunch before going back to the investigation.

It was a beautiful fall day, with the sun shining brightly and the temperature comfortable in the low eighties. The water on the Cedar Cliffs beach is on the harbor side of Nantucket Sound, so the waves lap slowly onto shore – not crashing down like they did on the south side of the island.

"That means we have to go and see Lily Munster or whatever her name is at The Beach House again," Teena said. "She won't be happy to see us."

I laughed.

"Are you afraid of Lily, Teena?"

"Aren't you?"

"I've never seen you intimidated by anyone."

"The woman's pretty scary."

"We have guns," I pointed out.

"I'm not sure bullets can kill her."

"We'll kill her with kindness."

It took quite a bit of kindness and a lot of prodding to get Lily to cooperate with us again. But Teena and I used all of our charm to eventually win her over. So there we were watching hours and hours of people coming in and out of the lobby and manager's office of The Beach House.

We watched the Lavelle family showing up and checking in for their vacation, looking happy and excited and with no clue of what horror lay ahead for them. We watched numerous other guests arriving and departing. We watched hotel employees moving around as they did their jobs through the day and night. It seemed to be a wasted effort. We kept watching all the way through until the time of the murder, when our mystery girl was led through the lobby and into the manager's office by Cedar Cliff police officers.

"Satisfied?" Teena asked, turning to me.

"Let's keep watching."

"The murder has already happened."

"Yes, and we've been looking for something unusual that happened beforehand. Let's see if anything unusual happened afterward."

Teena shrugged and the video kept playing.

The girl we found inside the Lavelles' rooms with the bodies was accompanied into the manager's office by one of the officers. The officer gave her something to drink, put a blanket around her and she sat down. She still had the same blank, unseeing stare on her face as I'd seen that day at the scene and later at the hospital. Like she was totally unaware of anything going on around her.

This went on for about fifteen minutes or so. Then the officer with her was summoned by a knock on the door. He left the office where the girl was, closing the door behind him. I realized this was probably the moment when I had arrived to see the girl.

But then, the moment the door closed behind him, everything changed with the girl. The blank expression was gone, she began looking around intensely until she found what she was looking for – a telephone. She picked up the phone on one of the desks, punched in a number and carried on a brief conversation with someone.

A few minutes later, the officer – accompanied by me now – returned to the room. By then, the girl was seated behind the desk again, with the blank, unaware of anything expression on her face once again.

"My God, she made a phone call!" I said.

"She was faking the whole time."

"So who did she call to tell what was happening?"

"That is the question, huh?"

Lily's cooperation had its limits, and we reached that limit when we told her we needed to go through the phone records for the hotel that day. She said she wasn't authorized to do that. She said we'd have to speak to the owner of The Beach House.

"Who owns the place?" I asked.

"Island Realty."

"Anyone special to talk to there?"

"Well, the president and CEO is Melvin Ellis. But his son has been doing a lot of the day-to-day operational work recently. His name is Mark Ellis."

"Mark Ellis?" I said with obvious astonishment to her.

"Yes, do you know him?"

I sure did know Mark Ellis.

Mark Ellis took me to my senior prom.

And Mark Ellis was the boy who for years I mistakenly thought was the one who had raped me on that long-ago prom night.

CHAPTER 33

"There's something weird going on here, Teena," I said afterward. "First, it turns out that the restaurant at The Beach House used to be the one owned by my family. Now I find out that The Beach House hotel and restaurant are owned by Island Realty. Which just happens to be run by the Ellis family. Specifically, at the moment, Mark Ellis. A person with whom, as you know, I have a long history with."

"What do you think it all means?"

"I don't know, but it seems like this case is getting very personal for me."

"Look, it's a small island. The Ellis family – Melvin Ellis and his son Mark – probably own half the businesses on it these days. The odds aren't that unusual that they turn out to be the owners of The Beach House."

"I guess."

"You're saying The Beach House used to be your family's restaurant. But it isn't really. Your father sold it to someone else who operated it under a different name for a while before the sale to Island Realty. Again, there's only a handful of restaurants that change hands on Martha's Vineyard and a handful of people who run them. So it's not really that unusual the way things worked out. It probably doesn't mean anything at all. I mean why would someone want to make it personal with you?"

I had no answer for that. But there was something else troubling me. Something I hadn't mentioned to anyone. About that slogan on the wall near the Lavelle bodies. The words "No One Here Gets Out Alive" written in the victims' blood. How that was something my old NYPD partner Tommy Ferraro and I used to say to each other on the street in New York City before Tommy died. Tommy had been a big Jim Morrison and The Doors fan, and it just seemed funny – or at least alleviated some of the pressure – whenever we went into a potentially dangerous situation.

Well, it seemed funny until Tommy died.

I had never thought much about the phrase again until it showed up on that wall. At the time, I assumed it had no connection whatsoever to me. But now I wondered. Was that aimed at me too? If so, the only people who knew about "No One Here Gets Out Alive" were other cops Tommy and I worked with back then. I didn't want to think that any police from my past could be involved in all this. So I kept that information to myself – at least for now.

Instead, I brought up the only explanation for all this that made any sense to me.

"You know, Teena, I got a lot of national publicity when I broke the big teenage sex/murder case here. I was all over TV cable channels. Written up in newspapers. Some of the stuff about me and my career even went viral on social media. Maybe some sick person became obsessed with me for some reason…"

"Obsessed enough to kill a family of five people and kidnap their daughter too just to get your attention?"

"Pretty crazy idea, huh?"

"Definitely crazy."

We talked some more about the strange connection, or whatever the hell it was, between my father's old restaurant the Vineyard Grille and The Beach House where the murders had taken place and where my old high school prom date Mark Ellis was now the owner.

No matter how many times we went over the details, neither of us had any idea what, if anything, this meant.

Or if it meant anything at all.

"What does Ellis say?"

"I don't know yet. I'm talking to him tonight. I'm supposed to meet him at the bar of the restaurant that's part of The Beach House."

"You're meeting up in a bar with the same guy you hated for practically your whole life because you thought he was the one who got you drunk and then raped you after your senior prom?"

"Yep."

"Well, that should be interesting," Teena said.

CHAPTER 34

There was a dark blue Buick sitting next to the Cedar Cliffs station when I left that night to meet Mark Ellis at The Beach House.

I noticed it because you don't see many cars that big on Martha's Vineyard. I didn't pay much attention to it then. But I noticed it again in my rear-view mirror once I pulled out of the station parking area and began driving down the road along the ocean toward The Beach House. That's when I began watching it carefully.

Of course, it could have just been another driver headed toward The Beach House or somewhere else south on the island.

But I was suspicious of the timing.

I kept glancing in the rear-view mirror at the Buick, which was staying behind me, moving at the same speed I was.

Just when I was considering whether I should make a turn off on one of the side roads to see if the Buick turned too and followed me, it changed its pattern on me and disappeared from the spot it had been in my rear-view mirror.

Instead, the driver had now speeded up and was passing me on the left side.

I slowed a bit to let the Buick get by and then watched its taillights disappear on the road in front of me.

But not for long.

A few hundred yards further down, I saw it parked along the side of the road. Its warning indicators were flashing so I couldn't miss it. I was pretty sure now the Buick had been following me ever since I left the station house. And whoever was driving the Buick was waiting for me up ahead.

I pulled my car up behind it, took out my gun and pointed it toward the vehicle as I approached it.

"I'm a police officer!" I announced in a loud voice.

There was no response from inside the Buick.

"Step out of the car and show me your hands," I said.

The door on the driver's side opened now, and a man stepped out. He had his hands in the air. At first, I couldn't see his face clearly. But, once I did, I recognized him right away. It was the security guy from Albert Ruggerio's house.

"You were following me," I said to him.

"Yes, I was."

"Not a very good job of it."

"What do you mean?"

"That's one of the worst tails I've ever seen. I picked it up right away. You couldn't have been more obvious."

"That's because I wanted you to see me."

"Why?"

"We need to talk, Detective."

"About what?"

"Can I put my hands down now?"

I nodded.

"And our conversation would be more comfortable if you weren't pointing that weapon at me while we talked."

I put my gun back in the holster and walked over to him.

"What do we have to talk about?" I asked.

"You need to stop harassing, Mr. Ruggerio." he said. "Sitting outside his house like you just did – or trying to talk to him. He knows nothing about these murders you're investigating or the girls who are missing. There is no reason for you to question him, and I cannot continue to allow you to keep trying. If you do, the consequences for you will be… well, unpleasant. This is not a course it would be wise for you to pursue, Detective Pearce."

"Are you threatening me?"

"I'm giving you a warning."

"Same thing."

He sighed.

"Let me tell you a story about another police officer that got involved with Mr. Ruggerio, who tried to interfere with his life and his business operations. This man became obsessed with Mr. Ruggerio, much like you seem to be. He kept coming after him, stalking him on the street and trying to find some way to arrest him. Nothing could convince this man that he was wasting his time. It became a real problem for Mr. Ruggerio and his business activities. Then one day this police officer left for work in the morning, got in his car and the engine caught fire and exploded. He was killed. There was barely enough of him left after the blast to put into a coffin. Very tragic, but it solved Mr. Ruggerio's problem."

I stared at him.

"Your boss blew up a cop's car?"

"I never said that."

"But…"

"I'm simply telling you a story to make a point."

"Which is that I have to worry now whenever I get into my car?"

"You seem like a nice woman, Detective Pearce. This is a nice island. No one wants any trouble here. I don't. Mr. Ruggerio doesn't. And I hope you feel the same way. Just walk away from this, Pearce. Mr. Ruggerio doesn't have any of the answers you're looking for. But he's going to become angry if you keep trying to ask him about the Lavelle case. And you don't want to make Mr. Ruggerio angry, believe me. I'm doing you a favor here, Pearce. Don't push him anymore or you'll be sorry you did."

He got back into his car. I guess he'd said everything he wanted to say. I walked around to the front of the Buick and looked at the license plate. It was a New York plate.

"Who owns this car?" I asked.

"Mr. Ruggerio."

"How long has it been on the island?"

"Oh, most of this year I guess. Why?"

"Tell Mr. Ruggerio he needs to get Massachusetts plates on it after six months here. Next time I see it, I'll be issuing him or you or whoever's driving it a summons that he'll have to appear in court to pay. That's my warning to you. Have a nice evening, sir. And drive safely. We take our traffic laws – and all of our laws, as a matter of fact – very seriously here on Martha's Vineyard."

He sighed.

"Anything else or can I go now?"

"Just one more thing."

"Yeah?"

"Tell your boss that I still want to talk to him."

I went back to my car then and watched the Buick pull away as he went back to Ruggerio's house to deliver my message.

CHAPTER 35

The bar at The Beach House restaurant was everything a beach bar should be. There was a window overlooking Nantucket Sound and quiet jazz playing in the background. The bartender came over and smiled. I smiled back. He put down a paper coaster in front of me and slid over a bowl of peanuts.

I loved all these little rituals in a bar. In the old days, the best moment would be when the bartender brought that first vodka for me. The ice cubes clinking pleasantly along the side of the glass. That first drink was always the best for me. Like a first kiss. Exciting, with the promise of so much more to come.

A few minutes later, Mark Ellis slipped onto the stool next to me.

A lifetime ago on Martha's Vineyard, Mark Ellis and I had been two different people than we were now. He was the handsome high school hunk I dreamed about being with and I was the shy girl who couldn't believe he'd asked me to the senior prom. But what should have been the best night of my life turned into the worst.

As it turned out, that wasn't his fault.

But it took me a long time to realize that.

Still, sitting with him here in a bar after all these years and memories of that night all seemed a bit weird for me.

"Thanks for coming," I said. "I'm hoping you can help me get some more background information on The Beach House that might help with our investigation into the murders that took place here."

"Happy to help any way I can, Abby. I assume you've already talked to Lily Knowlton."

"Yes. That's why I'm here with you now."

"Lily wasn't very helpful?"

"She seems more interested in when she can rent the place out again than she does in helping me solve the case."

"Lily is always very much about the bottom line. That makes her a good manager. But not always the easiest person to deal with. It's all about money with her. Just like it's always been about money with my father."

"And you don't care about money?"

"Like I said, Abby, I'll do anything I can to help you find out who did this. That's why I'm here."

He signaled the bartender for a Jack Daniel's on the rocks. The bartender came over with the drink.

"What are you drinking?" he asked, looking over at my half-empty glass.

"Diet Coke."

"You don't drink?"

"Not tonight."

"Did you stop drinking after everything that happened that night after our prom?"

"Oh, no. I've drunk quite a bit since then."

"When did you stop?"

"I'm not sure that I have."

"But you said…"

"I'm not drinking tonight, Mark. That's all I can tell you."

He nodded.

"Well, whatever you're doing, it works for you, Abby. You look terrific," he said, and I could tell he meant it.

"So do you, Mark," I said, even though I didn't mean it.

The pretty boy looks he'd had in high school were gone now. He had thinning hair, a noticeable paunch that hung over his belt – and he looked like an ordinary middle-aged man, not the to-die-for guy he'd been back when I was a teenager with a crush on him. Me, on the other hand, I knew I looked better now than I did back then. I looked pretty damn good. The years had been kinder to me than they had for Mark Ellis. And, even though I no longer hated him for what I wrongly thought he'd done to me, that still gave me a certain satisfaction.

I told him about the phone call the mystery girl, Susan Kirwin, had made from the office right after the killings – and said I needed to find out whatever information he could get about it from the hotel phone records. I asked him too for any other information about the Lavelle stay there that he could get from The Beach House office.

He took out a phone when I was finished and called the manager's office to talk to Lily Knowlton. I thanked him and we wound up talking a bit about our lives while we waited for some answers.

"I've been here for a few months now," he said. "I was working in Hollywood, as an agent and business manager, in the film industry. But I not sure I'm going back to Hollywood. I might just relocate here. At least for now."

"Why does a person leave the bright lights of Hollywood to come live in Cedar Cliffs?"

I asked.

He smiled.

"Why does a police officer leave the bright lights of New York and the NYPD to come work with the Cedar Cliffs police force?" Ellis asked.

"Good point," I said.

"I have a wife and two kids, just going into their teens," he said. "I just think this is a better place to raise them than Hollywood. And I wasn't that wild about working in Hollywood either. It sounds glamorous, but it's really not very fulfilling. So, when I found out my father needed some help here, I came back. How about you?"

"Oh, lots of reasons. My marriage broke up. I was having issues with my job on the NYPD. Anyway, I just felt like I needed a change of scenery, so I came back to this island where I grew up."

"Life always seemed so much simpler back here then, when were kids, didn't it?"

"Yes, I guess it did."

"So how has it worked out for you?"

"Well, life has been anything but simple here so far."

He laughed. It was a nice laugh. The truth was I kind of liked Mark Ellis now. I wasn't in love with him like I'd been in high school, and he sure wasn't a sex symbol for me anymore. But I liked him better. Maybe we could be friends. I could use some friends here. And besides, he had plenty of money, maybe he could buy me dinner sometime.

He was on his third Jack Daniel's and I was nursing my second Diet Coke when his phone rang. He answered it, listened for a while – then wrote down a phone number on a napkin and handed it to me.

"That's the number the girl called that day."

It was a 917 number. Probably a cell phone. It didn't seem familiar to me, but no reason it should. I'd check it out when I got back to the office.

"Thanks, Mark."

"There's something else…"

"Go ahead."

"I asked Lily to check out the Lavelle family registration information. To see if there was anything unusual there. Well, there was. Lily found out who booked the reservation for Thomas Lavelle and his family here at The Beach House. And it wasn't Thomas Lavelle or his wife."

"Who was it?"

"The reservation was made by Albert Ruggerio."

CHAPTER 36

The next morning Teena and I drove back to Albert Ruggerio's house in Menemsha. This time we had a warrant with us. It authorized us to enter Ruggerio's property, to search the premises if necessary and, most importantly of all, to question Ruggerio about any knowledge he might have concerning the Lavelle murders and the disappearance of their teenage daughter, Karin.

The phone number I'd gotten from Ellis turned out to be from a burner cell phone, so that didn't take us anywhere. But we were able to determine that the call had been made to a location somewhere on Martha's Vineyard. Did she call Ruggerio for some reason after the murders were done? We couldn't be sure, but that seemed to be a likely premise.

The big thing was the revelation that Ruggerio had been the one who set up the reservations for Lavelle and his family at The Beach House. Why did he do that? Well, the assumption – a reasonable one – was that he was luring Lavelle to the island to get revenge against him for mistakes in his heart surgery. I mean if this guy Ruggerio was willing to kill someone who messed with his garbage can, just imagine how mad he'd be with the surgeon who had messed up his heart.

Sure, there was a lot of speculation and supposition in this scenario but enough for us to get the warrant to compel Ruggerio to talk to us.

Ruggerio's security chief didn't seem to be surprised to see us when we arrived. I had the feeling he knew we'd be back. The guy had been around, and he knew the way the law worked. He could delay it for a while, but sooner or later he was going to have to allow Ruggerio to meet with us.

I held up the warrant for him to see. He didn't ask to read it.

"If you want me to read the specifics out aloud to you ..."

"Not necessary. I'm sure everything's in proper legal order."

"Then let us inside to speak to Ruggerio."

"I don't suppose it would do any good to ask you to surrender your weapons outside here first, would it?"

"That's not happening."

"What if I insisted?"

"Read Page three of the warrant. It specifically has a line about the police being authorized to carry weapons during the interrogation and/or also throughout any search of the premises. I specifically asked for that section to be added after you and your people tried to pull that on us last time we were here."

The security chief nodded. He knew that. I think he just wanted to make us go through all this before he eventually let us in.

"Be careful how you talk to Mr. Ruggerio. He's not a well man. I don't want you to say or do anything that might upset him and be injurious to his health."

"From what I understand, Mr. Ruggerio has done a lot of things that were injurious to other people's health."

He looked at me and smiled.

"You're an interesting woman, Detective Pearce. Maybe when this is all sorted out, you and I could get together off duty. Have a drink... maybe even a dinner in town. I'll bet we have a lot of things in common we could talk about."

"I doubt that. I'm a law enforcement officer, and you work for an underworld boss. Not much in common at all, the way I see it. Now please take me to Ruggerio."

Albert Ruggerio wasn't what I expected. He didn't look scary or intimidating at all. He looked like an old man. The man who was a feared killer in New York for so many years was in a wheelchair now and hooked up to some kind of oxygen machine that helped him breathe.

I told him what we wanted, but I didn't have to. He knew about the death of Thomas Lavelle and his family, he said.

"Is it true that Doctor Lavelle was the one who performed open heart surgery on you several months ago?"

"Yes, Doctor Lavelle is the reason I'm sitting here like this today."

That sounded ominous. I looked over at Teena. Maybe this guy was going to make some kind of deathbed confession to us.

"Were you angry at Doctor Lavelle because of this?"

"What do you mean?"

"Because you're in a wheelchair and on oxygen. You blame Doctor Lavelle for that, right? You were very angry at Doctor Lavelle for that and—"

"No, the opposite."

"Excuse me?"

"I was grateful to Doctor Lavelle."

"I don't understand—"

"I had a massive coronary. Virtually all the arteries to my heart were blocked. Other doctors said there was nothing that could be done. No one could save my life. But Doctor Lavelle did. He operated, managed to repair much of the damage around my heart and kept me alive. Ever since then, I've been getting better. This wheelchair, the oxygen is only temporary. They say I'll be up and moving around on my own soon. I owe it all to Doctor Lavelle. I owe my life to him."

That was pretty hard to believe. I told him that. But he stayed with the same story. How he wasn't upset with Dr. Lavelle over the heart surgery, he was thankful to him.

"Why did you bring Doctor Lavelle up here and book him and his family into The Beach House."

"I never did that."

"But your name is on the reservation."

"I know. Doctor Lavelle called me to thank me for giving him this free vacation here. Except I didn't do it. I told him that. But I think maybe he didn't believe me – like you probably don't believe me – when I say that I had absolutely nothing to do with bringing Doctor Lavelle or the members of his family to Martha's Vineyard."

"Then why is your name on the reservation?"

"Someone else must have used it to get him here – and then do this terrible thing."

"But that wasn't you?"

Ruggerio shook his head no.

"Did you really think I had this man murdered?"

"We have to pursue all possible leads," I said.

"And you seem like one," Teena added. "You have a reputation as a killer, Mr. Ruggerio. I'm sure you realize that makes you a prime suspect in the Lavelle murders, especially given your background and connections with him."

"Even if you believe I've had people killed, and I'm not saying I do, does this make any sense to you? That I would kill the man's entire family? Even young children? And that I would have had it done with a knife and all that blood and violence? Again, I'm not telling you I've ever done any killing like that. But, just hypothetically speaking, if I did such a crime that certainly wouldn't have been the way I would do it. Right?"

Yes, Ruggerio was right about that.

That had bothered me from the beginning about Ruggerio.

This didn't feel like a Mob hit.

And it really didn't fit that Ruggerio did this.

Something was wrong here.

Oh, I wanted Ruggerio to be the killer. It was so simple that way. Everything fell into place if we could arrest Ruggerio for the murder of Thomas Lavelle and the disappearance of Karin Lavelle.

It was what I was hoping I could do when I got the warrant to come out here and interrogate Ruggerio.

But now I was starting to have my own doubts.

Ruggerio's story of being grateful to the dead doctor and having nothing to do with him coming to the Vineyard was absurd and unbelievable.

But it was so absurd and unbelievable it was almost…

Well, believable.

And if he was telling the truth, that put me and this investigation in a spot I didn't want to be in.

Back at square one…

CHAPTER 37

Chief Wilhelm was flustered. And mad. Really mad. As mad as I'd ever seen him.

And, of course, he was mad at me.

"Wait a minute!" he said after I told him about our interview with Ruggerio at his house. "You've been telling me for days now that Ruggerio is the guy who did all this. Pushed me to help you get a warrant to force him to talk, even though you had no real hard evidence against him. But I finally let you get the warrant – the warrant you said would break the case wide open with Ruggerio – and now you tell me that he's innocent?"

"He's far from innocent," I said. "He's a bad guy. Really bad guy. He belongs in jail. They should lock him up and throw away the key, as far as I'm concerned. But I don't think he killed Thomas Lavelle and his family – or snatched their daughter."

"And yet you confronted one of the richest and most powerful people on this island and practically accused him of the murders."

"I thought then he did it. Now I don't."

"Because he told you 'I didn't do it'. And you believed him?"

"Uh, yes…"

"Jesus, Pearce!"

"It's more than just that. He convinced me he had no motive. That he wasn't angry with Lavelle. That Lavelle helped him, the same way he helped a lot of his other patients that we checked out. Without a motive, the case against Ruggerio falls apart."

"What about the reservation for the Lavelles that he made at The Beach House? You used that as the basis for us getting the damn warrant."

"I don't think that it was him who made the reservation. I think someone else used his name. They wanted to set him up as a suspect for us."

"Why?"

I shrugged.

"Ruggerio's an easy target. Anyone would believe he could do something so terrible as wipe out an entire family. Hell, I believed it too. But this isn't about Ruggerio. Oh, he's part of it for some reason, whether he realizes it or not. But someone else is out there pulling all the strings. We don't know who that is."

That's when Wilhelm really lost it.

"Goddamit, Pearce, you've come up with nothing on this case! I know you're supposed to be this hotshot ex-NYPD homicide detective. But I have to go the mayor and the city council now and tell them what we know. What am I supposed to tell them? They're not going to be happy with me."

I thought about saying to Wilhelm that he should tell the unhappy mayor and city council leaders how much he'd contributed himself to this investigation. That ought to give them a laugh.

But I bit my tongue instead. It wasn't easy, but I didn't want to take a chance of being suspended by him for insubordination or something. I needed to stay on this case, no matter what. Even though I wasn't exactly sure what to do next.

The hard truth was that I felt as lost on the Lavelle case at the moment as Chief Wilhelm.

There was a bar not far from my house in Chilmark that I passed every night on the way to my house.

I didn't really think about stopping inside there for a drink much anymore. But tonight that's exactly what I was thinking as

I drove home. I was thinking that I really needed a drink right now. God, I wanted a drink right now more than I had in a long, long time after that scene with Wilhelm.

It was far enough away from Cedar Cliffs that I wasn't likely to run into anyone from the force who knew me or might tell Wilhelm they saw me there. I thought about how I could go into this bar, have a drink or two – and no one would ever know about it. Not Wilhelm. Not even Teena. It would just be my little secret. Then I'd go home, feed and walk Oscar, get a good night's sleep and be back at work in the morning. It seemed like a good plan.

I walked into the bar and sat down on an empty stool. The bartender came over and smiled. I smiled back. I told him what I wanted. Vodka on the rocks. He nodded and brought me my drink. A vodka on the rocks. The ice cubes in the drink clinked pleasantly along the side of the glass. Hello, old friend. It's been a long time, huh? I sat there looking at it for a long time. Savoring this moment. Thinking about it.

And that's when my plan began to fall apart.

Because I knew what would happen if I drank that vodka. I would not stop after one drink. Or two drinks. Or maybe even ten. I would keep on drinking. I would not get home in time to feed and walk Oscar. Or get a good night's sleep. I would not be in good shape to go to work in the morning. I would be royally screwed, just like I was that night on the island when I started drinking vodka at a bar and wound up driving my car into a ditch.

I sat there with all these thoughts running through my mind as I stared at the drink in front of me. I'm not sure how long I did this. Five minutes. Fifteen. Maybe a half hour. Eventually, the bartender came over.

"You haven't touched your drink," he said.

"I know."

"Is there something wrong with it?"

"There's absolutely nothing wrong with this drink," I said.

I paid the bill, left him a big tip and walked out of the place without touching the vodka.

Another day without drinking for Abby Pearce.

CHAPTER 38

Lincoln came to see me the next night. That was nice. He played with Oscar for a little while in the living room, and then we played with each other for a lot longer in the bedroom. When we came out of there, he announced: "I'm hungry."

"I can see why you might have worked up an appetite from what you just did," I said.

"When the going gets tough, the tough eat."

"What's your preference?"

"Probably a little risky for us to go out in public to a restaurant, huh?"

"Yeah, the hotshot TV reporter and the lead homicide detective on the case he's covering… people might think there was something going on between us."

"How about we stay here? What do you have to eat in the house?"

We went into the kitchen. I opened the door of the refrigerator and checked out what was inside.

"It looks like we've got a carton of eggs, a few vegetables from my garden, plus lettuce, a hunk of cheddar cheese and also some kind of lunch meat that looks like it used to be salami in here," I said.

"What do you recommend?"

"That we stay away from the salami."

"You know, I've been known to whip up a pretty tasty omelet."

"Sounds good. I love eating eggs at night for dinner. And I'll make us a salad."

Lincoln took out some eggs and cheese, then started cooking at the stove. I worked on cutting up tomatoes and onions and a few other vegetables for the salad. When I was finished with that, I went over to the stove, came up behind Lincoln and put my arms around him.

"So how do you feel about everything?" he asked me.

"Okay."

"Just okay?"

"Yeah."

"Aren't you happy right now?"

"Yes and no."

"No? What aren't you happy about?"

"This damn case."

"Are you any closer to finding out who did it or why?"

He smiled.

"Off the record, of course."

I hadn't told Lincoln anything about Albert Ruggerio. Or how he was my best lead and chief suspect in the Lavelle murders. Or how we had uncovered a potential motive in the fact that Dr. Lavelle seemed to have botched the heart surgery operation on Ruggerio. I trusted Lincoln, but only to a certain point. He was a reporter, and he had his own job to do. The same as I had to do my job. But it seemed safe to tell him all that information now since the Ruggerio lead seemed to be going nowhere.

"I can't make head nor tail of this damn case, Lincoln. None of it – the mystery girl, the missing daughter, the mass murders themselves. I don't know if we'll ever be able to solve this one." I smiled. "All that's off the record too."

"Okay, that's the 'no' part. What about the 'yes'? Tell me what you are happy about."

"I'm happy that you came back to Martha's Vineyard."

"Did you really think I wouldn't?"

"The truth is I wasn't sure if I would ever see you again."

"Why?"

"I tried not to get my hopes up too high that we would get back together again. Not just because of you. Because of me too. I usually wind up disappointing the men in my life."

"Why do you put yourself down like that, Abby?"

"It saves other people a lot of time."

He laughed.

"Tell me more about your marriage," he said.

"Not much to tell. It happened when I was on the force in New York. He was a cop too. A state trooper. We lasted about three years together. Then… well, it all went downhill from there."

While we ate at the table, he couldn't help but notice the vodka bottle prominently displayed there. I explained to him what it was all about. How I wasn't drinking now, and this was just a reminder of what I didn't want to do with my life anymore. I wasn't sure if that made any kind of sense to Lincoln. But it made sense to me, which was all that mattered. I'd survived that close call at the bar last night, and that made me feel even stronger in my resolve now to stay sober.

"How long have you been dealing with this drinking issue?" he asked.

We'd talked about my drinking before, but never in any detail. Or about what happened to me the first time I drank. I didn't feel totally comfortable opening up about my secrets like this to a man I wanted to have a relationship with like Lincoln. But I didn't want him to feel that I was hiding secrets about my personal life either.

"Pretty much all my adult life. It started when I was still in high school."

"Damn, you really got an early start, didn't you?"

I told him the story of my high school prom. How I was raped after it. How I went through much of my life thinking that the person who did it was the boy I went to the prom with. How my mother and father lied to me about the real person that did it for their own reasons. Because the person who did it had been a family friend and also a big investor in my father's restaurant business. And how I'd never been able to forgive them for not telling me the truth about what happened.

"I just kept drinking after what happened to me that night in high school and everything that followed," I said. "Maybe I would have become an alcoholic anyway. Who knows? Hey, I could have stopped drinking on my own over the years if I tried. But I never really did. Until now. Until I met you. I haven't been drinking since I met you, whatever that means."

"I can't imagine you drunk," he said. "You always seem so poised on your job, so much in control of your life. At least that's the way I picture you. And the alcohol changes all that?"

"I'm not a pretty sight when I'm drinking."

"I hope I never see that."

"Me too."

After we ate, he wound up playing with Oscar some more, engaging in a tug of war with a chew toy that was one of Oscar's favorite pastimes. I watched for a while, then walked over to them.

"Were you serious when you talked about us getting married?"

"Of course, why else would I say it?"

"Just checking."

"So what do you think?"

"Let's talk about it again when this case is all over," I said.

He stood up now and kissed me.

I kissed him back.

Then we left Oscar with his chew toy in the living room and made our way back into the bedroom.

CHAPTER 39

I needed a break in this case. Something dramatic to happen. Sooner or later, that was what occured in most complicated murder cases I'd investigated in the past. And that's what did happen here.

Except when it did, it wasn't anything I expected.

"We've got a report of shots fired at a house out on the western end of the island," Meg yelled across the station house.

"Do we have an address?"

"Checking on that now."

She let out a loud gasp a few seconds later.

"My God, it's Ruggerio's house! The place out near Menemsha where you and Teena talked to him."

We headed out there in force as quickly as we could. Me and Teena in one car, Dave Bowers and more officers in other cars. It's about a thirty-minute trip, but with sirens blaring and going at top speeds on the winding roads of Martha's Vineyard we made it a lot quicker. On the way, we radioed a local police department, which was closer. Told them about the shots fired and said we'd meet them there. The cops were already there when we arrived, but standing outside the security gate looking in.

"What's going on?" I yelled as we got out of the car.

"Not sure yet," one of the cops said. "We haven't been able to get in. The security gate is locked. We keep buzzing and—"

"Can't wait any longer," I told them.

I began to scale the metal fence. It was tall, and not easy to climb. I just hoped there was nothing electrified on it or spikes or anything along the way. But when I was finally able to go over the top, I dropped down on the ground below inside the Ruggerio compound. It was a pretty steep drop, but I didn't break anything. Then I was able to open the gate.

I took out my gun and began walking toward the house, with Teena and the others.

Everything was quiet. If the call had come from someone inside the house, that meant that person might still be in there. Maybe the shooter too. Or maybe whoever fired the shots had already fled. One way or another, I wasn't taking any chances. I kept the gun pointed in front of me the whole time. Teena was right behind me, along with several of the other police officers.

When we got to the front door, I pushed it open. We moved inside and down the long hallway where I had been on my last visit here to see Albert Ruggerio. Then I walked slowly and carefully toward the living room.

"Police officers," I yelled as loudly as I could. "We're inside this house. Put down any weapons you have. This is the Cedar Cliffs Police Department. Please acknowledge that you hear us."

There was no answer.

I began moving further through the house, with the others behind me.

That's when I saw the first person.

Lying on the living room floor, covered in blood.

It was Ruggerio's security chief.

I raced over to him. He was still alive. I radioed for an ambulance, and then checked him out as best I could. There was a wound in his chest that appeared to be a stab wound. He'd lost a lot of blood, but he was still conscious. He started talking to me, as best he could in his condition, about what had happened there.

"It was a girl, a teenage girl," he said to me, struggling to get the words out.

Susan Kirwin. It had to be.

"She came to the front gate asking for directions. She seemed so innocent, just lost. I wasn't worried about her being any danger, so I let her in. Then she took out a knife, and she stabbed me."

"Where is she now?"

"She walked away – I guess she thought I was dead – and headed for the rest of the house. I managed to take out my gun and get off some shots at her. I think I hit her. But she kept going. That's when I took out my cell phone and called the police, saying there'd been a shooting and an attack here."

So it had been him who made the call to Meg.

We moved cautiously toward the bedrooms. I was totally prepared to find another body in there. But I was wrong. It wasn't one body. It was two.

Albert Ruggerio lay slumped in his wheelchair with stab wounds in his chest and head. He was dead.

Next to him lay the girl. She had been shot, apparently by the security guy. But somehow kept going and managed to stab Ruggerio to death before she died herself from the gunshot wounds.

She was lying face down. I turned her over. It was Susan Kirwin, all right. The mystery girl from the Lavelle crime scene who had escaped from the hospital. Now she was at another crime scene, only this time she didn't survive it. Did this mean she had done the killings at the Lavelle place too?

By the time I got back to the security chief, an ambulance crew was there and putting him on a stretcher.

"There's a pretty deep stab wound in his chest," one of the EMS people told me. "Barely missed his aorta, or else he'd be dead. He was damn lucky. Lucky you called us so quickly too. We stopped the bleeding, and we're taking him now to Martha's Vineyard Hospital. But it looks like he's going to make it."

The security chief was still conscious and able to talk.

"Your boss is dead," I said to him now.

"The girl killed him?"

I nodded.

"She's dead too. You hit her with one of your shots. But she still managed to stab your boss to death before she died herself."

The security chief shook his head.

"Ruggerio wasn't my boss," he said.

"You worked for him, didn't you?"

"Not really."

"I don't understand."

"That was just a way for me to get close to him. By pretending I was in the Mob and his bodyguard. While I gathered information about Ruggerio and his Mob friends and his dirty business and everything else about him back in New York City. I was actually working undercover."

"Undercover for who?"

"The NYPD."

I stared at him in amazement.

"Yeah, that's right, Pearce. I'm a cop too. We're on the same side."

CHAPTER 40

The security chief's name was Roy DeSantis. He told me at the hospital later – as he recovered from his wounds during the attack – how he'd been posing as a mobster with the Ruggerio crime family both in New York and later on Martha's Vineyard when Ruggerio moved up here. Except he was really working undercover for the NYPD's Organized Crime Control Bureau.

I couldn't find any record of a Roy DeSantis as a New York City police officer when I checked with the NYPD. Which didn't surprise me. If he really was working undercover, the department would not want to leave a trail or evidence which might expose him to anyone who checked up on his background.

Underworld organizations like the one headed by Ruggerio had informers everywhere, even within the police department. No information was safe from them. I'd learned that during my years with the NYPD, and I knew the organized crime people kept everything very top-secret and on a need-to-know basis.

Well, I had a need to know now.

And so, after numerous exchanges between me and Captain Wilhelm and top officials at 1 Police Plaza in New York, we were able to confirm that DeSantis was telling the truth. He was an undercover cop for the NYPD. He was posing as a mobster to get close to Ruggerio. And all of it was part of a massive investigation into Ruggerio's underworld dealings.

Neither the NYPD or DeSantis were happy about the way things turned out. But then neither was I.

"You really screwed everything up, Pearce," DeSantis told me from his hospital bed.

"What do you mean?"

"You were the one who came after Ruggerio on the Lavelle family murder case. I tried to warn you off, but you wouldn't listen. You seemed to have some idea that Ruggerio was involved in it. He wasn't, but that made him a target for this crazy girl that you found at the crime scene to go after him. Why did the damn girl do that?"

"I was hoping you could shed some light on that."

"Why should I help you after you blew up our investigation?"

"Well, for one thing, I saved your life."

"Huh?"

"You would have bled out if we hadn't gotten to you so quickly. That's what the doctors tell me. The only reason you're alive right now is because we got you medical help in time, DeSantis."

"Ah, right."

"You're welcome," I said.

"Okay, thank you." He smiled.

I asked him as many questions as I could think of about what happened back at Ruggerio's house.

"Like I said before, the girl seemed harmless at first," DeSantis said. "I had no idea who she was until you told me the story later. She wanted some directions, she acted scared and confused. I felt sorry for her. I invited her in and tried to look up on a map where she wanted to go, so I could help her.

"That's when she suddenly went crazy. Before I knew what was happening, she had taken out the knife, and she stabbed me in the chest. It was a really deep, well-directed knife blow too, like she was a pro at it. Okay, I know it was stupid for me to let her do that. But my guard was down, I wasn't expecting it from a teenage girl. Suddenly she was screaming about Ruggerio being a murderer and how he would now pay.

"I was lying on the floor and I guess she thought I was dead. But I managed to take out my gun and get off the shots that hit her. I wasn't sure at the time, because she kept moving. But I figured I'd at least wounded her, even though nothing seemed to stop her. She kept walking toward the bedroom where Ruggerio was. He was screaming at me from inside, asking me what was going on. I tried to warn him, but I guess my voice was too weak for him to hear.

"I managed to get out my phone and call your number. It was still on my phone from the last time you were here. That's why I called Cedar Cliffs police, not the local station out here on this side of the island. I got a few words out to whoever answered, and I was able to give them the address. Anyway, that's pretty much all I remember until you showed up and told me that both of them were dead."

"Where were the other security guards?" I asked him.

"They had left in the car about five minutes before the girl came to the front gate and rang the intercom. She must have been watching the house and seen them leave."

He asked me his own questions about the girl. But, other than her name, Susan Kirwin, and the family background, I didn't have much to tell him.

"Why did she kill Ruggerio?" he asked.

"I don't know."

"A teenage girl like that. First you find her at your mass murder scene at The Beach House, then she comes out to the other side of the island and kills Ruggerio. It doesn't make any sense."

I wanted to know more about the investigation by the NYPD into Albert Ruggerio.

"That's still classified, confidential information. What I can tell you is that Ruggerio had a long life of crime. But, as you saw when you came out here, he was pretty much finished now. Even if he hadn't died, he wouldn't have been able to maintain an active hold on his underworld organization. Still, we knew he'd done a lot of bad stuff in his time – loansharking, drugs, armed robbery, extortion, bribery and even murder. So we were hoping to get that information before he died. That's why I was there. And now…"

"What? I really was hoping you could tell me some more information about Ruggerio and his activities that might help me shed some light on his connection to the murders of the Lavelle family, the whereabouts of their missing daughter and how the mystery girl you shot fits into all this."

"Ruggerio's dead," he said. "My case is over. More than a year of undercover work down the drain. You work your own case. I'm going back to New York as soon as I get out of this place."

CHAPTER 41

"It's pretty clear now what happened," Chief Wilhelm said. "The girl was the one who murdered the Lavelle family, just like we should have known from the beginning when we found her at that crime scene. Then she kills Albert Ruggerio too, but she's shot dead by the NYPD undercover cop while she's doing it."

"We still don't know all that for sure," I told him.

"But what happened to the missing Lavelle girl?" he said, ignoring my hesitation to wrap up all the murders as quickly as he did. "We need to find Karin Lavelle. And we need to do it quickly."

"She's nowhere to be found, Chief. The FBI can't find her. The Massachusetts state troopers and other law enforcement agencies we've reached out to can't find her. And neither can we. She's just… gone."

"The media's going to want a better answer than that from me about Karin Lavelle," Wilhelm said. "What do I tell them?"

There was a big press conference scheduled for that day about everything that had occurred. The death of Albert Ruggerio and the girl and the rest of it.

"Once we solve the murders of the Lavelle family members, then Abby and I think that will lead us to the missing daughter," Teena said.

"We know now who committed the Lavelle murders. It was the girl at the scene. This Susan Kirwin."

"I'm not so sure," I said again.

"What do you mean?"

"Why would the Kirwin girl kill the Lavelle family?"

"She was crazy. We know that now. She killed her own family. Now she kills the Lavelle family."

"But why pick them? And why here? She wasn't even from Martha's Vineyard."

Wilhelm didn't say anything. He didn't have an answer. Neither of us did. There are sometimes unanswered questions left over in a murder case, but there were too many questions here.

I pointed out another one now.

"Even if she did kill the Lavelles, and I'm not convinced she did, at least not on her own, why did she kill Ruggerio too? What was the connection there? What was the motive for a teenage girl murdering an underworld boss?"

"You already found out about the connection between Ruggerio and Thomas Lavelle," Wilhelm said. "Ruggerio was Lavelle's patient. That's the connection. That's the link. You said so yourself."

"But we thought then that Ruggerio wanted revenge against Lavelle because he'd supposedly botched his heart surgery," Teena said. "Except Ruggerio claimed, and now the bodyguard/cop DeSantis confirms, that Ruggerio really was grateful to Lavelle for what he did. The dots just don't connect. So maybe something else was going on here."

"Let's run through a few of these questions we don't have answers for," I said. "First, if we believe the Kirwin girl did kill the Lavelles, then why? Because Ruggerio decided on revenge and got her to do it? Does that seem logical? Why would a top mobster like Albert Ruggerio, a man believed responsible for a slew of Mob hits, use a teenage girl to carry out a Mob hit for him?

"Second, why kill Ruggerio? Especially now that we know Ruggerio was happy with Lavelle for the heart surgery he did. The girl kills this prominent doctor, then goes and kills one of his prominent patients too for no apparent reason. Nothing about these murders fits together, Chief."

Wilhelm didn't look happy. This was not what he wanted to hear. He wanted the Lavelle murder case to be solved.

He wanted the Lavelle girl found.

And he wanted to take credit for this in the public eye.

But Teena and I were not going along with his plan.

"I'm going to speak at the press conference shortly," he said to us finally. "I am going to tell the media that we believe the Kirwin girl killed the Lavelles and that she later killed Ruggerio. And that the answers to why she did that – both crimes – likely died with her. I will also tell them we are continuing massive search operations for the missing Karin Lavelle. And we fully expect to find her very soon. That is our official position. It's the official position of the Cedar Cliffs Police Department, and everyone on the force involved in this case. Is that understood?"

The press conference went that way. At least for a while. Wilhelm talked about the scenario of what he believed had happened, and the press asked him a lot of questions – some of which he admitted he couldn't answer.

But the elephant in the room was the missing Karin Lavelle. Wilhelm didn't have any answers for that one.

But I did.

"I'd like to direct a question to Abby Pearce, who has been the lead detective on the case," one of the reporters stood up and said.

That reporter was Lincoln Connor.

I walked up to the microphone where Wilhelm had been standing.

"Detective Pearce, are you in agreement that this case has essentially been solved by the death of Susan Kirwin, the troubled girl you found at the Lavelle crime scene inside The Beach House?"

"Chief Wilhelm just stated the opinion for you of the Cedar Cliffs Police Department," I said.

"What about your opinion?"

"I am a part of the Cedar Cliffs Police Department."

"That doesn't sound like a very enthusiastic endorsement of what Chief Wilhelm has told us."

I didn't say anything.

We'd rehearsed this before the press conference, Lincoln and me. To make sure I got asked the question I wanted to be asked. So that I could give the media the answer I wanted them to hear.

"If Susan Kirwin is the only perpetrator in this case and no one else is involved, then what do you think that means for the fate of the missing Karin Lavelle now that the Kirwin girl is dead?" Lincoln said.

I took a deep breath. It was the moment I had waited for.

"Then I think Karin Lavelle would likely be dead too."

There was a loud gasp from the audience.

"But you don't believe Susan Kirwin acted alone, do you?"

"No, I don't."

"You think that Karin Lavelle is still alive out there with someone else. Is that an accurate appraisal of your position here, Detective Pearce?"

"I will continue to use all the resources of the department and anyone else I can get to help in an effort to find Karin Lavelle and bring her back safely."

"Meaning you think someone else is involved in this? Someone besides Susan Kirwin is responsible for all this? And that someone is the person who might now have Karin Lavelle with them?"

"I am going to find Karin Lavelle," I said. "I believe she is still alive. No matter what anyone else thinks. I will not give up the search for this girl. I give you my word on that. I'm going to get her back."

And, just like that, it was my sound bite not the ones from Wilhelm that led all the TV news and news reports from that press conference.

CHAPTER 42

I was back in the war room we'd set up at the station house and looking at the pictures and other information I'd posted on a big bulletin board there at the beginning of the case.

Looking for some sort of inspiration on what to do next.

There was a picture of Karin Lavelle. Another one of Susan Kirwin. Family shots of Thomas Lavelle with his wife and children. Crime scene photos from inside The Beach House. And lots of information I'd written on a chalkboard from all the interviews and searches we'd done on the island ever since the Lavelle bodies had been found and their teenage daughter went missing.

Now I'd added more material to the bulletin board. Pictures of Albert Ruggerio. Roy DeSantis. The Ruggerio house. And crime scene photos of the Kirwin girl lying dead next to Ruggerio as he lay slumped over his wheelchair.

It was an impressive amount of information. But none of it had helped us come up with any real answers. At least not so far. I kept looking at the pictures and everything I'd written on the board in the hope that something might click for me as a lead to pursue.

I picked up a piece of chalk and in big letters I wrote there: "MOTIVE?"

That seemed to be the biggest question of all.

If I could only figure out the motive, then maybe all of the other things in this case – the location of the missing Lavelle girl, the connection between the Lavelle family and Albert Ruggerio as victims, the mysterious killer girl who turned out to be Susan Kirwin – could fall into place.

Teena came into the room and looked at the array of material too.

"Wilhelm's not very happy with you after that press conference," she said.

"You think?"

"I assume you set that all up with Lincoln Connor so you could say what you wanted to say to the media."

"I have no idea what you're talking about." I smiled.

"Right."

Teena looked again at the display on the bulletin board. "Wilhelm wanted to be able to stand up in front of that press conference and announce that we had solved the case. He wanted to take credit for it all. He's going to want to take the credit too when – or if – we find Karin Lavelle."

"I don't care who gets the credit," I said. "I'm worried about what comes next if you and I don't come up with something. Will there be more killings like this? Is the Lavelle girl still alive? What made Susan Kirwin go to Albert Ruggerio's house with that knife? I keep coming back to the motive. That's the best way into this for us, Teena. Then maybe the rest of the pieces will start to fit together."

"It's got to be about the father," she said. "Doctor Thomas Lavelle. Someone in his past. A disgruntled patient or something like that. Okay, it's not Ruggerio. But it could be someone else. Someone who wanted revenge against the doctor for medical treatment that went bad. A vendetta that enraged them so much they lashed out not just against the doctor but his entire family too. I think we need to assume at this point that the daughter is probably dead too. I know we don't want to think about that, but it makes the most likely possibility."

"I'm not sure about that," I said. "If they were going to kill her, why not do it along with all the rest? I think having her disappear is making some kind of statement."

"What kind of statement?"

I shrugged.

"Gotta be about the doctor though," Teena repeated, looking at the picture of Thomas Lavelle.

There were several other pictures of the Lavelle family. The most poignant was one we'd found at The Beach House with the bodies. It was a photo they'd had taken of them all as they were getting off the ferry at Cedar Cliffs. Lavelle, his wife Nancy and their four children. Getting ready for a fun vacation on Martha's Vineyard. They were all smiling happily in the picture. With no idea of what lay ahead for them.

The picture of the little boy Steven got to me the most. Nancy Lavelle was holding Steven in her arms. I thought about how she'd altered her career to stay home and spend more time taking care of the baby and then be a stay-at-home mother for her other children too. A few days after this picture was taken, she would be lying dead on the floor at The Beach House – with the rest of her family. Everyone else except their missing daughter.

Staring at Nancy Lavelle now, I remembered how her wounds were different than the others. The rest of the dead members of the Lavelle family had been stabbed numerous times. But Mrs. Lavelle had only a single fatal wound.

Was that significant?

And then there was the unusual positioning of her hands in death. Like she was praying with them both clasped together.

"How much do we know about the wife?" I asked Teena.

"You know all that. We found it out from her family, the Hoods. Thomas and Nancy Lavelle had been married eighteen years. Good marriage as far as we know. She is, or was, an attorney."

"What kind of law did she practice?"

"Uh, criminal law."

"She was the only one who wasn't butchered by the killer," I pointed out. "He only stabbed her once. The others were stabbed repeatedly. But not her. Why was that?"

"You think maybe the killer didn't want her to suffer the ways the others did?"

"Maybe the opposite."

"What do you mean?"

"Think about it. What if she was the real target here, not the husband?"

"Huh?"

"And what if we got the timetable of the killing wrong? Maybe she wasn't one of the first to die, before her children. What if she had to watch it all happen before she died? Wouldn't that be the most cruel and heartless way to get revenge against someone? To be forced to watch their loved ones die and realize she was responsible for their deaths because of something she had done?"

Teena stared at me with amazement. I could see she was thinking the same thing I was at that moment.

"Then, after she had to endure that terrible thing, she was killed by a single knife wound," she said. "Because there was no reason to take a longer time like the killer did with her family while she was forced to watch them suffer and die."

"Right. The wife was the last to die, because she was the one someone really wanted to suffer the ultimate loss before that moment."

"Wow! That's an interesting theory."

"Let's find out more about Nancy Lavelle," I said.

CHAPTER 43

I knew something was wrong as soon as I pulled up in front of my house.

There was the sound of Oscar barking from inside the house. He never barked when I came home. Unless he was upset about something.

I pulled up in front, got out of my car and started walking toward my front door. As I got closer, I could see it was open. Someone was inside my house. Or else they had been inside and were gone now. I had no way of knowing for sure.

I took out my gun with one hand and held it in front of me as I made my way toward the door. With my other hand, I pulled out my cell phone and called the station. Meg was still there and answered.

"I need backup at my place in Chilmark," I told her. "It looks like someone broke into the house."

I gave her the address, even though I was pretty sure she already knew where I lived.

"Are they still there?"

"Can't be sure."

"Where are you?"

"Standing outside."

"Wait there until I can get someone over there to help you."

"My dog's inside."

"Abby, hold off for a few minutes until the backup gets there."

"I've got to find out if my dog is all right. I'm going in there to get Oscar. Once I have Oscar, I'll come back outside and wait for the backup to get here before I check out the rest of the house."

I clicked off my phone before Meg could tell me to wait again.

Oscar was still barking. Maybe he heard my car drive up, and he was trying to get my attention. Or was hurt. Who knows? All I knew was I had to get in there to make sure he was okay.

I carefully pushed the front door all the way open, with my gun still in front of me, and walked inside.

"I'm a police officer, and I'm armed," I said in a loud voice. "If there is anyone in this house, make yourself known to me right now."

No answer.

But Oscar was barking even louder now, presumably because he had heard the sound of my voice from wherever he was inside the house. So why hadn't he come running out to greet me? The answer to that was simple, but scary. Oscar couldn't come running out to greet me. He wasn't able to, for some reason.

I made my way down the front hallway into the living room, and that's when I got my next big shock. The living room was a mess. Someone had trashed the place. Chairs were overturned, drawers pulled out and their contents spilled all over the floor, books and even a TV toppled from the shelves.

I ignored that for now and tried to follow the sound of Oscar's barking. I figured out it was coming from the bathroom. I made my way there carefully, and saw the door was closed shut. I opened it and Oscar came bounding out. He jumped on me and began licking my face. He seemed okay.

I picked him up and began making my way back through the living room and outside again.

By the time I got there, the first police car had arrived. It was Teena, who lived not that far away from me. Meg must have called her at home. A few minutes later, two more squad cars pulled up with Bowers and other Cedar Cliffs cops in them.

I briefed everyone on the situation and then we made our way back into the house.

"What happened to your dog?" Teena asked me on the way in.

"Whoever did this must have locked him in the bathroom to keep him out of the way."

"Well, at least they didn't hurt him."

"Thank God. But wait until you see the housekeeping job someone did on my living room."

We made our way through the living room now – guns drawn. I shouted out again that there were armed police officers in the house. But nothing. I figured that whoever had done this was gone by now.

Teena and I stayed in the living room, checking out everything there, while the others fanned out throughout the house.

"Do you see anything missing?" Teena asked.

"Nope. Nothing at all."

"So you don't think this was a robbery?"

"Do you?"

"I have no idea what's going on here."

"Maybe they were looking for something," I suggested.

"Or else wanted to scare you by doing all this."

"Who would want to scare me?"

Teena shrugged.

"You're a police officer. You make enemies on this job. It happens."

"Well, it didn't work… I'm not scared."

"Okay."

"I'm mad."

Suddenly there was a shout from Bowers in another part of the house.

"Abby, you better get in here and see this. In the bedroom."

I made my way toward the bedroom. There were two of them in my house. The first one was empty and apparently intact. But it was in the second bedroom, the one where I slept, that I found Bowers and the others.

My bedroom was a mess, like the living room had been. Drawers open, clothes strewn all over. But that wasn't the most shocking thing I found there. It was what I saw written on the wall next to my bed. It wasn't done in blood like at the Lavelle crime scene; this was done with red spray paint. But the message was the same. It said: No One Here Gets Out Alive.

"Jesus," I said.

"There's more," Bowers said. "We found this here. On the pillow of your bed."

He gingerly picked up a white envelope with a pair of gloves to preserve any evidence on it.

"This is addressed to you," Bowers said. "There's a message inside."

A message for me.

From whoever had done this to my house.

But who was that?

Albert Ruggerio and Susan Kirwin were the two main suspects I had questioned about the murders and now this happens.

But it couldn't have been either of them – they were both dead.

There was someone else out there.

Someone watching me, and I had no idea who they were.

The one thing I did believe though: I had no doubt that all this came from the same person who had really massacred Thomas Lavelle and his family.

CHAPTER 44

The note was typewritten on plain white paper. I put on plastic gloves before I touched it so I wouldn't mess up any fingerprints that might be on the envelope or what was inside. Even though I knew there wouldn't be any fingerprints. Whoever was doing this hadn't left their fingerprints at the Lavelle crime scene or anywhere else. They were too smart for that kind of mistake.

Hello, Detective Abby Pearce

I thought it was time to introduce myself to you, Detective. Well, not by name. Not yet anyway. That will come later. You'll know who I am soon enough. But by then... well, it will be too late to matter. But more on that shortly. Yes, we'll all have a big laugh over that very, very soon.

Who did you think I was? Did you really believe big bad Albert Ruggerio did all those things to Thomas Lavelle and his pretty little family? (Although they're not so pretty anymore, huh? Ha! Ha!) Or that it was poor little Susan Kirwin who butchered them so horribly like that? Sure, she did it with Ruggerio. But the Lavelles... that was me. And Ruggerio was really me too. Yes, Susan plunged that knife in him, but it was me who sent her there with the knife and told her what to do.

I'm so enjoying watching you flailing around aimlessly trying to solve this case, Detective Abby Pearce. I've watched you on TV at the press conferences and read your quotes in news stories from papers and on websites. Oh, you've figured out a few things, which did surprise me. But there's so much more you don't know. So much you simply don't have a clue to understanding about me and about what is happening here.

What a shame for you. And after such a distinguished career. All the arrests in New York City. The awards and acclaim from the NYPD. And then all the wonderful publicity you just received by solving that teenage/sex murder case in your new job on Martha's Vineyard after you arrived in Cedar Cliffs.

You sure were riding high for a while.

But that's all over now.

You're not going to be getting any awards or acclaim this time.

Because I'm always one step ahead of you.

Here's the brutal truth, Detective Abby Pearce: You may think you're after me, trying to get me in your sights so you can catch me. But really it's me who has you in my sights. Did you actually think it was a coincidence that the Lavelles died at The Beach House, which now houses the restaurant your family used to own? Oh, yes, Abby Pearce, I've been watching you for a while.

If you don't believe me, here's the evidence.

There were a half dozen pictures that had been printed out on the next page in the envelope. They were pictures of me. Me in my car. Me on the street with Teena outside the station house. Me with Lincoln Connor. Me walking Oscar in my backyard. There was even one picture of me working in my vegetable garden.

Do you see how easy it is for me to get to you, Detective Pearce? I can do that anytime I want. Do you understand what I'm saying here? You're a target too. Just like the people in the Lavelle family and old Albert Ruggerio were targets. But the difference here is they didn't know they were in danger. Now you do.

I'd love to see you sweat about that, I'd love to see you be really worried for your own safety. And you should be. You see, the Lavelles and Ruggerio were only the preliminaries for me. Now I think taking out the lead detective on the case – the one case the much-ballyhooed star detective (that would be you!) couldn't solve – will be the fitting finale for this, don't you?

Oh, I know you'll probably be protected by other police and law enforcement people after this. But don't bother doing all that. It's a waste of time. Because you see I'm not stupid enough to come at you directly like that. No, I'm going to wait until you come to me. Which you will, sooner or later. So go ahead and solve the Lavelle and Ruggerio cases. Come find me. Try to arrest me. Then we can meet for the ending of all this. You and I, together. I am so looking forward to that!

There were two more pages in the envelope. The first page contained just a single paragraph. It said:

Let me leave you with one more thing to convince you this is all real, not some hoax. So I think I should show you one more picture. It's a picture of someone you've been looking for. I know you have a lot of questions about this person. Well, here is one answer for you. You're welcome!

The last page was another picture.

Not a picture of me this time.

It was a picture of a young girl. Sitting in a chair. It was difficult to tell the location, but it appeared to be some kind of a finished basement, with knotty pine paneling on the wall behind her.

She was holding up the front page of a newspaper, *The New York Times*, close enough to the camera so that I could read the publication date.

The date was today.

Proof that was when this picture was taken and that she was still alive.

The girl was not identified in the picture.

But I already knew who she was.

It was Karin Lavelle.

CHAPTER 45

"We have just received new evidence that Karin Lavelle, the missing fifteen-year-old daughter of the slain Lavelle family, is still alive," Chief Wilhelm told a press conference the next day.

"Last evening, an officer of the Cedar Cliffs police force – Detective Abby Pearce – had her home entered by an intruder. Detective Pearce was not present in the house when the incident happened, and she is thankfully unhurt. But whoever did this left a note and other evidence for Detective Pearce – who has been heading up the investigation of the murders of Doctor Thomas Lavelle and his family, along with the killing of Albert Ruggerio – indicating they were responsible for the killings.

"Most importantly, one item left for Detective Pearce was a picture of the missing Lavelle girl, Karin, that was taken during the past twenty-four hours."

The picture of Karin Lavelle holding up that day's newspaper was displayed on a screen.

There was an audible gasp from some members of the media when Wilhelm revealed this.

"So that means the girl is still okay?" one of the reporters yelled out.

"We're operating on that assumption, based on this picture."

"But she's being held by someone?"

"That appears to be the case."

It was an amazing turnabout for Wilhelm, who had told the media he believed the case was over. But now it was clearly not finished. Even Wilhelm couldn't still believe that teenage Susan Kirwin had been responsible for everything that happened. No, the real killer was still out there.

Wilhelm talked in some detail about the note and other things found at my house. This included the phrase "No One Here Gets Out Alive" on my wall. The same words as were found at the Lavelle crime scene. He also revealed the references in the note to my past cases, both here and previously in New York with the NYPD.

That raised a lot of questions with the reporters there – many of them aimed directly at myself.

"Chief Wilhelm, there have been relatively few major crimes that have occurred on Martha's Vineyard throughout its history. Certainly not anything like we're seeing now. But there were those missing teenage girls and murders recently here. Now we have a family massacred and a top underworld figure killed too. All of these major criminal activities began when Detective Pearce arrived here several months ago from New York City and a career with the NYPD. How do you explain that?"

"Well, I don't think Detective Pearce coming here has anything to do with these crimes."

"Then what do you think is happening here now and why?"

"I think the most logical explanation is that Detective Pearce received a tremendous amount of publicity for her work on the last big case. That must have attracted the attention of this person or persons. They decided to target her personally to gain more publicity for what they are doing."

The questions to me were tougher.

"So at this moment," one reporter said to me, "we have five members of a family dead; a mysterious girl at the scene who escaped from custody with you and was also killed; a Mob leader stabbed to death by that girl before she died; and a fifteen-year-old girl who remains missing, who it definitely appears now from that picture has been abducted. Have you made any progress at all on any of these things?"

"We are aggressively pursuing our investigation," I said. "We are using every resource at our disposal to find Karin Lavelle and bring whoever is behind this to justice."

"But at the moment you have nothing."

"We have a number of leads."

"Tell us about them."

"I can't divulge to you any specifics of our investigation at this point."

"I think you just answered my question."

But some of the questions were even worse than that.

I mean it got really personal.

"Detective Pearce, during your time with the NYPD you were described by some people as a tabloid and media star because of your police work. In other words, you got a lot of publicity. There was criticism from some that you engineered much of that publicity for yourself. Could that be what is happening here?"

"Are you suggesting that I made this up to get famous again in the media?"

"It does seem unusual."

"I won't even dignify your question with an answer."

"So you're not denying it?"

"Next question."

The next question wasn't any better. And it was more personal and closer to home than the suggestion that I had made up the break-in at my house and the note and the rest simply as some sort of bid to get attention.

"When you were in New York, you were involved in a controversy when your partner was shot and killed on the street. There was a question of whether or not you had been drinking prior to the incident, and if so whether or not that hindered your ability to back up and protect your partner from danger in that situation."

"I was not drinking when my partner, Detective Tommy Ferraro, died," I snapped. "That question was asked at the time, and my condition and my response was not determined to have played any part in my partner's death. Tommy Ferraro was one of the best police officers I ever knew – as well as a good friend – and I object to you bringing him into this conversation."

"But you are an alcoholic, right?"

I sighed.

"I've had issues in the past."

"Are you drinking now?"

"No."

"Have you been drinking at all since you became involved in this case?"

"That has no bearing on my ability to do the best of my ability on this case."

"Does that mean…"

"I haven't had anything to drink in a long while. Does that answer your question?"

My God, I'd gone from being a media star after the last big case here to now becoming a target for the media's barbs and criticism. There was only one way to escape that. By solving, or at least making significant progress, on this case. But I hadn't done that so far. I looked around for Lincoln in the media crowd. I spotted him in one of the seats. He didn't ask any questions of me though. I guess he figured that might be inappropriate.

That was too bad.

I would have liked to hear his voice right now.

Any friendly voice would be a nice change.

"In conclusion," Chief Wilhelm was saying now, "we are pursuing this investigation as vigorously as possible. And Detective

Pearce is spearheading that investigation. We will update you again when we have more information."

"And you're convinced that this personal involvement by Detective Pearce to the case is only because the killer or killers was attracted to her previous high profile in the media because of what happened with the teenage sex scandal and murders?"

"That's the most plausible scenario," Wilhelm said.

I sure hoped he was right, but I wasn't as certain about that being the reason as Wilhelm made it sound.

That this was only about my publicity from the earlier case.

Because someone had made this personal.

Someone was coming after me.

And the truth was I had no idea why.

CHAPTER 46

Mark Ellis had some new information for me on how the reservation was made for the Lavelle family at The Beach House.

"Someone called the office at The Beach House a few weeks ago and made the reservation," Ellis explained to me. "They said it was an anniversary present for Thomas and Nancy Lavelle. Their anniversary was coming up, and this person wanted to give them a special gift. The name of the person making the reservation was Albert Ruggerio."

"Or someone pretending to be Ruggerio?"

"It would seem so now. Why?"

"To lure the Lavelle family up here."

I asked him as many other questions about it as I could think of.

"Who paid for the Lavelles' stay?"

"The caller. The person who identified themselves as Albert Ruggerio. Sent a check for the entire amount."

"Was there a name on the check?" I asked.

Even though I was pretty sure there wouldn't have been any name.

"No. It was actually a money order."

"Didn't that seem a bit unusual?"

Ellis shrugged. "No problem once we were able to cash it. Which we did."

"Okay then, who talked to the person who claimed to be Ruggerio?"

"A young college kid that we've had working as an intern in the office. I spoke with her. That's where I got the information."

"And that's all she remembers?"

"Yes. She made the reservation, we received the payment and that was it. None of it seemed important until now."

"Did you ask the girl what this phony Albert Ruggerio sounded like?"

"She said the voice on the phone was kind of muffled. Hard to make some of the words out, she told me. Almost as if the person on the other end might have been trying to—"

"Disguise their voice?"

"That's right."

There were just too many pieces to this crime puzzle. It was hard to stay with a single strand of the investigation. Every time I went down one path, another one emerged. And I couldn't figure out how, or even if, they all fit together.

I mean we had a mass murder. We had a missing teenage girl. We had a dead Mob boss. We had another teenage girl who had been at both crime scenes, but she was dead now too. We had no real motive for any of this. Oh, and we still had a killer out there who seemed to have targeted me now. I'd never worked a case this confusing before.

"Let's go over the possibilities," Teena said back at the station house. "Thomas Lavelle and Albert Ruggerio both lived in New York. You were in New York on the force for a lot of years. Did you ever have any connection at all with Lavelle or his family or with Ruggerio back there?"

I shook my head no.

"The first time I heard of Lavelle was when these murders happened. I knew about Ruggerio from his reputation, but I never handled any cases he or anyone connected with him was involved in."

"There's also the business about the restaurant being the same one your father used to own here," Meg Jarvis added. "Plus, you said the phrase 'No One Here Gets Out Alive' – which was on the wall at the Lavelle crime scene and someone painted on your wall too – was one you were known for saying sometimes out on the street when you were in New York with the NYPD."

"There has to be a reason for that," Bowers said.

"What kind of reason?" Meg asked.

"Something personal," I said. "This is personal for them with me."

They all wanted to know why someone might want to make it personal with me. I had no answer.

Meg brought up the same possibility that had been mentioned by Chief Wilhelm during the press conference.

The obvious one.

"You got a lot of publicity here with that big case this summer, Abby. It could be as simple as that. You were all over TV cable channels. Written up in newspapers. Some of the stuff about you even went viral on social media. Maybe some sick person became obsessed with you that way."

"Obsessed enough to kill a family of five people and kidnap their daughter too just to get my attention?"

"Crazier things have happened," Teena said.

"Whoever it is, they're playing some kind of a sick game. A game they've made me a part of. And, if this is a game for them, that means it's not over. This person is still after something with me. And maybe more than me…"

My words out there in the air, I knew everyone realized what I was saying.

"You think more people may die," Teena said.

"Yes, unless we stop it first."

CHAPTER 47

"How are you doing after everything that happened?" Lincoln asked me.

"I'm okay."

"Those were some pretty tough questions thrown at you during the press conference about what happened at your house."

"Would have been nice to get a friendly question from you," I said.

"C'mon, I can't stand up as a reporter and lob some softball question at you, people would get suspicious."

I sighed. "I know that."

We were eating lunch at one of the restaurants with an outside dining room overlooking the harbor and marina. It was the first time Lincoln and I had eaten out in public. But I was tired of hiding behind closed doors with him, and so was he. We figured if anyone saw us, we'd say it was just a business lunch – he was interviewing me for a story. As long as we didn't lose control and have sex on the table, it should work.

We talked about the case awhile more, and then he went back to our personal lives.

"What's the situation between you and your husband?" Lincoln asked.

"Ex-husband."

"Okay, your ex-husband."

"Last time I talked with him was during the summer."

"How'd it go?"

"Not good. He told me he was getting married again."

"Were you shocked?"

"Yeah, I was. I sort of hoped for a long time that Zach and I had a chance of getting together again. But when your husband announces his wedding plans with another woman, well… that's pretty much the deal-breaker on your own marriage with the guy, right?"

"I'm glad he's getting married. Less competition for me. So now you and I can talk more about us getting married once this case is over."

"We're back on that topic again, huh?"

"Never left it."

There was a ferry docking below us now, carrying passengers in from Woods Hole on Cape Cod. No matter how many times I'd watched it over the years, I always loved seeing the ferries come in. Filled with tourists and their kids and dogs and bicycles. All excited about coming here to a beautiful vacation spot like Martha's Vineyard. Just like the Lavelle family had been that first day.

I watched some of the people as they began streaming off the boat, then turned to Lincoln.

"How about you?"

"What do you mean?"

"Tell me about Lincoln Connor."

"Not much to tell." He smiled.

"Everyone has a life story."

"Not much of a story for me. You wouldn't be interested. Trust me."

He smiled again.

"Well, you're a big-time TV reporter, I know that. But what about before you became a media star? How did you get to Boston? Where are you from? Why did you decide to go into journalism?"

"Let's talk about something else."

"C'mon, Lincoln, I opened up to you about some of the deep dark secrets in my past. I don't even know where you come from.

Is your family still around? Who was the last woman in your life before me?"

"Godammit, Abby, just stop it!"

He wasn't smiling anymore.

"Do you have to be a cop all the time? Stop asking me all these questions. Stop interrogating me like I'm one of your suspects or something."

I was stunned by his reaction. I certainly seemed to have touched some sort of sensitive nerve.

"Sorry," Lincoln said. "I didn't mean to snap at you like that. It's just that… well, I really don't want to talk about my past with you. Not right now. Not today. Let's just let it drop for now. Okay?"

"No problem," I said.

"Listen, I better get going. I've got a lot of work to do this afternoon. I'm sure you do too."

A few minutes later, he walked me back to the station.

"When will I see you again?" I asked.

"Very soon, I hope."

"Good to hear."

He kissed me even though we were standing in full view of people on the street.

I kissed him back.

It was nice.

But I couldn't stop thinking even as I did it about what was in Lincoln Connor's past that he didn't want to talk to me about.

CHAPTER 48

I'd asked Nancy Lavelle's parents to send us a list of client files from the New York City law firm she used to work at.

Is seemed to me to be the best lead we had to follow at this point.

We'd speculated at first that the murders must have had something to do with Dr. Thomas Lavelle's medical practices. Which was why we went through all his patient files. But that lead hadn't gone anywhere. Maybe we were looking at the wrong Lavelle. Maybe the reason for the murders had to do with someone from Nancy Lavelle's past in defending a variety of different criminals.

She had been a criminal attorney for a number of years. Plenty of time for her to make enemies. In the criminal community or elsewhere. Did she make any one of these mad enough to kill her – and her entire family?

It was awfully hard to imagine, but we still had no motive for the bloody massacre of the Lavelle family.

Why not her?

There was another aspect of the murder scene too that pointed to Nancy Lavelle as the potential target of the murderous rage.

The position of her hands in death – clasped together in front of her almost as if she was praying.

Meg had a new idea about this.

"I did some research on it," she said. "There's a lot of historical data and lore – as well as a bit of superstition – about why people fold their hands together like this when they pray. And it's not only about praying in some cases.

"There's a common belief that this hands-folded position – like we saw with Mrs. Lavelle – comes from a Roman tradition symbolizing submission. Like shackling a prisoner's hands together. In ancient Rome, a captured soldier sometimes would put his hands together like that to show he was surrendering. It was an acknowledgement of another's authority and the captured soldier's submission to that authority. Maybe that's what the killer was trying to show here with Nancy Lavelle."

"Wait a minute," Teena said. "Somebody takes time in the middle of a mass murder to go through all this to send some kind of crazy message. Why?"

"Because it was a statement kill," I said. "We know that now. Everything about it – from the 'No One Here Gets Out Alive' message on the wall, all the way to the letter at my house."

"And you figure the clasped hands in front of her was part of that statement?"

"Whoever did this wanted to sign their kill. To leave a statement about these murders. Nancy Lavelle was part of the statement. She was the only one with her hands in that position. That's got to be significant."

"Which means Nancy Lavelle – not her husband – was the reason for the murder of her family," Bowers said.

"I think so. Now we have to find out why."

According to the information we had been able to dig up on her, Nancy Lavelle was a very successful criminal attorney. At least she was until she stepped away from her job with a big New York City law firm to have their last child and then become a stay-at-home mother for him and her family. Which made it even more poignant, of course, that the child was now among those who died along with the rest of this family that seemed to have so much going for it until they came to Martha's Vineyard.

Many of her clients were certainly not of the highest moral character. She represented a variety of unsavory people in many of her cases. She didn't seem to care much about whether her clients were guilty or innocent, as long as they paid her legal fees.

I found an old speech she gave at a conference of attorneys in which she defended this approach. "My clients aren't always upstanding citizens," she said. "They aren't victimized unfairly by the law or the justice system, they frequently are responsible themselves for the legal mess they are in. But that doesn't matter to me. They deserve the right to a legal defense. A competent legal defense. That's my job as a lawyer. At least, I feel that's my job. Guilty or innocent doesn't really matter to me. I simply represent my client in the best way that I can."

With a client list like that, it certainly seemed possible that a disgruntled client, prone to violence anyway, might have decided to seek revenge against her if he was unhappy with the legal representation he received.

Except there was a problem with that theory.

She seemed to win most of her cases.

Still, that appeared to be the best trail to follow and so Teena and I, with the help of Bowers and Meg when they could, went through all the past clients of Nancy Lavelle looking for some obvious clues from the names to jump out at us.

And we found one.

A real obvious one too.

Or at least we thought so at first.

"She represented Albert Ruggerio!" Bowers shouted out to us as he read from one of the files. "Three years ago. On an extortion and attempted robbery charge."

"That's exactly what we're looking for!" Teena said.

"What happened?" I asked.

"It involved a bookmaking rival. Ruggerio was running a gambling and bookmaking operation in Washington Heights.

Then a local thug started to try to cut in on his turf by booking his own bets. Ruggerio was so infuriated he showed up in person to confront the guy. Like we heard, he had a bad temper. The confrontation got out of hand and turned physical. Ruggerio hit the guy in the head with a metal crowbar, and he nearly killed him. The cops arrested Ruggerio, and it turns out Nancy Lavelle was the lawyer who represented him."

"Did she win the case?" I asked.

"Yes, she did. She was able to convince a jury that Ruggerio – believe it or not – was acting in self-defense after being attacked by the other man. So he was acquitted on the attempted murder charge. As for the extortion threats, the victim suddenly decided not to pursue that charge."

"Sounds like he got bought off or threatened by Ruggerio to do that," Meg said.

"Maybe, but it was still a big legal win for him, keeping him out of jail, all thanks to Nancy Lavelle."

Which was the problem, of course.

"It's just like it was with Doctor Lavelle and Ruggerio," Teena said. "We know now that Lavelle saved Ruggerio's life at the time. The wife did a good thing for him too. She got him off on the criminal charges. So why would he be mad at her? Ruggerio would have no motive for killing her and her family. So where does that leave us?"

"Yep, I agree, Teena," I said. "Also, this happened a few years ago. If there was some kind of revenge from Ruggerio, why wouldn't it have happened then? Whatever set these killings off must have occurred a lot more recently."

Teena nodded.

"Still," she said, "there's got to be some kind of connection here with Ruggerio. I mean Nancy Lavelle represented him, then her husband treats him for heart problems. The most likely scenario, I suppose, is that Mrs. Lavelle knew Ruggerio, and he reached out to her when he needed a heart surgeon. But then what? How did that lead to the bloody massacre here – and for what reason?"

I called Nancy Lavelle's parents again. The timing of all that bothered me too. And there was something else. Nancy Lavelle had stopped working for the big city law firm as an attorney a year before she died. Or did she? Because, when I reached her mother, Elizabeth Hood said that wasn't totally true.

"Nancy was still working as a lawyer," she told me. "She didn't go into the city every day anymore. She wasn't with that firm anymore. But she still represented clients and appeared in court on her own. She ran the practice from her home. Not a lot of clients, but some here and there. She liked it that way so she could spend more time with the children."

"Would those cases be in the files you sent me?"

"No, not the more recent ones."

"How can I see them?"

"She kept them at home. I've been cleaning out the house after everything that happened. I'll get them to you. I want to do anything I can to help you find out who did this to my family."

"That would be of great help. Thank you."

I was busy when these more recent files arrived, and Teena and Bowers went through them before me. There weren't nearly as many of them as we'd gotten from the big law firm in the city she previously worked for. Like the mother had said, Nancy had cut down on her workload when she was working from home, but she was still handling a limited number of cases.

"She really must have been a good lawyer," Teena said when I walked in on them. "She won most of these cases too. There's no real motive here, nothing I can see. Most of these people got off because of her. Why would they want her or her family dead?"

She was right about that.

Was this going to be another dead end too?

"How many cases were there in her home files?"

"About a dozen."

"And you didn't recognize any of the names?"

"Nope. Nothing significant in any of her clients that I can see."

She shoved the stack of files over to me. I looked down at them, wondering if I should bother to go through them myself or if that was just a waste of time.

There was a list of the names of the clients Nancy Lavelle had represented over the past year stuck onto the cover of the first file.

I looked at the names.

And that's when I saw it.

A name Teena wouldn't recognize, but I sure did.

Richie Briggs.

Richie Briggs was the man who shot and killed my partner Tommy Ferraro.

CHAPTER 49

Richie Briggs.

Nancy Lavelle had been representing Richie Briggs before she died.

Trying to appeal his murder conviction on some legal technicalities, according to the file. There wasn't a lot of information in the file. And the last entry had been made several weeks earlier. About some court hearing Nancy Lavelle was seeking on the murder conviction appeal. These personal files of hers we'd gotten from the mother weren't nearly as complete as the previous ones from the law firm – presumably she didn't spend as much of her own time keeping them up to date. But just the fact that Lavelle was representing Briggs was mind-boggling to me.

I'd thought a lot about Richie Briggs since that horrible night in Chelsea. Not as much now, of course, as I did in those days and weeks after Tommy Ferraro died. But the memory of Richie Briggs, and what he did and how it changed my life so irrevocably, still haunted me. And I'm sure it always will.

All the memories were coming back to me now. The shooting. Tommy lying there dead on the street next to me. The controversy about my drinking. The arrest of Briggs later. His trial. And then all the difficult times that came afterward until I finally left the NYPD and returned to Martha's Vineyard.

Briggs had gotten away after he shot Tommy, but he was captured not long afterward. He had been identified by witnesses who had seen him rob the sporting goods store, which led to Tommy and me chasing him to that building where he was hiding. It took another day or two after that to find him, but he was soon located, arrested and charged with murdering a police officer, Tommy Ferraro.

At first, the case against Briggs seemed simple. He even confessed to the shooting, in an effort to avoid the maximum sentence. But then a lawyer convinced him to deny he did the shooting or that he was even there and claim that the confession was coerced out of him illegally.

There was a trial, which was very difficult for me to deal with. I was still reeling from Tommy's death, and my inability to save him, when the case went to court. And, as the only person who was present at the time of the shooting, I became a key witness during the proceedings.

The defense made a big deal about my alcoholism and the controversy over whether or not I was drinking when Tommy died. Even though I hadn't been drinking that night, and a departmental panel confirmed that, the lawyer for Briggs hammered away at me on the stand about my history and background as an alcoholic. There were numerous incidents of me being under the influence of alcohol – most of them off-duty, but damaging – that I had to admit to during my testimony.

All this talk about my drinking so soon after losing Tommy made me want to drink even more. I did my best to control that urge during the Briggs murder trial. But, stressed out by the grilling interrogation I was undergoing on the stand, I actually took a few drinks before testifying one day. Just to calm myself down. I felt guilty about that, but it helped me get through the ordeal.

Then, after the trial was over, I really started drinking heavily again, trying to forget about Tommy being dead and the damn trial and everything else. I would drink off and on again sporadically after that. But I was on a downward spiral that eventually led me back to Martha's Vineyard.

The good news was that Briggs was convicted of murder. His previous lawyer's tricks and courtroom maneuvers didn't work in the end. The jury found him guilty, and the judge sentenced him to life in prison. He was serving his sentence at a prison in upstate New York. I felt good about that, and I'd managed to put Richie Briggs to the back of my mind. At least most of the time.

I still dreamed about him though.

And Tommy too.

There were different versions of the dreams, but the basic scenario was always the same.

I was back on the street with Tommy, and he was alive. Richie Briggs was there too. Not hiding in the building this time, but standing there with us on the street. He was smiling. No, it was more than a smile. Richie Briggs was smirking. And that made me hate him even more than I ever did. I wanted to warn Tommy about Briggs, because I knew what was about to happen. But I couldn't get the words out.

I never could do that in my dream.

No matter how hard I tried.

The rest of the dream was pretty predictable, I guess. Briggs had taken out a gun. Tommy didn't seem aware of it. I tried to grab the gun away from Briggs, but I couldn't do it. I tried to pull Tommy away to safety, but I couldn't move to do that. And, no matter how many times I tried, I couldn't get my gun out of my holster to protect Tommy from what was about to happen to him.

That's the moment when I always woke up.

I never saw Tommy actually lying dead on the street in the dream.

But, when I did wake up, I realized all over again that he was dead and wondered why I hadn't been able to do something to prevent it from happening.

I didn't pay a whole lot of attention to Briggs after his conviction. But I always hoped the life term he was serving in prison was painful and horrible for him to endure. Briggs was a small guy in stature and never seemed very tough. I figured a guy like that would be a real victim in prison for other inmates who could make day-to-day life there a living hell for Briggs.

It wouldn't bring Tommy Ferraro back, or ease my own guilt about Tommy's death, but the thought of Richie Briggs suffering in prison always made me feel a lot better.

The bottom line though was that Richie Briggs was in my past.

He was a part of my previous life back in New York City before I left the NYPD and changed my life by returning to Martha's Vineyard.

Except now he suddenly showed up in this case here.

Just like all those other things from my past were somehow connected to this case.

But why?

What did any of this have to do with Thomas Lavelle and his family or Albert Ruggerio or Susan Kirwin or any of the rest of it?

And why, especially after that letter I received, had this whole case suddenly become about me?

CHAPTER 50

I called Rikki Ferraro, Tommy's widow. I was also hoping she might have heard something or knew anything that could explain how the killer of her husband suddenly showed up in my murder case here.

"I miss him so much," she said to me now when I got her at her home on Long Island. "You'd think it would get better after all this time, Abby. I mean he's been gone for a year and a half now. But I still wake up in the morning and think he's going to be lying next to me. When I'm cooking dinner at night there's a part of me still expects him to walk in the door and start talking about his day on the job. It's only a fleeting second or two for these thoughts. Then I remember the truth. Tommy is dead, and he's not ever coming back again. I wonder if I'll ever really be able to accept that."

I wasn't exactly sure what to say. I'd never suffered grief like that. When my father died, I barely remember feeling any grief because of my anger at him for so many years. And even with Tommy, my grief was as much for myself as it was for him – I was consumed by how my actions, or inactions, had played a role in his death.

"I miss him too," I said finally.

"I know, Abby. He was your partner. I understand that bond between partners on the force. I was a cop's wife long enough to realize the trust he had in you and vice versa. But he was my partner in life. My husband. Father to our children. And now that's all gone in just a few seconds. No goodbyes, no closure, no nothing."

"He talked about you a lot, Rikki," I said, hoping that might make her feel better. "And the kids too. He loved you all. Right up to the end. He said going home to you at night was the best part of his life."

"That's nice to hear, but it makes me miss him even more than ever."

I wasn't sure what to say.

"You know what I think about a lot?" she said. "That last day before he left for work. I can't remember very much about it at all. What we said to each other. Did we kiss goodbye? Did I walk him to the door or even barely acknowledge him leaving? I've tried. I've tried to remember those kinds of little details about those last moments we shared together. But there's nothing.

"I guess that's because it was just another day. We assume life is going to go on the way it always does, so we don't give a lot of thought to things like that when they're happening. But then... well, it can all end, everything in our world that matters can end, in an instant. That's what happened with Tommy.

"I sometimes wish I could have just one last chance to talk to him now. Five minutes maybe, or even a minute. To have some kind of goodbye, some kind of closure."

"What would you say to Tommy?" I asked.

She sighed. "I'd tell him that I loved him, of course. And then... then I'd tell him how damn mad I was at him doing what he did and getting himself killed. Does that make any sense?"

I told her it did.

She said the best thing for her now was keeping busy with her therapy work and taking care of her family.

"I'm throwing myself into my therapy work," she said. "That really helps me deal with the grief. I want to make the world a better place to grow up in for the children. I can't do anything about Tommy being gone, but this is what I can do right now. I think Tommy, wherever he is, would be happy to see that for me.

I believe he is still there for me. I know it sounds strange, but I feel him by my side whatever I do, Abby."

I waited until she was finished before bringing up the real reason for my call.

Richie Briggs.

I told her how his name had turned up unexpectedly in my investigation.

"I don't understand," she said.

"I don't understand either. That's why I was hoping you might remember something about Briggs that might give me some kind of lead in connection with this. All I have now is that one of the victims had been representing him as a lawyer in some legal action. But that's it."

"I try not to think about Richie Briggs," she said. "It upsets me too much."

"Me too. This is weird though. I can't figure out why Briggs suddenly popped up in my murder case."

"Do you have any theories?"

"Not really. The simplest one is that Richie Briggs killed the Lavelle family for some reason just like he killed Tommy. But that's not possible. Since Briggs is in jail for the rest of his life."

"No, he isn't."

"What do you mean?"

"You didn't hear?"

"Hear what?"

"Some lawyer, I guess maybe that lawyer you talked about, got him sprung from prison not long ago. I couldn't believe it. The final insult for Tommy."

"You mean…?"

"Yes, that son-of-a-bitch Richie Briggs isn't behind bars anymore… He's out."

CHAPTER 51

Richie Briggs suddenly emerged as the top suspect in everything that was going on here on Martha's Vineyard.

Briggs knew Nancy Lavelle. She had represented him as his lawyer recently. I still wasn't sure what that meant, but because of their connection Briggs jumped out at me now as the big lead I needed to follow.

My own background with him might explain too why I was being targeted so personally in this case.

So where was Briggs now after his release from prison?

Was he here on Martha's Vineyard?

According to New York State Correction Dept. records, Briggs had been released from Attica – the legendary maximum security penal facility located in upstate New York. This came after his attorney – Nancy Lavelle – was somehow able to convince a judge that his constitutional rights had been violated both during his arrest and also at the subsequent trial.

One of the key issues was the video confession he had given at the beginning when he was arrested which he later claimed had been coerced from him. There were other procedural matters including whether his Miranda rights were read to him promptly enough and whether or not he had suffered police brutality in those first days he was in custody out of revenge because they believed he had killed a police officer.

His appeal also was successful because of alleged improprieties by the prosecution and the judge during his trial. All of these things were based on technicalities. But the case wound up in front of a sympathetic judge who had ruled against the police in numerous other cases and clearly had conflicts with the NYPD. The judge agreed that Briggs had not received a fair prosecution and ordered a new trial.

And, until the prosecution completed that process, the judge ruled that Briggs could be freed on bail.

"How could they let a killer go out on bail?" I asked Teena when she tracked down this information on Richie Briggs from court records of the case.

"Crazy, I know. But it sounds as if the judge has a big chip on his shoulder about cops violating the rights of suspects. He decided that's what happened here."

"What about Tommy Ferraro's rights?"

"Abby, I'm just telling you the facts of this."

"How much is the bail?"

"Five hundred thousand dollars."

"How did a creep like Richie Briggs raise that kind of money?"

"He only had to post a fifty thousand dollar bond up front."

"Where did he even get that much money? This was a guy who robbed a sporting goods store for twenty-six dollars. How did he get his hands on fifty thousand dollars?"

"I don't know, but Nancy Lavelle posted the bond and he went free."

"Damn, Nancy Lavelle must have been a pretty good lawyer. Well, I hope he had a tough time while he was in jail. Attica's the toughest prison in New York. Murders, rapists, street-gang leaders – they all get sent there. Hopefully, a guy like Briggs would be a real target – a victim – of them all. Maybe that would be a little bit of payback for what he did in killing my partner."

"Actually, from what I see here, he managed pretty well during his time in prison. Clean record, no problems. Supposedly he was a model prisoner and a trustee in the prison library. That was one of the factors that figured in the judge's decision to let him out on bail the way he did. No fights, no reprimands, no nothing on his record. It seemed like everyone left Richie Briggs alone in prison."

"So let's see if we can put him back there again," I said to Teena.

"You really think he could be the one who did all this? Murdered the Lavelle family?"

"I do."

There were some problems with that theory though.

Why would a lowlife like Richie Briggs kill anyone else now that he'd lucked out like this on the murder rap for Tommy Ferraro? And there was an even bigger problem: motive. What would be his motive for coming to Martha's Vineyard and killing Nancy Lavelle and her family?

It was the same motive problem I'd had with Albert Ruggerio in the end. We'd assumed at first that Ruggerio was angry at Dr. Thomas Lavelle for the medical treatment he received. But later it turned out that Ruggerio was grateful to Lavelle for performing the heart surgery that had saved his life up to that point. So the motive for murder by Ruggerio wasn't a viable motive at all.

And the motive here simply didn't work either. No matter how many ways I looked at the facts, I couldn't put them together in any logical way.

Nancy Lavelle had turned out to be an amazingly successful lawyer for Briggs. She'd managed to get him out of jail after killing a police officer, which no one believed would ever happen. She did a great job. Which meant there was no reason he would want to see her and her family dead.

Unless there was something going on between Briggs and Nancy Lavelle that we didn't know about.

All I knew at this point was that I needed to find Richie Briggs.

CHAPTER 52

The last record the New York State Corrections Dept. had for Richie Briggs was his release from Attica prison several weeks earlier. After that, all the information about him went to another agency that was required to monitor his activities while he was out on bail. We weren't able to reach anyone there quickly. But I found an address in the court records for a place in Washington Heights, which was where he had apparently been living when he was arrested for Tommy's murder. I couldn't find any newer address, so I decided to start there while I waited for more information.

I'd spent some time working in the precinct that covered Washington Heights in Manhattan when I was a patrol officer on the street in my early years with the NYPD. Before I made detective.

I called the precinct now and hoped I'd find a sympathetic voice on the other end.

As it turned out, I did.

His name was Sgt. Bruce Weber, and he remembered me from my days there. He was a desk sergeant now, which I guessed was a permanent position for him until retirement. This was good for me. Weber was happy to hear from me and eager to find out more about how I was doing in Martha's Vineyard.

"Why did you wind up going to a small force like that?"

"It's my hometown. I grew up here. I guess I just wanted to come back home to this place for a while."

"How's that working out?"

"Well, basically I came here looking for a quieter life than being a homicide detective in New York City. But it hasn't been that way. At least so far. Which is why I'm calling. I'm working on a big murder case up here. I could use your help in tracking down someone from Washington Heights who could be crucial to this new murder investigation."

"Sure. Who?"

"Richie Briggs."

"Briggs? The one who killed your partner?"

"The one and only. His name has come up in my investigation."

"What does he have to do with anything you're working on up there in Martha's Vineyard?"

"That's what I'm trying to find out."

I told him how the Correction Department records indicated his official New York City address still seemed to be the one in Washington Heights where he'd been at the time of his arrest after Tommy's death.

"Yes, Briggs lived with his mother," Weber said. "Never left there until he went to prison, then returned to it after he got out recently. Can you believe that? I hated the fact that the guy who killed a cop was back living in our precinct again. It made my blood boil every time I thought about it. But he got some hotshot lawyer who sprung him, thanks to an anti-cop judge. It made me sick when I heard that. I assume you felt the same way."

"I need to talk to Briggs, Bruce. Could you send someone to check the address and find out if he's there? If not, maybe put out an APB that he's wanted for questioning in another murder case. I can explain the details later, but right now I need your help in tracking Briggs down so I can question him."

"Oh, that won't be hard. The tracking down part, that is. The questioning might be a bit tougher."

"What do you mean?"

"You haven't heard?"

"No, what?"

"Richie Briggs' new residence is in a coffin. He's buried in a cemetery here. Got himself killed not long after he got out of prison. Not too many people are going to miss him. Lots of us are glad to see that guy dead."

I sat there in shock, trying to take this all in.

"What happened?" I asked finally.

"Weirdest thing. He went out to a deli to buy some beer, and someone attacked him there. Stabbed him in the chest. A couple of times. But it didn't really matter how many stab wounds there were, the first one was enough to kill him. Dead straight into his heart. Guess he was just unlucky. But, like I said, I don't think too many are going to shed any tears over the death of Richie Briggs."

"Did you arrest a suspect?"

"No, the killer got away before police got there."

"Any idea who it is?"

"We got a description."

I sighed. Descriptions at the crime scene from witnesses was notoriously unreliable and could fit half the population.

"Don't tell me," I said. "Male, average height, 160-175 pounds, no distinguishing features—"

"Nah, this one was different. It was a woman. Well, really a girl. A teenage girl, people said who saw her. This teenage girl just walked up to Richie Briggs at the deli and stabbed him to death. Then she fled. But – and this part is really weird – before she ran away, she took time to place his hands together in front of him on the body. It was almost like he was praying. Crazy, huh? No one had ever seen this teenage girl before or had any idea who she was."

"I think I know," I said.

CHAPTER 53

"Susan Kirwin killed both Albert Ruggerio and Richie Briggs," I said to Chief Wilhelm.

"Which means she killed the Lavelle family too?"

"Not necessarily."

"But they were all stabbed so…"

"I still can't quite figure out how a sixteen-year-old girl would subdue an entire family of five people – two of them adults, two of them young girls near her own age – while she stabbed everyone to death. She was able to do it with Ruggerio because he was in a wheelchair and not able to defend himself. She stabbed the bodyguard, Roy DeSantis, by surprise – he never expected she would be a danger. The same thing probably happened with Briggs in the deli. But with the Lavelles… well, I think she would have needed some sort of help. Maybe she did do it, but with someone else. Or someone else did it all. That was the same person who broke into my house and left that note and the writing on the wall. It has to be someone else we don't know about. That stuff at my house happened after Susan Kirwin was dead."

"Are you sure? It still might be someone who was just attracted by all the publicity you got on that last case, like we thought…"

"What about the missing girl? What about Karin Lavelle? She was alive the day the break-in happened. We know that from the newspaper she was holding. Whoever did that is who has her."

Wilhelm sighed. He knew I was right. But he desperately wanted this to be over. To get this case solved quickly. There was a new mayor in Cedar Cliffs, and I knew he was getting impatient for results. Wilhelm's career, which he had painstakingly put together through long years of dedicated service with the Cedar Cliffs police force, could be in jeopardy.

And he knew the only thing that could save him was me.

He hated that.

But I took no particular satisfaction in the possibility that Chief Wilhelm could be fired. As bad as Wilhelm was, I might wind up with someone worse if he lost his job. I'd seen that happen before. No, all I cared about was solving this case. The rest of it would fall into place if I could do that.

"Take me through it all again," he said. "Everything we know at the moment."

I did. I told him all about the Richie Briggs connection to me and also to Nancy Lavelle who had gotten him released from jail. I ran through everything else I knew too. Including the fact that the girl had put Briggs' hands together in front of him – as if he was praying in death. Another statement murder. I told him Meg's theory about this being a sign of submission or surrender to the power of the murderer.

"Just like with Nancy Lavelle," I said. "The girl didn't have time to do it with Ruggerio before she died herself. But someone is 'signing' these murders, Chief – making sure we know they're out there doing this."

"What does it all mean? Who's doing this?"

"I don't know."

Wilhelm's frustration boiled over at this point. "Dammit, Pearce, all you do is keep coming up with more dead ends, more leads that don't help us."

"That's the way a murder investigation works," I told him. "There's a lot of dead ends and leads that don't go anywhere until they finally do. I've done this before, you know."

I wanted to add that he hadn't ever run a murder investigation before, but I didn't.

I didn't have to.

He knew that as well as I did.

And it was another reminder for Wilhelm that he needed me. I was his only way to solve this case for him.

Teena and I sat in our makeshift "war room" at the station afterward and went through it all one more time.

"I see a couple of possible scenarios here," Teena said. "Want me to run through them?"

"Go ahead."

"Scenario one: The Kirwin girl did it all. Killed Briggs, killed Ruggerio, killed the Lavelle family. All by herself."

"Doubtful," I said.

"Okay, scenario two: There were two different teenage girls. One of them, Kirwin, killed Ruggerio. Another separate teenage girl for some reason attacked and stabbed Richie Briggs to death in New York. They just both happened to be teenage girls who stabbed different people for different reasons. Simply a coincidence."

"Even more doubtful."

"Scenario three: There's someone else behind this. A mastermind. They seem obsessed with coming after you now, just like they were obsessed with killing Briggs and the Lavelles and Ruggerio. Which means you need to be very careful, Abby. Because this is the scenario I'm betting is the right one."

I ignored the warning and concentrated on something else.

"The girl, Teena. The missing girl. Karin Lavelle. If we find her, then I think everything else will fall into place."

"So let's find the girl," Teena said.

She looked up at the sign on the wall of the station that said: "Get your ass out of your seat, go knock on doors."

"I'm getting off my ass and going back to work," she said. "How about you?"

But I didn't. Not right away. I sat there for a while after Teena left looking at all the pictures and documents and other evidence that was posted on the wall.

Everything we had was there. The crime scene photos. Pictures of the victims – Thomas Lavelle, Nancy Lavelle, Janet Lavelle, Eileen Lavelle and Steven Lavelle; Albert Ruggerio and his bodyguard (who I now knew was an undercover cop from the NYPD) Roy DeSantis; Richie Briggs, the man I'd hated ever since he murdered my partner and changed my life forever; and, most compelling of all, a picture of Karin Lavelle, the only one here who was still alive. If I could find her in time.

I stared at one of the pictures of Karin Lavelle for a long time. It had been taken on the first day she and her family arrived on the island. She was standing on the beach looking happy and eager and full of life. Without any clue of what lay ahead for the Lavelles on this seemingly paradise island. A dream vacation that would quickly turn into a nightmare.

I looked again through all of the other pictures we'd put up on the wall.

Desperately looking for some kind of inspiration.

The Lavelles. Ruggerio. Briggs. What tied them all together? Okay, I knew the connection between Thomas Lavelle and Ruggerio. And the connection between his wife Nancy Lavelle and Richie Briggs. But what about Ruggerio and Briggs? They'd both been stabbed to death the same way, presumably by the same person – Susan Kirwin. Was there some connection there that I was missing?

I stopped now at one of the pictures and stared at it intently.

Not a picture of one of the dead victims.

This was one victim who had survived.

Roy DeSantis.

DeSantis had told me his story of being an NYPD undercover cop working inside the Mob to get information about Albert Ruggerio. And DeSantis' story about that had checked out.

But I was pretty sure now that he hadn't told me the whole story.

It was time to go back and talk to Roy DeSantis again.

CHAPTER 54

"They say I should be getting out of this place pretty soon," Roy DeSantis told me when I went to see him at the hospital.

"You were lucky."

"Tell me about it. Docs said that you getting an ambulance as quickly as you did also probably saved my life. So, if I didn't say this before, thank you, Detective Pearce."

"I was only doing my job."

"Good job." He smiled.

There were remains of a meal on a tray next to his bed. It looked like some kind of tuna casserole, a dish of green Jell-O and a cup of coffee. It didn't look particularly appetizing. Hospital food never is. DeSantis looked over at the tray now and shook his head.

"First thing I'm going to do when I get out of here is have a decent meal," he said.

"I'll bet."

I asked him to run through everything he remembered from the Ruggerio house. He gave me pretty much the same story as he'd told me before.

The public story everyone still believed was that DeSantis had been Albert Ruggerio's security guard. No one else knew about his real identity except me, Teena and Chief Wilhelm. He said he wanted to be able to keep his cover as a Mob guy, even though Ruggerio was now dead.

"That's a helluva story, Roy," I said when he was finished talking. "But that's basically the same things you told me before. There's more to the story than that, isn't there. You can tell me the rest of it now, right?"

"What are you talking about?"

"I want to know what you found out about Ruggerio while you were working for him. Everything you know from those months as his security guard. Because something there could be important, it could give me a lead into his murder and how it might connect to all these other murders. Tell me what the organized crime force of the NYPD learned from your undercover work."

"I can't do that."

"Why not? I'm a police officer."

"Yeah, you're a police officer on a rinky-dink force in a rinky-dink town. This is big-time police stuff I'm working on with the NYPD. Way above your pay grade. I'm sorry to put it like that, but it's the truth."

"I used to be with the NYPD. If I was still with the NYPD, would you tell me?"

"No. I'm not going there with you. I'm not telling you secret information. So don't even try to get it out of me."

"Look, I know you want to stay undercover as a Mob guy when you go back to New York," I said. "I'm happy to cooperate with that. But at the same time, I'm asking you to cooperate with me on a murder investigation. If you help me, I help you."

"Wait a minute, what does that mean? Are you threatening to expose me if I don't talk with you about this? You can't publicly expose me as being a police officer. You'd get yourself in trouble if you did that."

I was never going to reveal the identity of an undercover officer like DeSantis. I told him that. But I still wanted that information he had gathered with Ruggerio. I had a feeling that it was somehow crucial to this case, even though I wasn't sure how or why.

"I really need your help, Roy," I said. "I'm asking you cop-to-cop. One police officer to another. Yes, I know I work for a rinky-dink force in a small town, just like you said. But I'm still a police officer, like you are. And I need to stop a mass murderer before more people are killed. Will you help me do that, Roy?"

DeSantis sighed.

"You're a real piece of work, Pearce. You know that, right?"

"Well, I did save your life. That ought to be worth something." He smiled.

"You figure that the Kirwin girl who stabbed me was the same person who killed the Lavelles?"

"I think she was involved."

"But she had help?"

"Yes."

"Someone you have to find before they kill again."

"Right. What can you tell me about Ruggerio? That might help me figure it all out."

I hadn't told him anything about the stabbing death of Richie Briggs by a teenage girl in New York because I couldn't imagine what it might have to do with Ruggerio. And we hadn't even gone public with that yet for the same reason. So I was focusing on the Ruggerio and Lavelle family stabbing deaths with DeSantis.

"Okay, let me make a phone call," he said.

I left the room while DeSantis called someone. Presumably the people he worked for back in New York at the NYPD as an undercover police officer. A few minutes later, DeSantis called out to me to come back into the room.

"The information I'm about to convey to you is just between you and me," he said. "Not your partner. Not your chief. No one else. But, if you can use it to help your murder investigation, I'll give it to you personally. But this can never be connected to me. Is that acceptable for you?"

"Acceptable," I said.

"Okay, we have a deal. I have your word on that, right?"

I nodded.

"We weren't just trying to take Ruggerio down," he said. "I was trying to get other information from him too before we made our move on him. Before we put him in jail. That was my assignment. That's why I was there undercover pretending to be an underworld security guard."

"Why wait? Wasn't arresting a Mob boss like Ruggerio enough. If you already had enough evidence on him, then why were you still working undercover for him?"

"Because we were trying to bring down the rest of his operation too. We wanted to nail some people that were doing something just as bad – maybe even worse – than Ruggerio. That was my job there working undercover. To find out who those people were working with Ruggerio and expose them."

"What's worse than what Ruggerio did?"

"NYPD police on his payroll. Taking payoffs to protect him and other Mob guys. That was our real target. We needed to find out who they were."

"Jesus!"

"That's right. We were out after dirty cops."

CHAPTER 55

"Ruggerio was a strange guy," DeSantis told me now. "Moody, I guess you might say. Actually, it was more than just moods. I mean he could be the most cold-blooded person, ordering people to commit all sorts of violent and ugly crimes, and he'd be the nicest guy in the world a few minutes later.

"But, at the end, he'd gotten a lot more mellow. I guess he sensed his own mortality or whatever. I'm not sure what would have happened if he lived. Sooner or later, we would have closed the law enforcement net around him, and he would have been arrested. I guess he would have died in jail.

"With me, he was always friendly and nice. I guess that's because he knew he needed me. He never had any idea of who I really was, I'm certain of that. Otherwise, he wouldn't have talked so much about all his business dealings with me. He told me a lot of bad stuff that we could have used against him. Still can use that information, to put away the rest of his Mob organization.

"Funny thing is I kind of liked him. Especially at the end. He seemed grateful to be alive after his heart surgery. What I told you before about that was true too. He credited Lavelle with saving his life. He told me that a number of times. So there was no way he would have had anything to do with whatever happened to Lavelle and his family.

"It wasn't Ruggerio who had Lavelle and his family killed. No, someone else wanted them dead. But I have no idea who. I've thought about it, I really have, and I can't come up with anything to help you in solving these murders, Detective. And that's the truth."

I asked him about Ruggerio having NYPD cops on his payroll.

"How many cops?" I asked.

"Too many."

"Yes, even one is pretty shocking."

I tried to imagine what kind of a police officer would sell himself out to someone like Albert Ruggerio and his Mob pals. It was unthinkable. Or at least I couldn't think of anyone I ever knew on the force who would do something like that.

"What did these cops do for Ruggerio?" I asked DeSantis.

"They protected him. Gave him a heads-up on any police activity involving his Mob business. Looked the other way when he extorted someone or had someone beat up or whatever. Or, on a few occasions, a key piece of evidence against one of his people who'd been arrested disappeared from a secure area that only cops and other law enforcement people had access to. Most of the cops on his payroll weren't pushing the line too much, just a little bit here and there. But that's too much."

"Why would they – the dirty cops, that is – jeopardize their career and do something like that?"

"C'mon, you know the answer to that as well as I do. Money. You don't get rich being on the police force. Some of them needed the cash to support bad habits like gambling or drugs. Some wanted to put away money for their family or their kids to go to college. Hard for cops like that to get along on just their salary. So along comes Ruggerio asking for a few favors and offering to pay them well for that service. It probably seemed harmless, at first. But once you're in with the Mob, you can't just get out. The favors they want you to do start out small, but then they get bigger and bigger. It's a slippery slope. Didn't you ever know any dirty cops when you were with the NYPD?"

"Not really. I mean I suspected a few cops might be on the take, but I never knew for sure. I guess I really didn't want to think about it too much. I couldn't believe a cop, no matter what his troubles, would ever do something like that."

"You'd be surprised," DeSantis said. "In some cases, the dirty cop's family and friends and co-workers – even his partner on the street – didn't even know what he was doing."

"That's hard to believe. I had a few partners, and we always laughed about how we shared the same brain. Each of us always knew what the other one was thinking and doing. No secrets. We were that close."

"Sounds like you had good partners."

"Did any of these cops who went on the take ever change their mind?"

"You don't quit the Mob. The worst case was a cop who got second thoughts, gaining a conscience, I guess. Was thinking about coming to us at organized crime and telling all. Only Ruggerio found out about it before he could do that. And Ruggerio had him killed so he couldn't talk."

"My God!"

"Yeah, Ruggerio told me about that one just before he died. I was going to look into it further when this happened and I got laid up here. All I know is that this guy was killed in what looked like a line of duty shooting but it was really someone Ruggerio sent to assassinate him. I don't know a whole lot more about it yet. Like I said, I just got this information out of Ruggerio before he died. About how they killed this cop to keep him from talking. I do know he worked out of Chelsea…"

"I worked out of Chelsea. What was his name?"

"Tommy Ferraro."

CHAPTER 56

I didn't tell Roy DeSantis that I knew Tommy Ferraro. I didn't tell him that Tommy was my friend. My mentor on the force. My idol as a police officer. Hell, most of all, I didn't tell DeSantis that Tommy had been my partner.

He would find that out soon enough when he began looking into the details of Ferraro after getting the information from Ruggerio before he died.

But I'd worry about that later.

Right now I had two important questions to deal with. Was Tommy Ferraro really on Ruggerio's payroll when we were on the street together? And, if Ruggerio actually did have Ferraro killed, then how did Richie Briggs fit into the picture?

Was I wrong about Tommy Ferraro? How did I not see that or suspect anything during my long time working with him? Or was this all some kind of horrible mistake and the dirty cop on Ruggerio's payroll was someone other than Tommy?

I didn't talk about this shocking news that DeSantis had told me with anyone at the Cedar Cliffs station when I got there, not even Teena. But I thought about it the rest of the day until I went home.

When I got home, there was a message from Lincoln asking me how I was doing. Should I tell Lincoln? Well, if I wasn't going to tell my partner Teena, I sure wasn't ready to share this with Lincoln Connor. Besides, I'd been uncomfortable ever since that scene at our lunch when he got so defensive after I asked him about his past. I knew I would have to bring that up again with him. I just wasn't sure how or when to do that.

I decided to take a bike ride now. Riding a bike in Martha's Vineyard sometimes helped me clear my head and relax. So, after I fed and walked Oscar, I started pedaling from my house to a road that took me along the beaches on the northern side of the island.

It was a scenic route, and especially so now in the early fall. The leaves hadn't really started to turn on the trees yet, but there were patches of red and brown and yellow all around that made the landscape even more spectacular than usual. I tried to focus on the beauty around me as I rode.

But the memories of Tommy Ferraro kept flooding back to me.

I'd been on the street with Tommy Ferraro for nearly two years before he died. I remembered that first day on the job with him, how I was so nervous and how he put me at ease right from the start. About all the conversations we had together as partners and the fun and the good times.

There were some not so good times too, but he always helped me through those.

Tommy always had my back, always stood up for me. A lot of guys in our precinct – on the whole force actually – didn't like the idea of a woman detective on the street. There was a lot of sexist harassment.

Tommy got mad when anyone did stuff like that. I said it came with the territory of being a woman cop. But Tommy never accepted that. And, even though I was never sure exactly what he said or did to some of those other cops at our precinct, the harassment against me stopped afterward.

But the best thing about me and Tommy was that we trusted each other.

He trusted me.

And I sure always trusted him.

"Never go against your partner," he told me that first day we were together on the street. "Always trust your partner. If you can't trust your partner, you can't trust anyone. No secrets between us, partner."

So did Tommy Ferraro keep a secret from me? That he was taking payoffs from an underworld boss? I'd never have believed he was capable of doing something like that until I talked to DeSantis. I used to be sure that Tommy would never lie to me about anything. Now I wasn't so sure.

I'd arrived at the beach. I got off my bike and sat in the sand, looking out at the water. The northern side of the island was on the harbor, shielded by Cape Cod a short distance away. It was really a pretty sight, but it didn't match the ugly thoughts going through my mind as I sat there.

Even if I thought that Tommy really had been a dirty cop, what did that have to do with his death?

I mean I knew who killed Tommy. It was Richie Briggs. Briggs wasn't some professional underworld hit man. He was a low-life loser in the world of crime.

So it wasn't Ruggerio or any of his men who shot Tommy.

It was Richie Briggs, after a robbery gone wrong.

That just didn't fit with the scenario DeSantis had told me about Tommy deliberately being taken out by the Mob so he wouldn't talk about his relationship with Albert Ruggerio and the Mob.

I sure couldn't see a connection anyway.

Or was I missing something?

When I got home again, I pulled out a scrapbook of pictures and other stuff that I keep from my days in New York.

There were a number of photos of Tommy and me there. At the Chelsea station house. In our car. Hanging out on the street. One from a family picnic outing, which had both me and my husband Zach posing with Tommy and his wife Rikki. We all looked so happy in the picture. I had no idea my marriage to Zach would implode because of my drinking. And Rikki Ferraro had no idea her husband wouldn't come home from work one night.

Happy memories and tragic ones too.

But I knew now that's all they were.

Memories.

"Never go against your partner." Yep, that's what Tommy told me that first day we were together on the street. "Always trust your partner. If you can't trust your partner, you can't trust anyone. No secrets between us, partner."

But now those secrets – from a man whose death had haunted me for a long time – were emerging and pulling me into an even worse nightmare than I could have ever imagined.

Even worse than Tommy's death.

Because I was afraid now that other lives might be at stake here.

And one of them could be mine.

CHAPTER 57

I tried to call Tommy's wife Rikki the next morning.

I wasn't exactly sure what I was going to say to her. I mean I wasn't planning on asking her directly if her husband was on the Mob's payroll when he died. But since I'd been talking to her anyway since I'd moved to Martha's Vineyard, I guess I hoped I'd pick up something from her voice or the conversation if I brought up Tommy.

Especially knowing what I knew now.

In any case, it didn't matter because Rikki Ferraro didn't answer the phone. My call went right to her voice mail. I didn't leave a message. Because I wasn't sure what to say to her. But, whatever that did turn out to be, I wanted the conversation to be live and not a message on a voice mail.

I tried my last partner Vic Gelman next. Would he know anything about Tommy being on the take? Not likely, since I didn't even know. Still, I wanted to sound him out some more about Tommy and the rest. But he was in court testifying on a case, I was told. I left a message this time, asking him to call me back when he could.

Then I called Nancy Lavelle's parents, Walt and Elizabeth Hood. I wasn't sure why I did that either. I was just flailing around here for some kind of lead. But their daughter had represented Richie Briggs. Briggs had been stabbed to death too, just like Ruggerio and the Lavelle family. Maybe the Hoods would come up with something that could help me.

"Nancy never talked to us about her cases," Walt Hood said to me when I reached him. "She didn't like to talk about her work. I think she was embarrassed by some of the clients she took money from. And frankly, my wife and I didn't want to know too much about some of the unsavory ones ourselves."

"So she never mentioned a client named Richie Briggs to you?"

"No. Who's he?"

"Your daughter represented him. She got him out of jail."

"What did he do?"

"He killed a police officer."

He sighed. "My daughter had too many of those kinds of clients, in my opinion. Nancy knew her mother and I didn't approve of them. Do you think this Briggs person had anything to do with what happened? Did he kill her and Tom and our grandchildren?"

"No, Briggs is dead. Since before your daughter and family were murdered."

I asked him about Albert Ruggerio.

"The underworld boss?"

"Yes. Did your daughter ever talk about him?"

"Not my daughter. But my son-in-law did. Tom was his doctor. Performed heart surgery on him. I was worried about that too. But I couldn't tell my son-in-law who to treat or not treat as a patient, any more than I could with my daughter and the undesirable people she represented as a lawyer."

"Your daughter represented Ruggerio as a lawyer several years ago too."

"Do you think that had something to do with all this?"

Yes, I did, but I had no idea how or why.

Teena came in after I did all this. I told her all about it. Everything. I'd been thinking about this ever since I talked to DeSantis. If it was true that Tommy had kept his involvement with Ruggerio and the Mob from me, then he'd broken the number one rule he'd taught me. Always trust your partner. No secrets from your partner. Tommy used to be my partner, but Teena was my partner now.

So I told her how DeSantis said Tommy Ferraro had been on Ruggerio's payroll.

I could tell she was stunned and confused by everything I told her, the same as I was when I first found out. But she didn't show any outward emotion. Teena rarely did.

"What's the connection between Ruggerio and Briggs?" she said. "All we know is they got killed the same way – and by the same person."

"Let's go through everything we have about Richie Briggs and Nancy Lavelle one more time," I said.

The Briggs file I'd gotten from Lavelle's law records with the help of her parents was still on my computer. I read through it all again now.

It was the same as I remembered. A lot of details about all the legal moves Lavelle had made to win Briggs' appeal and get him out of jail. About how his rights had been violated and he'd been subjected to police brutality along the way. It made me angry just to read this stuff again. Because of this woman, a cop killer had gone free.

Nancy Lavelle might have been a very good lawyer, but I didn't think much of her as a human being.

I realized something new though after I finished with the file. A question I had before that had never been answered.

"How did Briggs get the money for bail?" I asked Teena.

"He didn't need to put up the whole amount. All he had to do was post a bond for ten percent of it."

"That's fifty thousand dollars."

"Okay."

"Richie Briggs didn't have fifty dollars to his name, much less fifty thousand."

"A bail bondsman?"

"He'd need to have some kind of collateral to put up for any bail bondsman. Briggs had nothing, from what I've been able to find out."

"Then somebody else must have put the money up for him."

"Who?"

I scrolled to the last page of the file. The part where it talked about how Briggs had been released from prison several weeks earlier. It said that there had indeed been a fifty-thousand-dollar bond that was posted by someone for his release. The money came from a company called Binstock Associates.

"What's Binstock Associates?" Teena said.

"And why would they front fifty thousand dollars for a loser like Briggs?"

It took a while to figure it out. The financial trail to Binstock Associates was a tangled one. Someone had deliberately made sure of that. It turned out be the name for a different company, which was in turn a front for another one. It took more time to get to the real people behind Binstock Associates.

But then, when we finally did sort everything out, we got the answer we were looking for on Richie Briggs' release from prison.

"The chairman and CEO of Binstock Associates is – or was – none other than…"

"Albert Ruggerio?"

"Bingo."

CHAPTER 58

Teena and I were back at the Black Dog Bar. We both decided we needed to take a break from work. So, of course, we were mostly talking about work at the Black Dog.

"What do we do next?" Teena asked me.

"We wait."

"That doesn't sound like us. Shouldn't we be out chasing suspects or something?"

"Who do we chase? Everyone is dead. Ruggerio. Briggs. The girl, Susan Kirwin. And all the Lavelles."

"Except for the missing daughter."

"Do you think she could have done all this?"

"No way."

Teena thought for a second.

"What about this Roy DeSantis guy? He's still alive. Can he be trusted? Is he telling you the truth about what he did or didn't do?"

"I checked DeSantis out. He's who he says he is. An NYPD cop working undercover. DeSantis is telling the truth about who he is and what's he's been doing."

"Which means there's another player in all this. A brutal, cold-blooded murderer who likely will kill again. And we have no idea who this person is or where to look. A very scary scenario, huh."

"That's why we have to wait for the killer to come to us."

"Could be dangerous to do that."

"I'm the next target. Not you. The letter left at my house made that pretty clear."

"Yeah, well, I'm your partner. If someone comes after you, they're going to have to come after me too. I'll be there with you."

"Good to hear, partner." I smiled.

Teena was drinking her third Heineken beer. I was sipping on a Diet Coke. She looked over at it now.

"What would happen if you had like one beer with me here, Abby?"

"You want me to drink a beer?"

"Not really. But I'm curious. I don't really understand about being an alcoholic. Would you go crazy if you did that – and just keep on drinking?"

"Probably not. I could very well drink one beer and be fine."

"But you won't?"

"No, I won't. Not tonight."

"Why?"

"Because I can't be sure that's what would happen. And I can't take the chance. Not now."

Teena nodded.

"I think it's a good idea for you stick with the Diet Coke then," she said.

She asked me then about Lincoln Connor. I explained how we were having a clandestine romance at the moment. How we planned on keeping our relationship a secret, at least until this case/story was over. But I also told her about the strange moment when I'd brought up questions about his background and family.

"Did you ask him why he was upset over that?"

"He didn't want to talk about it anymore."

"That is weird."

"Yeah, I tried to check up on him afterward and couldn't find much. I mean there's a lot of stuff about him doing stories on the Boston TV station. But I can't find any background material. About his family. His hometown. Nothing like that at all. It's almost like he dropped in from outer space or something."

"Interesting."

"Kinda disturbing to me, too. Is he hiding something?"

"What are you going to do?"

"Keep seeing him. Whenever I can. And maybe try to find out more about him and his background too."

"Well, you are a detective…"

"I did find out a bit more about Richie Briggs, though," I told her. "I talked again with the cop I knew at the Washington Heights precinct. He said he went back and talked to the mother of Briggs again after our last conversation. The mother said her son was a kind of a gangster wannabe. Always dreamed about somehow getting into the Mob and becoming a professional criminal. Some aspiration, right? But there's nothing in his record to indicate any Mob link. Until the end when he got sprung from jail by Albert Ruggerio's company."

"You figure Ruggerio hired Briggs to kill your partner Tommy Ferraro to keep Ferraro quiet?"

"Looks like it to me. That way no one would connect Tommy's death to Ruggerio. Everyone just assumed Tommy was killed by a fleeing holdup man, not in retaliation by Ruggerio and the Mob so he wouldn't talk to the NYPD. Of course, Briggs wasn't supposed to get caught. When he did, Ruggerio convinced him to stay with the holdup story. That's the likely reason no one messed with Briggs in prison. Ruggerio was the one making sure he was protected in there. I also checked out Nancy Lavelle's rates as a lawyer, she was very expensive. No way Briggs could have afforded Lavelle on his own. It was Ruggerio who put up the bond to get Briggs out of jail. It all fits, Teena."

"And then, after Briggs was freed from prison, maybe it was Ruggerio who had Briggs killed – to make sure he didn't talk about doing the Ferraro shooting for him," Teena suggested.

"Why would Ruggerio do that? He was the one who got Briggs freed from prison. Presumably as payback for carrying out the

Tommy Ferraro killing for him. Hell, Briggs was finally going to get what he always dreamed about. The opportunity to be a part of Ruggerio's Mob organization. Besides, Briggs was killed by a teenage girl – not a Mob hit man. And then Ruggerio gets stabbed to death the same way a few weeks later? No, Ruggerio and Briggs were both killed by the same person. Just like the Lavelles. But why?"

"I still don't like the idea of us just waiting around for something to happen. What if someone else – someone besides you – is the killer's next target?"

"I did do something. I reached out to the local police in the two towns where Mrs. Lavelle's parents and Tommy's wife and family live. I asked the local cops to keep tabs on them because of these other murders that might be related. Suggested they leave a patrol car outside the Lavelle and Ferraro houses if they could do it."

"You think both of those families are in danger?"

I shrugged.

"This person killed a year-old boy and two young girls for no reason other than they were related to one or both of the targets in the Lavelle family. Maybe the killer goes after the parents next, for some bizarre reason. The same with Tommy's family. If Tommy Ferraro really is somehow at the center of this, well… I don't want to be responsible for losing his wife and kids too. I already feel responsible about Tommy. It can't hurt to keep an eye on them all."

"What about Karin Lavelle? That kid is still out there. She's certainly in danger… assuming she's still alive."

"I know. We have to believe she is still alive. At least she was a few days ago when that note was left for me. Hopefully, there's a reason the killer didn't murder her too. And that she'll be kept alive – until we can find her."

"But where do we even look for Karin Lavelle?"

"I'm betting she's not on the island anymore. We've searched everywhere."

"But you don't know that for sure."

"No, I'm not sure."

I wasn't sure where Karin Lavelle was – or what had happened to her.

I wasn't sure who murdered her family.

I wasn't sure about much of anything right now.

CHAPTER 59

If you want to find out anything about a person these days, it's not hard to do. You don't need to have the resources of a big law enforcement organization like I used to when I was with the NYPD. It's all there on social media.

I typed in Lincoln Connor's name along with a few other facts like location in Boston, age in the early thirties and a few other facts I knew, then punched in the search key and waited to see what happened.

Like I'd told Teena, most of it was stuff about him being a Boston TV news personality. He'd gotten to the station about a year ago, and since then Lincoln Connor had broken and covered a lot of high-profile stories on the air. Before that, he'd worked at a couple of smaller stations – a few years at one in New Hampshire and then more time at another station in Springfield, Massachusetts, until he made the big move to Boston. But I couldn't find anything else. Usually there was information about a person's hometown and education and family members, etc. But there was nothing like that for Lincoln Connor.

One of the things that's fascinating about social media these days is how searching for one thing can quickly lead you to other similar choices. Like when you friend someone on Facebook and get a list of other people that you might want to friend.

I came across a list like that while I was looking up information on Lincoln Connor. It suggested I try some other names that I might be interested in too. I noticed that one of the names had appeared on a previous piece of background information on Lincoln I'd called up. An item on that bio said: AKA (or may also be known as) Lawrence Cranston.

Lincoln Connor.

Lawrence Cranston.

Close enough that it could be more than a coincidence.

I started looking up information on Lawrence Cranston. There were several people with that name around the country, but only one in New England. He was located in a small town in New Hampshire called Hillsboro. I checked a map, and I discovered that Hillsboro was not far from the place where Lincoln Connor had his first TV job.

It took a while but I finally found a picture of Lawrence Cranston with a social profile. It looked like Lincoln. A few years younger, of course, but it was him. Which meant he had changed his name at some point from Lawrence Cranston to Lincoln Connor. Nothing wrong with that, I guess. He was a public media figure, and maybe he figured Lincoln Connor was a better air name for him – better for his career in the media – than Lawrence Cranston. It could have been no more than that.

Except there was more.

The bio I found along with his picture said Lawrence Cranston was married.

And that he was the father of two children.

I stared at my computer screen trying to figure out what to do next. Finally, I located a phone number online for Lawrence Cranston aka Lincoln Connor at the Hillsboro, N.H. address.

Then I called the number. A woman answered the phone. I wasn't sure what to say, I didn't have a real plan so I said the first thing I could think of.

"Is Lincoln Connor there?" I asked.

"No, he's not," the woman said.

There was no hesitation, no question about the Lincoln Connor name. Lincoln and Lawrence Cranston were obviously the same person. I knew that now. What I didn't know was who the woman was.

"Do you expect him soon?" I asked.

"Who is this?"

"Uh… I work for his office at the TV station in Boston. We need to reach him."

The woman didn't say anything.

"Just for my records, who am I speaking to," I said.

"Barbara Cranston."

"And you are?"

"His wife."

There was another long pause on the line.

"You're not really from his office at the station, are you?"

"No," I said numbly.

"What did he tell you?"

"Excuse me?"

"Did he promise to marry you?"

"What?"

"That's what Larry does. He asks all the girls he's running around with to marry him. You're not the first, honey. Believe me. He's told a lot of women he wants to marry them. But there's one little problem with that. A little detail he leaves out. Larry's already married. He's got a wife. And that wife is me."

"It's not what you think," Lincoln said to me.

"Are you married to a woman named Barbara Cranston?"

"I am."

"And are you the father of two children?"

"That's right, but—"

"Just tell me when we get to the part where it's not what I think it is."

We were sitting on a bench overlooking Nantucket Sound, a half-mile or so east of the Cedar Cliffs ferry station and the police station next to it. I'd asked him to meet me there, and when he arrived I confronted him with what I knew. I wanted answers.

"How about you let me tell you the story, Abby? Instead of interrogating me again. Like I said that night at the restaurant, I don't want to feel like I'm some kind of a suspect or someone in one of your cases."

"Good idea. Tell the story. You're good at telling stories. Like the story about how you wanted me to move to Boston, where you and I could get married and live happily ever after. That was a helluva story, Lincoln. Only thing is you left something out of that story. The fact that you already had a wife, and she damn sure wasn't me."

There was a ferry slowing making its way through the water to the Cedar Cliffs docks. Filled with tourists on their way to Martha's Vineyard. I could see some of them on deck now, waiting early for the boat to get there. I thought about how many times in the past I'd sat here near the Cedar Cliffs ferry station and watched the boats pull into the island. Both when I was growing up as a teenager here and more recently too. It sure was a beautiful sight. And Martha's Vineyard was a beautiful island. It seemed incongruous to me that a place so beautiful could also have been the site of so much pain and trauma for me. Now here it was happening again, no matter how grown up I was and how far I'd come from those long-ago days.

"Okay, I deserved that," he said. "And everything – all of it – is true. The wife. The family. I'm still married, I support them – so in that way I am a husband and a father. I never really lied to you about that. But I didn't mention it either. So I understand why you feel like I've been hiding the truth from you."

"You asked me to marry you," I pointed out.

He sighed.

"In my mind, I'm not married. I haven't been married for a long time. I was very young when I met Barbara. Then she got pregnant. I thought it was an accident, until I found out later she planned the whole pregnancy so she could convince me to marry her. Which is what I did. It seemed like the right thing to do.

"Then we had a second child too, in hopes of keeping the marriage working. I tried to convince myself that this was the life I was going to lead, married to Barbara and a father to our children. But I could never quite convince myself of that. I always knew I wanted something more.

"I was working then as a sales representative for a pharmaceutical company. Sounds boring, right? Well, it was. I was good at the job of selling though. That's when I realized I had the ability to connect with people. At some point, I wound up joining an actor's workshop in our town, and I was so successful that I thought about trying to be a professional actor.

"Mostly though I was doing the acting workshop because I wasn't happy at home. Barbara was very possessive, almost obsessively, and was constantly accusing me of cheating on her with other women. I wasn't, but she never believed that.

"Then one day I decided I wanted to try my hand at being a TV news reporter. I watched other people doing the news on TV, and I knew – or at least I convinced myself I did – that I could do a better job at it than them. I answered an ad for a tryout at a small local station near where we lived in New Hampshire. I got the job, and I was very successful. After that, I moved up to the station in Springfield – and finally made it to the big time with this station in Boston.

"But, when I moved up to the Boston station and became more popular, Barbara became more and more upset with me. She wanted me back in my old job with her and the family. She refused to move to Boston with me. She was jealous that other women would see me on TV and well… like I said she was almost obsessed with this idea of possessing me only for herself. She didn't want me to have any life outside of that. It was an untenable situation. I couldn't live like that anymore."

"Why didn't you just get divorced?"

"She wouldn't divorce me. No matter how many times I tried. She said she was my wife. That I'd never have another wife except her. She said there was no one else for me, that I'd realize that sooner or later. She was not leaving me, and she wasn't letting me go from our marriage either. It was really sick, but I didn't know to deal with my life anymore as Larry Cranston.

"So I started a new life. I changed my name to Lincoln Connor. Became a TV news star in Boston. I pretty much forgot about my life back in New Hampshire. Oh, like I said, I tried to be a father to my children as best I could with Barbara acting like she did. And I still support them. But I wanted something more out of life. And that's when I met you."

Some of his story made sense, but not all of it.

"I don't understand why you asked me to marry you and move to Boston. You knew that couldn't happen because you were already married. What if I had said yes to you?"

"That's why I asked you, I guess," he said with a small smile. "I knew you'd say no. I knew enough about you to realize you weren't going to give up your job and career here to be with me in Boston. It was really more of a fantasy for me. The fantasy of you and me together like that. I enjoyed the fantasy, Abby. After a while, I guess I forgot it was a fantasy. And that's all of it. I'm sorry. I should have told you the truth from the beginning. You deserve that. But I was afraid if you knew the truth about me, I would lose you. I didn't want to lose you. I still don't want to lose you, Abby. That is the truth."

People were getting off the ferry now. People with bikes. Some with backpacks. There were families with kids and animals. Everyone looked happy to be here. I wished I could be that happy. But that wasn't a possibility for me right now.

"What do we do now?" Lincoln asked.

"You're going to keep covering the story. And I'm going to keep investigating until I solve the case."

"And how about us?"

"I don't know. I need time to think. And right now I just need to find out who murdered Thomas Lavelle and his family and took his teenage daughter."

CHAPTER 60

Walt and Elizabeth Hood were stunned when I told them how we were putting them under police watch from their local law enforcement until the killer was caught.

But, after I explained the latest details and my concerns for them, they agreed to do everything they could to cooperate with me and their local authorities. They would remain at home, with regular police checks outside. And they would not let anyone they didn't know into their house for any reason.

I think they were happy and also relieved to know all these security precautions were being put in place after my warning that they could be in danger.

"What about our granddaughter?" Mrs. Hood asked. "If you feel we're in danger, she must be in even greater danger."

"Maybe not. The killer could have murdered her that first day at The Beach House, but didn't. There has to be a reason. Whatever that reason is, it's kept her alive so far. And hopefully will be able to keep her alive now until we find her."

"Do you have any more any leads on where she might be?" her husband asked.

"Not yet. But we will find her. I promise you that."

I wasn't sure why I "promised" them we'd find Karin Lavelle. I mean I wasn't certain about that. There were a number of things, mostly bad, that could have happened since that picture was taken of her alive with the newspaper a few days earlier. But I wanted to keep the Hoods as calm as I could. And I wanted to keep myself in the most positive frame of mind about Karin Lavelle too.

I did have one more question for the Hoods.

"Is there anyone else in your family or in your son-in-law's family that we should be concerned about for their safety? His parents are dead, right?"

"Yes. And he's an only child. We're really the only family."

"What happened to his parents?"

"They were killed in a car crash."

For a second, I wondered if that could somehow be related to the case too. But Walt Hood quickly dismissed that possibility for me.

"It happened a long time ago. More than ten years. A truck driver fell asleep at the wheel and hit their car head-on while they were on the New York State Thruway. It was a terrible tragedy."

That meant the only two families whose safety I needed to be worried about were the Hoods and Tommy's wife and children.

I was actually more worried about Rikki Ferraro than I was about the Hoods at the moment. That's because I still hadn't been able to reach her.

It was time to tell Wilhelm everything I knew, which is what I did.

"If the Hood and Ferraro families are in danger from this killer, then you could be in even more danger, Pearce," he said when I was finished. "I need you to acknowledge that. And we need to protect you better. I'm going to assign a car to remain outside your house and make sure you have twenty-four-hour police surveillance and backup with you."

"I can't work like that, Chief."

"Well, we can't leave you out there alone as a target."

"How about using Teena for more protection?" I said. "Have her stay with me. She could even sleep over at my house. I have an empty bedroom. And, if we're looking for someone to protect me, there's no one better I can think of than Teena."

I wasn't sure I really wanted Teena living with me for the foreseeable future.

And I wasn't sure how Teena would feel about that either.

But it seemed like the one scenario that was the most acceptable for me.

"Okay, you tell her," Wilhelm said.

Well, that should be fun…

I was still thinking about Tommy's wife and kids when I got back to my desk. Were they really in any danger? I called Vic Gelman, my ex-NYPD partner again. He told me he talked to Rikki Ferraro after Briggs' shocking release from prison. Said she was furious about Briggs walking free. Just like he was. Like I was too.

"And that's when you told her about Briggs getting out of jail?"

"Well, there were two calls. That one, where I told her about Briggs being free. And then a second one later after he got killed. I thought she should know that too. I called her as soon as it happened. She was very grateful to me for doing that. As upset as she was when Briggs got out of jail, she was really happy to hear about his death. And why not? She said no one had ever deserved to die a horrible death more than Richie Briggs, after what he did to Tommy."

Wait a minute…

There was something wrong with what he was telling me.

I'd talked to Rikki Ferraro following that last phone call after Briggs' death and she never said anything about Briggs' stabbing. Only about him getting out of jail and what an outrage that was.

"Maybe she forgot to mention it to you," Gelman said. "She's had so much trouble. I can imagine she's having a hard time dealing with everything."

"You mean she's never gotten over Tommy's death?"

"Oh, that too. But all the rest of it. Especially losing her daughter after that the way she did."

"What happened to the daughter?"

"She died not long ago. Only a teenager. But the girl never really was able to deal with her father's death, she went into a tailspin and had all sorts of emotional problems. Started doing a lot of drugs to ease the pain. And then one day they found her dead in bed from a heroin overdose. Sad, sad story."

"How old a teenager?"

"I'm not sure… about fifteen or sixteen."

My blood suddenly ran cold.

Because I realized now what that meant.

She was the same age as Susan Kirwin, the girl at the The Beach House crime scene.

And Karin Lavelle too.

CHAPTER 61

You think you know someone until you realize you don't know them at all.

That was certainly the case with Rikki Ferraro. Of course, my image of her had been formed through her husband talking about her during that time we spent on the streets for the job. But the picture we began putting together now of the real Rikki Ferraro was a much more shocking and terrifying one.

I knew she and Tommy had met when he was in the army, but I didn't realize she'd been in the army too then. She was a special forces operative like Tommy. They had served in Afghanistan together, and she did a tour of Iraq after that.

When Tommy left the army and joined the police force in New York, she got her military discharge at the same time. Raised their two children in the years afterward, but also ran a business. Actually two businesses. She was an instructor at a karate school, where she held a black belt. She also did some kind of therapy sessions with children who came from broken families.

I wasn't sure what the second one meant, but the first one was pretty clear: As a black belt, this was a woman who knew how to take care of herself. And presumably could handle other people too. No reason to think she wasn't proficient enough in martial arts to subdue the Lavelle family that day at The Beach House.

There was more: An article in a local paper on Long Island talked about her speaking at women's groups on how to defend yourself against rape or other sexual attacks. Her advice was to carry a knife at all times. She then gave a demonstration of how a knife could be used to immobilize an attacker, either by killing him instantly with a stabbing wound to the right spot or by inflicting damage to other parts of the body. The article talked about how she'd learned to use these techniques with the Army Special Forces as a trained combat soldier in Afghanistan and Iraq.

"Damn, this woman is a real piece of work," Teena said. "You never knew any of this?"

"I only met her a few times for dinner. Tommy talked about her, but not about this stuff. Or, if he did, I didn't really hear it. You know how it is when someone is talking about their husband or wife or partner. You're sort of listening, but not totally."

The financial records were intriguing too. The house she and Tommy had on Long Island cost $1.5 million, more than a police officer could be expected to afford. They also had two expensive cars and even a boat.

"Ruggerio's money to your old partner," Teena said.

"I'm afraid it sounds like that."

"He was living too big a lifestyle for a cop's salary."

"Tommy did talk sometimes at the beginning about how his wife complained he didn't make enough money. Said she kept pestering him to get a job that paid more."

"Sounds like he did. Working for Ruggerio."

I kept hoping there might be some other explanation for all this, but it seemed to be true. Tommy had been on the Mob's payroll. The only thing I could hold on to in his favor was that, according to DeSantis, he was trying to quit Ruggerio. Maybe Tommy's conscience finally got to him. Maybe he really was a good man in the end. But that got him killed by Ruggerio's hit man, Richie Briggs.

The time since Tommy's death had been difficult for Rikki Ferraro, we discovered from the information about her. Not only was she grieving for her husband, but she also soon had to deal with the loss of her children. Both of their children.

The son Thomas Jr. had quit school after Tommy was shot and joined the army, saying he wanted to carry on his father's mission somehow now that he was dead. But he never really got the chance. He died in a helicopter crash that killed him and six other recruits during training at Fort Benning, Georgia.

Even more devastating was the death of her daughter, Christina. Christina Ferraro fell into a deep depression after losing her father, and she started using drugs. She overdosed one day from a heroin injection. Her mother was the one who found her dead in bed.

"Her whole life is turned upside down in a period of a year or two," I said. "She loses her husband Tommy first. Then her son and daughter. Neither of them would have likely died if Tommy was still alive. His death was what started all this despair and tragedy for her. So maybe she goes looking for revenge against the people she perceived as being responsible for that. The Lavelle woman, Ruggerio, Briggs and—"

"You."

"Right. Because I didn't save Tommy that night. That's my sin. I let my partner – her husband – die. I felt guilty about that for a long time too. I eventually convinced myself I wasn't responsible for Tommy's death. Except what if Rikki Ferraro thinks I was responsible? Which is why she wants to finish this off by killing me."

Teena shook her head.

"We still don't have a slam-dunk case against this Ferraro woman. We could use some kind of evidence linking her directly to the murders."

"I've gone through the records of Susan Kirwin," Dave Bowers said. "I mean we knew she was the girl at the Lavelle scene and now that she killed Ruggerio and probably Briggs too. But what was she doing and where was she before that? Well, she had been confined to a juvenile detention center after the deaths of her parents. Then she got adopted. Or at least given over to a foster parent with the possibility of adoptions. There were several foster families she was placed with and she went through a lot of therapy. In fact, Susan Kirwin's current therapist is…"

"Rikki Ferraro," I said.

"How did you know?"

"I should have figured it out earlier."

CHAPTER 62

Teena and I flew to New York, then drove to the town on Long Island where Rikki Ferraro lived. I originally wanted Teena to stay behind on Martha's Vineyard and keep working the case from there, but she said Bowers and the others could handle things while we were gone. She said she wasn't going to let me confront the Ferraro woman without her there to back me up. I don't win many arguments with Teena, and I sure wasn't going to win this.

We had notified the local police on Long Island, who we'd already been talking to about her. They said they had sent regular patrols to check on Ferraro, knocking on the door and peering in windows – but there was no sign of her inside the house. The local police said they weren't prepared to forcibly enter the house. But we were.

I explained that we were looking for a suspected murderer and that she might be holding a kidnapped teenager with her. That was enough. A short time later, we arrived at the Ferraro home with a contingent of officers and equipment to break in, if necessary.

The house looked the same as I remembered it from the few times I'd been there for dinner with Tommy and his family when we were partners. At least from the outside it did. It was a white stucco house with black trim and a big front yard at the end of a cul-de-sac on a quiet-looking suburban street.

One of the Long Island officers walked up to the front door, rang the bell and yelled loudly: "Police, ma'am, open up!"

There was no answer.

I tried it too. I yelled out who I was. "Rikki, this is Abby. Abby Pearce. We've been trying to reach you. Please open the door if you're in there. Otherwise, the officers are going to have to use force to enter your house. Please! Are you in there?"

Still nothing.

One of the Long Island officers looked at me. I nodded and told him to go ahead. They took out a battering ram and used it to smash open the front door of the Ferraro house. By this time, a group of neighbors had gathered to see what was going on. One of the officers stayed behind to hold them back from the scene. Teena and I and the other local officers took our guns and carefully made our way into the house.

I wasn't sure what we would find. The first place we walked into was the living room. I remembered the last time I'd been here with Tommy and Rikki and their kids, talking and having a good time after we'd had dinner. It all seemed to be the same as it was then. Even though Tommy was dead now and Rikki Ferraro could be a mass murderer.

Next we made our way into the kitchen. Everything seemed okay there too. I felt a little ridiculous for a second standing there with a gun looking for a killer in the kitchen of my dead partner's wife. It all seemed normal. But then I realized again that there was nothing normal here at all. Rikki Ferraro had inexplicably gone over to the dark side. She was no longer the loving wife of Tommy, my partner. She had turned into a deadly monster. I was certain of that. What I didn't know for sure was where this woman was right now.

We moved slowly to the master bedroom. The bed was unmade, but that was the only thing that seemed out of place. I'd noticed some dishes and plates left out in the kitchen along with a half-drunk cup of coffee. As if someone had left in a hurry. Presumably Rikki Ferraro. Unless there was someone else involved here.

There were a couple of other bedrooms. I assumed they had been occupied by the kids – when they were living here. They looked untouched since then. We finally got to a final bedroom. This one was locked, so we needed to break the door down just like we had with the front door. Which is why I figured there must be something important inside. But I had no idea what that would be until we went inside.

It was a room that had once been Tommy's office. He had a desk there, a filing cabinet and mementos from his days on the force. Rikki Ferraro had turned it now into a sort of shrine for her dead husband. Awards, newspaper articles about big cases he'd solved and a lot of pictures. One of them was the picture of Tommy that was my favorite. Tommy standing by the door of his car, gun and badge on his belt, looking so much like the tough, terrific cop that he was.

But that wasn't what really shocked me. It was what I found on one of the other walls in this room.

There was a big picture of Albert Ruggerio. Another one of Nancy Lavelle. Plus one of Richie Briggs that looked like it had been taken from a mugshot of him somewhere along the way. Each of these pictures had huge Xs drawn over their faces.

There was another picture too.

A big picture of me.

There was no X on my picture.

Not yet.

The message was clear.

She had dealt with the others, everyone she blamed for her husband's death.

Now I was next.

The last place we checked was the basement. I remembered that from my visits here too. Tommy had finished the basement and turned it into a kind of rec room for him and the kids. There was a pool table in there, a big TV and other stuff like that. It was a large room, tastefully furnished and with very distinctive knotty pine wood on the walls.

The same kind of knotty pine wood I'd seen in the picture sent to me of Karin Lavelle.

I hadn't made the connection then, no reason to think of the Ferraro home.

But now it jumped out at me.

This was the place Karin Lavelle was being held!

So where was she now?

I shouted her name, hoping she was still here. At first, I heard nothing. Then I thought there was some kind of slight scratching sound. We tried to determine where it was coming from. Calling out Karin Lavelle's name over and over again. The scratching got louder and louder. And then we heard a faint knocking coming out of the wall.

It didn't take long after that.

We found a door hidden in one of the walls.

It was locked, but we were able to quickly batter it down.

On the other side, in that basement of Rikki Ferraro's house, was a tiny room. It was dark and sparsely furnished, with just a simple cot. But someone was lying on that cot.

She was very frail looking.

And barely conscious.

But she was alive.

It was Karin Lavelle.

CHAPTER 63

"What happened to my parents? My sisters and my brother? Are they all right?"

Those were the first words Karin Lavelle said when she was able to speak.

"Let's just worry about you right now," I said.

"She was going to kill them…"

"We're going to get you to a hospital now, Karin."

"But…"

"What do you remember?"

"I was there when they came in…"

"They" must mean Rikki Ferraro and Susan Kirwin together.

"And then… then I woke up here."

"That's all?"

"Tell me about my family."

"We'll talk about everything when we get you to the hospital."

"My family…"

Her voice was becoming weaker now, and she began losing consciousness. She had somehow rallied with all her remaining strength in that basement room to scratch and knock on the wall to get our attention. Then, once we found her, she was able to get out those few words – mostly questions about her family. But that was the extent of it. The doctors would discover that she was suffering from malnutrition and dehydration and had also been given drugs that kept her weak and docile.

An ambulance arrived, and the EMTs put her on a stretcher and then into the back of an ambulance for the ride to a nearby hospital. I got in and rode with her, while Teena stayed behind at the house with Long Island police looking for any other leads or evidence about Rikki Ferraro or where she might have gone.

I didn't want to let Karin Lavelle out of my sight. Maybe she would tell me something more about what happened to her. But she had an IV in her arm now that was giving her some kind of sedative, which put her to sleep for the trip.

Later, at the hospital, she talked about everything she had been keeping inside her since that fateful day on Martha's Vineyard at The Beach House.

"All I know about that day was I heard a commotion coming from the living room. I ran there and saw my father battling with a woman. The woman who owns this house here, I found out later. When I went to help my father, someone else – a girl just about my age – grabbed me from behind. Then I felt some sort of needle prick in my neck. And that's all I remember. When I woke up, I was tied up and blindfolded in the trunk of a car. I was then taken to that house, where I was held after that."

That all worked with what we knew. The murders happened in the afternoon, but they weren't discovered until the maid entered the rooms the next morning. That gave Ferraro plenty of time to hide Karin in the trunk of her car and drive back to Long Island with her.

But why did she leave Susan Kirwin behind?

It was almost as if she was exchanging one girl – Susan Kirwin – for the other.

That became even more clear when Karin told me some of the things Rikki Ferraro said to her during her captivity.

"She told me how her family had been destroyed. She'd lost her daughter, her son and her husband. And that now everyone who played a role in their deaths would pay for it. Including my mother. I didn't really understand most of it. I mean she seemed crazy.

"Sometimes she would be nice to me. Like she was trying to win me over, playing some kind of mind control games with me. But when I resisted she locked me away in that room and took away most of my food and water for a period of time. For instance, when I agreed to pose for that picture you saw in the basement rec room, I hadn't been fed in three days. Afterward though, she brought me a nice meal. It was some kind of behaviorist conditioning, I guess.

"Then, a few days ago, she locked me again into that room. She left me some food and water this time. But she said she was leaving because she had a job to do – and that I better hope she was successful. Otherwise, if she didn't come back, I'd die in that little room because no one else knew I was there. Well, I was in a constant state of terror about it ever since that moment. Terrified no one would ever find me. Thank God you showed up."

But the most traumatic moment came when Karin Lavelle finally found out the truth about her family.

Her grandparents arrived at the hospital soon after she was brought there, and then stayed by her bedside the whole time.

They were the ones who broke the horrible news to her.

"Karin, honey, we're going to take you home to live with us when you're well enough to leave the hospital," Elizabeth Hood said to her granddaughter when the Hoods first got there.

"Why can't I go home?"

"Well…"

"Why aren't my mother and father here?"

"That's what we need to talk to you about…"

I was in the hospital room when that happened. Standing there and listening to the Hoods tell Karin Lavelle that her entire family had been murdered.

Karin began to cry as they told the story, first softly and then with gasps of grief and despair.

And now I had a job to do.

To find the woman who was responsible for this.

Before she found me…

CHAPTER 64

"Where do you think she is?" Teena asked me now.

"You know where she is."

"Right here. On Martha's Vineyard."

"Yep. It's the only thing that fits. She's killed everyone she blamed for the death of her husband. Everyone except me. And then, when she figured out I was on to her, she disappeared. She wants to kill me next, and there's only one place for her to do that. Right here on Martha's Vineyard."

"And we're supposed to just wait around while she tries to kill you?"

"Unless we find her first."

We were back on Martha's Vineyard after the whirlwind of events on Long Island. There'd been a big press conference down there about the rescue of kidnapped Karin Lavelle that made all the national news shows. Then we'd had another press conference after arriving back here where I talked about all the aspects of the case, including the fact that I was probably a target of the killer.

Chief Wilhelm had met with me as soon as I got back to discuss protection scenarios for me. He wanted me to move out of my house and into a hotel, with a twenty-four-hour police guard on me. Yes, Teena had moved into my house to provide protection for me, but Wilhelm said that was no longer enough.

I appreciated his concern. I really did. But I told him again that I couldn't do my job under those conditions.

"I need to catch that crazy woman before she kills again," I said. "I can't do that locked up in a hotel room."

"But she wants to kill you."

"All the more reason that I need to be out there doing my job and trying to stop her."

He finally agreed we'd stay with the plan of Teena living with me full-time at the house for protection – along with having regular police patrols check up on me regularly there as a backup.

Wilhelm seemed different. Friendlier to me. I think he was impressed by what I'd done in New York by finding the missing girl. It made me look good to the public, which made him look good to the public, too. Which was fine with me.

"You did a good job down there, Pearce," he said.

"Thank you."

"I'm glad you made it back safely."

"You won't get rid of me that easily, Chief." I smiled.

We did keep trying to do our job the best we could under the restrictions. I reported to the station every day, went out on assignments and cases with Teena. No question about it though, I kept looking over my shoulder the whole time for any sign of Rikki Ferraro. But we never saw a thing.

"Why do you think she hasn't made a move yet?" Teena asked.

"Maybe she wants to make me sweat first."

"Are you sweating?"

"Profusely."

"Well, I still think we should do something."

"We've looked for her everywhere on the island we could think of."

"So what else is there?"

"Somewhere we haven't thought of looking yet."

We were sitting in my kitchen after eating dinner. I'd made a salad from some of the vegetables in my garden, but it was Teena who did the real work. She was a great cook. And she'd put together some kind of lasagna that was maybe the best Italian food I'd ever eaten. We were actually getting along very well being together full-time like this, Teena and I, since she'd moved in to protect me.

She'd lived by herself for a few years after the death of her husband, so I think she liked the company. I was fine living alone with just Oscar most of the time, but the truth was I liked her company too. After months of only talking to Oscar in this place, it was nice to have someone I could have a two-way conversation with.

Teena asked about Lincoln Connor and I filled her in.

"And you're buying his story?"

"Some of it."

"You don't need to have both parties agree to a divorce, Abby. It's harder to do if the wife refuses to end the marriage. But it can be done. Except your boyfriend Lincoln hasn't done it."

"I'm aware of that."

"Which means…"

"There's more to the story that he's not telling me."

"Any idea what that might be?"

I shook my head no.

"Just another unsolved mystery in my life."

We had settled into a kind of regular routine since she moved in with me. After dinner, we took Oscar out for a walk in the woods behind the house. It was still light out late at this time of year, so we usually made it a long walk. There were a lot of trails for Oscar to follow, and plenty of squirrels there for him to chase after.

"You ready to go?" Teena said, reaching for Oscar's leash.

"Go ahead without me. I want to look through some of the stuff in the file one more time about Rikki Ferraro."

"You've already gone through it a hundred times."

"Maybe I'll find something I missed."

"Are you going to be okay alone?"

"I'm fine."

"Call me if anything seems wrong."

"Have a nice walk with Oscar. Don't worry about me."

Except it wasn't long after she left that I noticed something was wrong.

Two things actually.

First, Teena had forgotten to take her phone with her. It was still sitting on the kitchen table. I wondered if she'd realize that and come back. No big deal. She'd be back soon enough after the walk.

The other thing I noticed wrong was more disturbing though. The bottle of vodka I kept prominently displayed was gone. I looked around the kitchen to see if Teena had moved it to another spot for some reason. But it was nowhere there.

Where the hell did that bottle go?

I walked into the living room to see if I could find it there.

That's when I heard something behind me and turned around.

It was Rikki Ferraro.

Holding the bottle of vodka.

"Looking for this, Pearce? Want to get drunk again? Like you did the night you let my husband Tommy die in the street?"

CHAPTER 65

She was holding a knife in her hand. A large knife, with a curved and serrated metal blade. It looked different than the knife we'd found in the woods behind The Beach House. This was the real murder weapon Rikki Ferraro had used to slaughter the Lavelle family. I knew that now.

I didn't have my gun with me. It was still back in the kitchen, sitting in the holster that I had left draped over the chair I was sitting in while I ate dinner. My phone was in the kitchen too, so I couldn't even try to call for help.

Rikki Ferraro was standing about ten feet away from me. I was pretty sure, based on her military background and the way she'd managed to subdue the Lavelle family before killing them, that there was no way I could get into the kitchen for either the gun or the phone. She'd cut me down before I got there.

All I could do was try to keep her talking until I saw how this played out.

"There's a police patrol outside," I said, "You'll never get away with this."

She laughed.

"The police patrol checks out your house every hour during the evening. Stops to make sure everything inside is all right with you. They were here fifteen minutes ago. So I know I have at least forty-five minutes to do what I need to do and get away before that. Also, that woman that's been living with you just took your dog for a walk a few minutes ago. You and her never walk that dog for less than thirty minutes. I wouldn't count on anyone getting here in time to help you."

"You've been watching me."

"What else would I be doing?"

"Why?"

"To make sure I picked the right time to show myself to you."

"No, I mean why are you doing this? Why do you want to kill me so badly? I thought we were friends."

"Friends? My husband is dead because of you. My children are dead because of you. I can't bring them back, but I can avenge their deaths. Make the people responsible pay for taking them away from me. The rest of them have all paid that price now. Everyone except you. Now it's your turn…"

She laughed loudly again. It wasn't really a laugh though. It was some kind of scary sound coming out of her mouth. I wondered if she had always been this crazy, even during the years with Tommy and raising the kids. Or did she go crazy after Tommy's death and then losing both of her children? Plus, the release of the man who killed Tommy?

"Why did you take Karin Lavelle?" I asked, even though I had a pretty good idea now of what her answer would be.

"She was going to be my daughter. They took away my real daughter, along with my son. So I decided I would have her as my daughter. She was going to become Christina Ferraro. I wanted to turn her into the perfect daughter. She would replace the Christina that was taken from me. That's what was supposed to happen. I could have made that happen too. But you ruined everything. You took this daughter away from me too. Now I want to make you pay."

I tried my best to ignore the threat and focus on keeping her talking.

"What about the Kirwin girl? You could have just kept her?"

Another crazy laugh.

"That girl was a mess. I didn't want her. I only wanted to use her. And I did. I had her kill Briggs for me. And then Ruggerio. She helped with the Lavelles too. I figured I'd do Ruggerio myself, which is why I left her back there at the Lavelle murder scene. I figured that was the best way to start playing with your head, Pearce. Trying to figure out who this girl was and why she was there.

"But she managed to get away and then kill Ruggerio herself. I think she wanted to please me. She was very malleable. I could get her to do anything I wanted. Which was to help with the killing. She was the one who got us into the Lavelle place by posing as a maid. She looked so innocent that Thomas Lavelle never even hesitated to let her in. Of course, I was right behind her and killed him.

"It wasn't him I wanted though, as you know. I wanted his wife. The bitch who got the man who killed my husband out of jail. I made her watch while I slaughtered her family."

I remembered how there was very little blood in the little boy's room, but a tremendous amount of blood around Nancy Lavelle, even though she'd only been stabbed a single time.

"You brought the little boy from the bedroom out to her – then put him back into the bedroom after they both were dead," I said. "That's what happened, right?"

Rikki Ferraro smiled at the memory.

"I wanted her to pay for what she did. I wanted her to see it all. I wanted her to suffer like I've suffered. The more she screamed, the more I enjoyed it. Then I told her how I was going to take her other daughter with me, and I was going to become her mother. That was the final moment of terror for her. Right before I finally plunged the knife into her, and I killed her."

She boasted then about leaving the "No One Here Gets Out Alive" slogan and the clasping of hands together in death poses for Nancy Lavelle and Richie Briggs as part of a "spiritual message" she was sending to Tommy that his death was being avenged. She said Susan Kirwin was supposed to do that with Ruggerio too, but died before she could. She showed no remorse over the death of the Kirwin girl. She was a crazy woman on a crazy mission, and that mission was all that mattered to her.

"I wanted Briggs killed first because he was the one who murdered Tommy. Then the Lavelle woman and her family because she got him out of jail – that's what convinced me I had to do this. That was the final straw for me. And then, of course, I figured out that Ruggerio was behind my husband's death because he was afraid Tommy was going to talk about taking payoffs from him.

"I don't know why Tommy had to do that – I begged him not to, to keep taking the money – but he insisted it was something he had to do. Even if he was afraid Ruggerio would come after him like he did. So that's why Ruggerio had to pay too. They all had to die, and they all had to suffer.

"I wanted to leave you until last. I wanted you to see all the others die first. I couldn't believe the way everything fell into place for me to do that. I mean I knew you were back on Martha's Vineyard. So when I heard about Ruggerio being here too, it seemed like a message from some greater power – a sign from God – of what I needed to do.

"I remembered Tommy talking about how your family owned a restaurant. So I found the restaurant, tracked down who owned it now – and decided that would be the scene of the Lavelle murders. I lured them up here with that phony invitation from Ruggerio. I did it all so that my Tommy – and my children – could rest in peace. First with Richie Briggs. Then Nancy Lavelle and her family. Then Ruggerio. And now you.

"Let me tell you what's going to happen. I could end it very quickly with a simple jab into your carotid artery. You would bleed out very quickly that way. But I want you to suffer, I'm going to keep stabbing you. You'll lose a lot of blood, but not enough to kill you. Not until I'm ready for you to die. And then I'll deliver the final blow as payback for the way you let my husband die on that street in front of you."

I didn't know what to say, but I had to say something.

"I loved Tommy. Not like you did, but he was my friend and my mentor. He was my partner. You have to believe me."

She shook her head.

"Time's up, Pearce."

She raised the knife high above her head. I took a look again at the kitchen and wondered if I should make a desperate dash to get there to try for my gun. Or else try to take her on directly in a fight as she came at me with the knife. Either way I didn't figure I stood much of a chance.

And then suddenly I heard something.

It was a dog barking.

Oscar.

Rikki Ferraro turned for just a second to see where the barking sound was coming from. She had put the vodka bottle down on an end table next to where she was standing. There was no other choice. I dove for the bottle, picked it up by the neck and swung it as hard as I could at her head.

She went down.

But she still had the knife in her hand.

"Hey, Abby," Teena was saying now, "I forgot my phone. Did you happen to see it anywhere…"

Teena had walked in the front door now and saw Ferraro.

The rest of it seemed to happen in slow motion.

Teena grabbed for her gun.

Rikki Ferraro got up on her feet with the knife still in her hand.

Teena yelled at her to drop the knife.

Ferraro raised it instead and flailed it around in the air.

She kept coming after me, ignoring Teena and the gun.
Killing me was all that seemed to matter to her.
I felt the blade of her knife on my neck.
Teena yelled one final warning.
Then she pulled the trigger and shot Rikki Ferraro dead.

CHAPTER 66

I was lucky. Rikki Ferraro's knife had just nicked me and made only a small incision on the side of my neck. The sudden arrival of Teena and Oscar had startled Ferraro and made her hesitate before trying to stab me and that threw her off her game. It was what had saved my life, the doctors said.

One of the first people to come see me at the hospital was Lincoln Connor.

"Did you come here hoping to get an exclusive interview with me for your story?" I asked him.

"I came to make sure you're all right, Abby. It freaked the hell out of me when I heard about what happened. Thank God it ended the way it did. That's why I'm here. I'm here to support you and be with you."

"But you'd take an exclusive interview with me if I gave it to you, right?"

"Well, I wouldn't turn it down." He smiled.

We didn't talk any more about us. I knew we didn't have a future together but I hadn't been able to admit that to myself until now. Marriage was hard enough to make work under ideal conditions; it would be impossible with a man like Lincoln who was still living a lie. I would tell him that. Not today, it was nice that he had come to see me. But soon, once I was out of the hospital. It was time for me to move on in my life past Lincoln Connor.

Chief Wilhelm came to see me, too. That was a surprise. But he was a veteran police officer at heart, I guess, and Wilhelm appreciated what I had done in the end – despite all the tension and bad feelings between us. He even told me that as he sat by my bed in the hospital room.

"I know I've been tough on you, and I'm sorry about some of that," he said. "Yes, you can be a pain-in-the-ass sometimes, but it will be good to have you back on duty soon. You really are a helluva detective, Pearce."

We still had a lot of issues to work through, but he was there for me now at this moment. I appreciated that. We could deal with the rest of the unresolved baggage between us later, Chief Wilhelm and me.

Teena stayed with me the whole time I was at the hospital, then drove me home afterward.

"Are you gonna miss having me live there with you now that you're safe again?" she asked.

"I won't miss you, but I will miss that lasagna you made. You're a helluva cook."

"You can still stop by my place and pick it up for takeout."

We drove in silence for a while, headed west across the island toward Chilmark. The leaves on the trees were really starting to turn now, giving the area a gorgeous color that you didn't see until this time of year. I understood why people liked to visit Martha's Vineyard in the fall. I was glad I lived here again.

"So are you gonna say it?" Teena asked me finally.

"Say what?"

"You know."

I sighed.

"Thank you, Teena."

"You're welcome."

"Seriously, you saved my life."

"Hey, you saved my life in that shooting incident a few months ago when I almost died."

"Then I guess we're even now, huh?"

"For now."

EPILOGUE

Justice is an elusive goal. And too many times it is the innocent who pay the greatest price. I have learned that many times during my years as a police officer. And yet I am still haunted by the memory of the victims.

I can't go to sleep at night without thinking about Thomas Lavelle, Nancy Lavelle, their three children – and the future that was snatched away from them for no real reason. I do not grieve for Albert Ruggerio or Richie Briggs, but I do wish that justice had been meted out to them in a different way.

Martha's Vineyard is a beautiful place – an island paradise to many. But sometimes evil even comes to a place like this. When it does, I have to stop it. That's my job.

And, when I find myself gripped with despair over the innocent lives that were lost, I remember the one I saved.

Karin Lavelle is alive today because of me.

That gives me hope.

I cling to that hope each day when I go to work at the Cedar Cliffs police station.

Even as I wonder when the evil will return to this island…

A LETTER FROM DANA

Dear reader,

I want to say a huge thank you for choosing to read *Silent Island* – and hope you enjoyed the book. If you want to keep up to date with all my latest releases, just sign up at the following link. Your email address will never be shared and you can unsubscribe at any time.

www.bookouture.com/dana-perry

This is the second thriller I've written featuring Abby Pearce, a former star homicide detective in New York City who returns to the small town on Martha's Vineyard where she grew up to work on the police force there, in an attempt to escape the demons of her past. For me, the Abby Pearce series is a wonderful opportunity to write about two places I know very well – Martha's Vineyard and New York City. I've worked in New York for most of my life as a journalist/author, and I have vacationed many summers on the beautiful island of Martha's Vineyard off the coast of Cape Cod. I love writing the Abby Pearce character and hope you enjoy her, too!

If you have time, I would be very grateful if you could write a review of *Silent Island*. Reader reviews on Amazon, Goodreads and anywhere else are crucially important to an author and can spread the word about Abby to new readers. If you'd like to contact me personally, you can get in touch via my Facebook page or Twitter.

Thank you for reading *Silent Island* and spending time with Abby Pearce.

Best wishes,
Dana Perry

 DanaPerryAuthor

 @DanaPerryAuthor